Unstoppable IN A KILT

Other Books by Anna Durand

Dangerous in a Kilt (Hot Scots, Book One)
Wicked in a Kilt (Hot Scots, Book Two)
Scandalous in a Kilt (Hot Scots, Book Three)
The MacTaggart Brothers Trilogy (Hot Scots, Books 1-3)
Gift-Wrapped in a Kilt (Hot Scots, Book Four)
Notorious in a Kilt (Hot Scots, Book Five)
Insatiable in a Kilt (Hot Scots, Book Six)
Lethal in a Kilt (Hot Scots, Book Seven)
Irresistible in a Kilt (Hot Scots, Book Eight)
Devastating in a Kilt (Hot Scots, Book Nine)
Spellbound in a Kilt (Hot Scots, Book Ten)
Relentless in a Kilt (Hot Scots, Book Eleven)
Incendiary in a Kilt (Hot Scots, Book Twelve)
Wild in a Kilt (Hot Scots, Book Thirteen)
Lachlan in a Kilt (The Ballachulish Trilogy, Book One)
Aidan in a Kilt (The Ballachulish Trilogy, Book Two)
Rory in a Kilt (The Ballachulish Trilogy, Book Three)
The American Wives Club (A Hot Brits/Hot Scots/Au Naturel Crossover Book)
Brit vs. Scot (A Hot Brits/Hot Scots/Au Naturel Crossover Book)
A Novel Secret (A Hot Brits/Hot Scots/Au Naturel Crossover, Book Three)
The Dixon Brothers Trilogy (Hot Brits, Books 1-3)
One Hot Escape (Hot Brits, Book Four)
One Hot Rumor (Hot Brits, Book Five)
One Hot Christmas (Hot Brits, Book Six)
One Hot Scandal (Hot Brits, Book Seven)
One Hot Deal (Hot Brits, Book Eight)
One Hot Favor (Hot Brits, Book Nine)
Natural Obsession (Au Naturel Nights, Book One)
Natural Deception (Au Naturel Nights, Book Two)
Natural Passion (Au Naturel Trilogy, Book One)
Natural Impulse (Au Naturel Trilogy, Book Two)
Natural Satisfaction (Au Naturel Trilogy, Book Three)
Fired Up (standalone romance)
Echo Power (Echo Power Trilogy, Book One)
Echo Dominion (Echo Power Trilogy, Book Two)
Echo Unbound (Echo Power Trilogy, Book Three)
The Janusite Trilogy (Undercover Elementals, Books 1-3)
Obsidian Hunger (Undercover Elementals, Book Four)
Unbidden Hunger (Undercover Elementals, Book Five)
The Thirteenth Fae (Undercover Elementals, Book Six)
Cyneric (Undercover Elementals, Book Seven)

Unstoppable IN A KILT

Hot Scots, Book Fourteen

ANNA DURAND

JACOBSVILLE BOOKS · MARIETTA, OHIO

Prologue

Fiona
Two Years Ago

What happens when two Scots meet at a nudist resort and swiftly fall for each other? Fireworks, that's what. The sort that fill up the sky and blind everyone for miles away. I have never been the type of woman who falls for a man instantly, but Domhnall Sterling stirred feelings inside me that I still don't understand. The moment I met him, I should have realized he would be trouble with a capital T and the thickest black line underneath it, not to mention several exclamation points and a series of firecracker emojis.

I should have told him to sod off and then walked away.

But I couldn't do that. I sensed something in him that I recognized—pain and longing. He might have behaved like a *tolla-thon* at the time, but even then, I'd seen glimmers of goodness. Domhnall is not an ersehole at heart.

He's doing a perfect impression of one, though.

The day I arrived at the Au Naturel Naturist Resort in Oregon for Alex and Catriona's wedding, I could never have guessed how my life would change. My sister married a Brit, but that wasn't the pivotal moment. No, the turning point came a wee bit later on the same day, when I was in the dining hall making the final seating arrangements for dinner that evening.

When Domhnall Sterling sauntered into the room, everything changed.

He made me laugh, though not on purpose, when he informed me that my brother Rory had threatened to give him his head in his hands to play with, literally. The Scottish saying meant that Rory would beat him up. My brother wouldn't really do that. He was only making sure Domhnall wouldn't cause too much trouble.

Domhnall smiled a wee bit when I laughed.

But when our eyes locked, I felt a strange sensation like nothing I'd ever experienced with any other man. I wanted him to kiss me. I knew next to nothing about the man, yet I felt a powerful attraction that I didn't even try to fight. Something in him triggered something in me, and the connection felt too good to resist.

The second time we crossed paths, Domhnall was trying to force Jessica O'Connor to talk to him. She is not a woman who can be easily cowed, which meant Domhnall could never get what he wanted from her. He had followed Jessica to the caretaker's house, where Eve and Val Silva lived. They own the resort, and Val had intervened when Domhnall tried to push his way into the house to force a conversation with his former girlfriend. Aye, Domhnall is a man with serious issues. Deep down, we all know he didn't mean to harass Jess. He was frustrated and heartbroken.

When Val slammed the door in his face, Domhnall slumped against the wall, closing his eyes, clearly intending to wait for Jessica to leave so he could pester her again.

And for reasons I still can't explain two years later, I approached him. "Having a good morning, are ye?"

Domhnall couldn't have overlooked the sarcasm in my tone. But when he opened his eyes, he didn't squint at me or scowl. Instead, he roved his gaze over my body with clear interest. He even licked his lips when he noticed the wee bit of cleavage my dress revealed.

"Well, are ye having a good morning?" I asked. "Since you stalked Jessica over here like a wolf tracking a deer, I'd say you aren't feeling particularly good today."

"Fuck," he hissed under his breath.

I couldn't help laughing softly. "You're head's mince for sure."

Domhnall clearly didn't appreciate that I pointed out he seemed extremely confused and unable to sort out his problems. How did I know he felt that way? Because the *bod ceann* gritted his teeth and slanted toward me while grinding out the words he spoke. "Away and boil yer head."

And I couldn't help but laugh even more. "I have three brothers, and two of them can be very intimidating—to other people. If I can deal with them, I can handle you. Snarling doesn't work on me. Neither does a steely glare or Gaelic swearing. And honestly, I'd expect a mature man to do better than 'away and boil yer head' if he wants to offend me."

I can still see his expression in my mind, as clearly as if it happened this morning. He had gaped at me like I'd just suggested he should literally boil his head. There was a hot spring nearby, so I suppose he could have done that.

Then a strange impulse grabbed me, and I shuffled closer. "You're a braw man who could get any woman he wants. Why are you banging your head into a brick wall trying to make Jessica love you?"

Would he have told me the truth? I'll never know, because he spotted Grey Dixon coming out of the guest house on the other side of the main resort area. Domhnall's demeanor changed in an instant. His expression hardened. His body stiffened. Then he shoved himself away from the wall of the caretaker's house and snarled words at me.

"Keep your bonnie wee nose out of my business."

Sighing, I shook my head. "If you want to keep banging your skull on those bricks until it caves in, it's your choice."

I casually walked away.

But that was hardly the end of things. I couldn't stay away from that gruff, grumpy man. Maybe I noticed a similar pain in him that I felt in myself, though I had never let it show and certainly never told my family about it. I suppose that's why I kept after Domhnall. I wanted to help him. I wanted him, full stop. Though I kept catching glimpses of Domhnall after that, I tried to stay away from him as much as possible. A damaged man who's still hung up on his ex-girlfriend? No, that wasn't the sort of situation I wanted to get tangled up in, no matter how sexy and intriguing Domhnall Sterling was.

Then one day I went for a walk, with no particular destination in mind, and wound up at the lake that lay within the resort's land. As I was hiking back up the path, I saw a familiar figure wandering down an offshoot trail. That was Domhnall. I shouldn't have been able to recognize him from his backside alone, but I might have studied him surreptitiously whenever he came into my view, always from a distance but close enough to intrigue me.

Did that pigheaded lout even know where he was going?

I decided he most likely didn't and headed down the offshoot trail after him. Domhnall was a good distance ahead of me. By the time I reached him, he had sat down on the ground and leaned back against a tree, shutting his eyes.

He didn't even notice when I approached him. The man seemed ill at ease, or perhaps actually ill.

I studied him briefly, then announced my presence. "Are you unwell?"

Domhnall cracked one eye open but didn't speak.

"Well?" I asked. "Are you ill? I can get help if you need it."

"Not unwell," he growled through gritted teeth. Then he opened both eyes. "Are you following me?"

"Arrogant, aren't you? Assuming I ran after you, like I'm a stalker or I'm smitten with you." I planted my hands on my hips. "I went for a hike on my own, and I saw you on my way back from the lake. Pardon me for stopping to make sure you're not dying."

"I'm fine. You can leave now."

Oh, aye, he seemed quite fine. Men often get testy when they're in a good mood. No, they didn't do that. Domhnall was a liar.

He made a dismissive hand gesture. "I said go."

As if that would stop me. I settled onto the ground beside him, sitting cross-legged. "What have you done this time?"

"You're a bloody annoying woman. Do you know that?"

"Aye. Now tell me what's fashing you."

In the conversation that followed, Domhnall shared surprisingly personal information with me, revealing more than I ever would have expected. He told me that his ex-wife had cheated on him for years. But his most surprising admission was when he confessed to his behavior when he was with Jessica. His ex-wife had started ringing him, wanting to get back together. She even rang Domhnall while he was on holiday with Jess.

And he took those calls. But he muted Jessica's mobile so Grey Dixon couldn't call her. Domhnall thought I should be horrified by his behavior, and he couldn't understand why it never bothered me. He insisted he was a *bod ceann* through and through.

"You might be a dickhead," I had told him. "I can't speak to that. But as I told you before, I'm not put off by men who act like erseholes, not when I can tell they've got pain and tenderness underneath the prickly surface."

That statement had baffled him for sure.

But Domhnall showed sincere regret when I mentioned that my dress shop had gone out of business. An irredeemable *bod ceann* wouldn't give a toss about that. Maybe that explains why I had sex with him during the wedding week.

Why have I stayed with Domhnall Sterling for two years? Not for his body. Not for his money. Not for any other superficial reasons. I stayed because I love him and see things in him that he never lets anyone else even glimpse for a split second. I allowed him to keep his secrets, but that time is long gone now. I need to know why he won't commit to marrying me and why he won't tell me about his past before he got involved with Jessica.

Oh, aye, he told me a few things about his ex-wife, but I need to know everything. Our relationship can't survive in the dark, and I'm done waiting for him to open up to me. Either he does it now, or we are done.

This is our last chance.

Chapter One

Domhnall

Go away, you stubborn, obnoxious, pigheaded *bod ceann*," Fiona shouts at me as she closes the door almost all the way, leaving only a few inches of her face visible between the jamb and the door. "I've said all I want to say to you, Domhnall. There's nothing left to talk about. Get your bloody erse out of my house and never come back."

"But Fiona—"

She slams the door shut.

I wasn't in the house, but she ordered me to leave it anyway. Women are irrational when they get angry, especially Fiona. I love her fire and spirit, but not when she tells me to go away and never come back. I can't do that even if I wanted to obey her command.

So, I suck in a deep breath and shout, "Fiona! Open the bloody door. All my clothes and things are still in there."

"I don't care." Her shout is muffled somewhat by the door, but she must not have gone far since I can clearly understand her words. "I'll put your things in a rubbish bag and leave it on the porch for you."

"Dinnae be an eejit."

She yanks the door open and squints at me. "I am not a moron, Domhnall. And I'm done trying to get you to open up and explain yourself. Your behavior has become impossible to tolerate. We are over. For good."

I lean in until our noses are inches apart and lower my voice to a husky murmur. "We belong together, *gràidh*. And ye can't deny we have powerful chemistry."

"Hot sex is not a good reason to stay with a brute like you."

"But ye used to call me your hero."

She rolls her eyes. "I said that after we had sex. That doesn't count."

Now that I have her talking, how far should I push? Subtlety has never been my strong suit. I set my hands on the door jamb and lean in a wee bit more until our noses brush against each other. "We have more than sex keeping us together. You've threatened to throw me over half a dozen times, but you never can do it. Can you?"

Fiona stares into my eyes without blinking for so long that I begin to wonder if she's had a stroke. But then she blows a breath out through her nostrils. I watch as she gradually narrows her gaze and puckers her lips. "Mhac na galla. You sneaky, conniving, arrogant, bastard. Never again will you trick me into loving you."

She takes one step backward and slams the door.

It smacks into my nose, and I curse under my breath.

That woman is the most stubborn, intractable female I have ever met. She curses at me. She refuses to listen. Aye, all right, maybe I do share those traits with her. And maybe that's part of the reason that we argue. But no, it is not my fault that Fiona insists on always getting her way, and it is definitely not my fault that she kicked me out of the house.

Any other man would probably walk away and forget about her. But I cannae do that. I love that stubborn woman, and this time, I will not give up no matter what it takes. I will be unstoppable. Munro MacTaggart had told me that months ago, when Fiona and I were having trouble—*be unstoppable*. I believe he's right, which means I need to think of a plan to win back Fiona.

For the moment, I'll execute a strategic withdrawal from the battlefield. Aye, getting her back will require a battle. Two pigheaded eejits can't simply kiss and makeup.

I turn and walk away, jumping into my pickup truck. Though I start driving, I don't have a bloody clue where I'm going. My subconscious must have an idea, since it compels me to drive straight through town, away from the home I've shared with Fiona, and to a different house on the far side of the village. Once I've parked along the street, I sit in the truck for several minutes, gripping the steering wheel in both hands. My gaze flits to the house repeatedly. Should I knock on the door? Or should I drive away? What if the man I've come to see refuses to speak to me?

Mhac na galla. I've become a coward.

No, that will never happen. I leap out of the vehicle and stalk up to the front steps of the house, then punch the doorbell.

A moment later, the door swings open.

"What are you doing here?" Munro MacTaggart asks. "Must be more trouble with Fiona, aye?"

"That's right."

Munro pulls the door wide open and spreads an arm in invitation. "Best come in, then. Any talk about Fiona takes at least an hour."

I can't deny that. Why Munro continues to help me, I cannae explain. Fiona is his cousin, after all, and the MacTaggarts are fiercely loyal to each other. I've never asked Munro why he speaks to me. Maybe I should do now.

He leads me into the living room, and we both sit down on reclining armchairs. Munro folds his hands over his belly and crosses one ankle over the other knee. "Tell me what's fashing you this time."

"Ah, before I do that..." I resist the impulse to squirm. It's a bloody stupid thing to do. "I need to ask you a question."

"Go on."

"Why do you still speak to me? I am the bastard who tried to steal Jessica O'Connor away from Grey Dixon, and I'm also the bastard who drives Fiona off her head and makes her miserable."

Munro shrugs. "I dinnae take sides. As a *bod ceann* myself, I have no standing to criticize your behavior."

"Are you saying you'll give me advice?"

"That depends on what you're asking me about."

I'm starting to feel like we're on a carousel that will never stop spinning. Munro is usually direct, almost to the point of rudeness, yet he seems to be deflecting right now. I suppose that's because Fiona is his cousin.

"Fiona won't even speak to me," I say. "She tells me I'm hiding my feelings from her, but that's not the case. I just dinnae like talking about myself."

"Most men don't, especially MacTaggarts."

"I'm not a MacTaggart."

He narrows his gaze and growls like an irritated dog. "You are not listening to me. Do ye want my advice or not?"

"Aye." Though I want to snarl right back at him, I restrain that impulse. I am asking for his help, after all.

Munro sits forward, resting his arms on his knees. "Listen carefully. The way to get Fiona back is to..."

I wait, counting the seconds until he finishes his statement. One, two, three, four, five, six, seven—"Bloody hell, Munro. I'm about ready to batter you if you don't stop being so fucking dramatic."

He smirks. "I'll be direct, then. The way to win her back is to stop acting like a *fanaidh bàlaichean* and do whatever she tells you."

I squint at him. "Is that how you deal with your wife? Can't picture you prostrating yourself before Natalie."

"No prostrating is necessary. Just make the lass happy."

This conversation is not giving me any insight. What did I expect from Munro "Wild Man" MacTaggart? He knows all about whitewater rafting but nothing about women. I've heard the stories of how he behaved like a grumpy ersehole when he first met Natalie.

I shouldn't have come to him for help. But I'm desperate.

"You're *tiamhaidh*," Munro says. "Best get used to that feeling. When your woman is unhappy, you will be too."

"Maybe I am *tiamhaidh*. Must be a way to convince Fiona."

"Convince her of what? That she needs to apologize?"

"Well, aye."

Munro slaps his hands on his knees and bursts into a fit of laughter. "Good luck with that, Domhnall."

I've had enough of this. "Thank you for your help, but it's time I go."

Munro walks me to the door and pulls it halfway open, halting so that I can't move past him. "You know, there is another MacTaggart who might be able to help."

"Dinnae say it."

"Say what? You're a mind reader now?"

I feel my jaw tightening and take a slow, deep breath to calm myself. "I am not going to talk to a psychologist."

"Then you best get used to celibacy and living alone." He cocks his head to one side. "Where are ye staying?"

"I, ah, don't know. Fiona booted me out of the house, and I came straight here. Maybe the Loch Fairbairn Arms has a vacancy."

Munro shakes his head slowly. "Haven't you noticed? Kirsty and her sisters are hosting a metaphysical festival in the village starting tomorrow. The Loch Fairbairn Arms is fully booked for the week. Then there's the Highland games Rory and Emery have arranged at Dùndubhan. All the surrounding villages are having events of their own too, so you aren't likely to find accommodations anywhere."

"*Mhac na galla.*"

He pats my shoulder. "Relax, Domhnall. I'm sure we can find you a place to stay. Go straight to Jack's house, and I'll call right now to let him know the situation."

"I do not want you or any of the menfolk in your clan to be meddling in my life."

"Oh, we wouldn't do that." He places a hand on my back and virtually shoves me out the door. "We leave the meddling to the American Wives Club."

He shuts the door.

Well, at least Munro didn't smack it into my nose.

As I jog to my pickup truck and climb in, I begin to feel a strange slithering sensation in my gut. Why? Because I know full well what the American Wives Club does to "help" their friends and family. They have made meddling an Olympic sport. Aye, they have done some good and helped couples through their relationship issues. I was tangentially party to some of that meddling when I crashed the wedding of Alex Thorne and Catriona MacTaggart at a nudist resort in Oregon. My plan to steal Jessica O'Connor away from Grey Dixon had gone down in flames as spectacularly as a Viking funeral.

Maybe I should take Munro's advice and at least hear what Jack might say. He bollocksed up his relationship with Autumn but still managed to win her heart again. They had a baby recently, so he must know something about the topic of second chances.

I start up the engine and head for Jack's house. Everyone knows where the only psychologist in the village lives. I own a pickup truck, but it's the high-end sort that's as close to a sports car as I care to get. That means it takes only a few minutes to reach Jack's home, though I might have driven a wee bit too fast. What's the point of driving a high-performance vehicle if I don't give the beast its head once in a while?

The tires screech as I stop in front of the house where Jack and Autumn live. I hadn't meant to slam on the brakes. It's possible I am a wee bit anxious about what the psychologist might tell me. A greeting of "*go to hell, ye bloody cacan*" wouldn't surprise me one bit. Everyone loves Fiona, and MacTaggarts are fiercely loyal.

I knock on the door.

A baby starts crying inside the house, and I can hear muffled voices. Then footsteps approach, and the door swings open.

Jack lifts his brows at me. "So, you're needing a right good mental cleaning, eh? Like dentistry for the soul."

Oh aye, that sounds brilliant. Maybe I should leave. But I don't get the chance.

Jack clamps a hand on my shoulder and all but drags me into the house. "Come in, Domhnall. We'll go into my office to talk."

I see Autumn on the sofa with their bairn, a wee baby boy. He smiles and almost seems to be waving at me. No, he's probably looking at his father.

"He likes you," Autumn tells me. "Michael has good taste."

Fortunately, I don't need to respond to that statement because Jack shepherds me into his office and shuts the door. He waves for me to sit down on the window seat, where I can see the flowering bushes in the garden. He settles onto a high-back chair, facing me.

Jack clasps his hands over his belly. "So, Domhnall, tell me all the ways you've been behaving like a *bod ceann*."

Oh aye, this will be torture.

Chapter Two

Fiona

A phone rings, and I leap out of my chair to race over to the sofa where I'd left my mobile. My heart is racing, but only because I rushed to get over here. I am not excited by the prospect that it might be Domhnall ringing me. No, I simply don't want to miss a potentially important call. So, while the mobile rings for a third time, I take a moment to calm myself. Then, I answer.

"You sound out of breath," my sister Jamie says. "Did you and Domhnall kiss and make up? Ooh, I love make-up sex. Don't you?"

"Haud yer wheesht, Jamie. Domhnall and I have not reconciled. He's a flaming ersehole, and I don't care if he literally kisses my feet. I will never take him back."

"I see. Didn't you say the same thing a dozen times over the past few months?"

Maybe I did. But my little sister has no right to sound so smug about it. "You threw Gavin over and refused to speak to him. So dinnae be telling me how to handle Domhnall. He's a much bigger ersehole than Gavin."

"But not as big a *bod ceann* as Alex. Catriona whipped him into shape."

Jamie is glossing over some very important facts about Alex and Cat's relationship, but I know she's trying to sneakily convince me that Domhnall can change and wants to do it. Alex had been adamant in his belief that he didn't deserve another chance with Cat. Gavin went along with what my brothers insisted he must do to please them and was determined to change

Jamie's mind about him. Alex is nothing like Domhnall, while Gavin shares traits with him. They both served in the military, after all. All three men were outsiders when they courted MacTaggart women, and my brothers wanted to batter them.

They haven't put Domhnall through the Three Macs test. Not yet. They've been surprisingly supportive of our relationship. Aye, that makes me very suspicious.

My brothers only recently started calling their harassment the Three Macs Test. I think they invented the term just for Domhnall. Gavin and Alex both submitted to the same trials, but without the official title for it.

"You are the oldest sister," Jamie says, her tone sly. "Doesn't that mean you're supposed to be the mature, level-headed one? You aren't acting that way, Fiona."

"I just tossed Domhnall out of the house an hour and fourteen minutes ago. You don't know yet how I'll behave post-Domhnall."

"An hour and fourteen minutes?" Jamie laughs. "If you're counting the minutes, that means you are not over Domhnall. Did you count the seconds too?"

"No, you cheeky *smuilceag*."

Jamie laughs again. "Oh-ho, you're calling me a chit now. I might be flippant and a wee bit cocky, but only because I know you and Domhnall belong together."

A sigh blusters out of me, and I slump down onto the sofa. "We don't belong together. I cannae live with a man who won't share himself with me. Domhnall Sterling keeps too many secrets."

"What sort of secrets?"

"He won't discuss his ex-wife. I doubt I would know anything about his relationship with Jessica O'Connor if I hadn't been there when he tried to get between her and Grey Dixon."

Jessica is now a good friend, and she told me a few things about living with Domhnall. But she wouldn't tell me everything. I never expected she would. It's personal information. But I remember one specific thing she told me, though I still haven't figured out what it means.

I've always known Domhnall kept his past to himself, but I have no idea why. When he finally meets the woman who can crack him open, you'll see a new man.

What secrets? I'm clearly not the woman she described, because I can't get Domhnall to open up to me. After two years of trying, I've given up.

A sharp whistle shoots straight out of my mobile and into my ear, making me wince. "What the bloody hell are you doing, Jamie? I think you shattered my eardrum."

"You're being overly dramatic. I needed to get your attention. I asked a question, and you said nothing. I waited forty-five seconds before I whistled."

"You're counting? I bet you know how many milliseconds it was too."

I suddenly realize I've puckered my lips and scrunched my eyebrows, a sure sign that I want to shout at Jamie. But I am the mature oldest sister, which means I don't behave that way. So, I take a deep breath and exhale the anger. "Thank you for sharing your opinions, Jamie. But I don't need any help dealing with Domhnall."

"You're going to talk to him, then."

"Aye. Eventually."

She says nothing for several seconds, then clears her throat in the most deliberate way. "*How* eventually? Dinnae want to wait too long and lose your Prince Charming."

I hold the mobile away from my face and stare at it. And aye, I'm probably scrunching up again. Prince Charming? No one in my family would ever call Domhnall that. He has a sweet and loving side, though he hides it well from everyone—sometimes including me. To hear Jamie refer to him that way... It makes me very suspicious.

"What are you doing?" I ask her. "No MacTaggart has ever referred to Domhnall as Prince Charming."

"But he used to be that to you, didn't he?"

No, I will not answer that question. Not until I get the truth out of her and learn what her ulterior motive is. "This conversation had better not be the prelude to a round of insanity spearheaded by the American Wives Club."

"Would it be so bad if it was? Everyone loves you and wants to help you."

"Are you referring to just me? Or me and Domhnall?"

Jamie hums tunelessly. It's a dead giveaway that she's figuring out how to phrase her response without lying or telling the truth. "You and Domhnall are a couple, so there's no difference."

"Of course there's a difference. Either you support me, or you support Domhnall."

"You don't honestly believe that. Once you've calmed down from your barnie with Domhnall, you'll realize it too. And then, maybe you'll let us help you."

"Jamie—"

"Goodbye, Fiona."

My sister hangs up on me.

I sit here for several minutes, just ruminating on all the ways my life has become a gigantic mess. Was I wrong to get involved with Domhnall so soon after the debacle with Grey and Jessica? I had never been the sort who throws herself into a relationship the instant she meets a tall, braw man with big muscles. But if I'm one hundred percent honest, his physique was never the main thing that made me want him. I loved his determination. His intelligence. His willingness to try to be friendly with my brothers.

But lately, he seems to have given up.

Ugh. Am I going to huddle on the sofa for days or weeks thinking about that man? No. I have a life beyond Domhnall Sterling. Today is Saturday, but though I often work on the weekend, I have today off. My cousin Kirsty had given me a job at her metaphysical shop. I could go there anyway, for something to do.

Aye, that will show Domhnall.

I throw my head back and moan. No, it won't prove anything except that I have no direction in my life anymore.

Bloody hell.

I get up and find my shoes, which requires me to go into the bedroom—the one I've been sharing with Domhnall. I feel an odd pang in my chest when I look at the rumpled sheets and man-size boots on the floor. My eyes sting. I swipe at them, though I'm not crying, as if I can stave off the tears that way. To hell with Domhnall. He brought this on himself.

With a strange resolve, I snatch up every last piece of clothing that belongs to *that* man and dump it all into a rubbish bag the way I'd told him I would. His running shoes and hiking boots go in there too, along with his toiletries. I lug the lot into the living room and hunt down a piece of notepaper. On that, I scrawl two words—"Domhnall's rubbish." Then I tape that to the bag and haul it out onto the porch so I can shove it over to the side where it won't be obvious from the street.

I do feel a wee bit childish doing this. But it feels necessary. Why? I haven't got a clue.

Once I've finished my task, I get in my car and drive straight to Kirsty's shop.

The chime above the door jingles as I walk inside. I see several people milling about and one couple chatting to Kirsty. Her husband Luke, an American, stays behind the counter fiddling with knows what. Luke is a psychophysicist, which means he studies human behavior with the aid of technology. I doubt whatever he's doing now has anything to do with the wares Kirsty sells.

I hang about in the far corner until the customers leave. Then I approach the counter. "*Madainn mhath,* Kirsty."

"Aye, *madainn mhath,* Fiona. Though it's almost twelve o'clock, so you should probably say *feasgar math.*"

How could it be almost noon already? It seems like moments ago that I slammed the door in Domhnall's face. I hope I didn't injure his nose. It's one of his best features.

Kirsty grins. "You're thinking about Domhnall, aren't you?"

"I don't want to talk about him."

"That's understandable." She waves toward the area behind the counter. "Why don't you come back here? We can sit down to talk."

"I don't want to blether. Just needed to get out of the house." But I do what she suggested and go around the counter to perch on a stool beside Kirsty. "I kicked Domhnall out of the house."

Her expression shifts into something softer and more sympathetic. She lays a hand on my knee. "I know, and it's awful that you two are having troubles."

"You know? How? The only person I've spoken to was Jamie."

"And she told Catriona, who then rang Emery, and—"

"Enough. I know how the MacTaggart grapevine works. By now, everyone in the Highlands knows that I'm done with Domhnall."

Kirsty's brows hike up. "Done with him? I see no evidence of that."

I throw my head back and moan. "Please dinnae tell me that your *dà-shealladh* showed you that we belong together."

"Oh, no," she says with a laugh. "It wasn't my second sight. It was Emery who told me that."

How could Emery know anything about my relationship with Domhnall? It's utter rubbish.

Kirsty pats my knee. "You seem confused, Fiona. That's understandable. But we've all been discussing you two for months, ever since your troubles started. And we are all determined to help."

"No meddling."

She sighs, though I see a canny glint in her eyes. "Everyone says that. But in the end, you will thank us."

I know they've helped other couples, but Domhnall is nothing like my brothers or sisters or cousins. He's far more pigheaded than any of them. Besides, I have a plan. Maybe I invented it a few seconds ago, but it's still a valid strategy.

So, I straighten and give Kirsty a curt, decisive nod. "I know exactly how to deal with Domhnall. I will ignore him and move on with my life. Working here was always a temporary situation, and it's time I looked for something permanent. That means I'll need a new job and a new house."

"Why would you want a different house?"

"Because I need to eradicate Domhnall Sterling from my life."

A throat-clearing draws our attention to the man hunched on the floor in the far corner behind the counter. Luke's expression turns pinched. "Sorry. I didn't mean to eavesdrop, but I was over here before you guys started talking. Didn't want to interrupt."

Kirsty swivels her stool to face him. "You had something to say, *gràidh?*"

"Yes. I was thinking that maybe Fiona should get a new job. Not because of Domhnall, but because she's a very smart lady who should have a career that really means something to her. You love this shop. But for her, it's just a paycheck. Am I right, Fiona?"

"Aye. But how did you know that?"

He taps his temple. "My scientific brain told me."

"I would love to find a job like I used to have—being a manager for a regional supermarket chain. It was more rewarding than selling trinkets." I wince as I look at Kirsty. "I don't mean that your job isn't rewarding."

"Aye, I know what you meant. And Luke is right. You should find something that suits you better."

Luke rises and stretches, then he gets a devious look on his face. "And I know exactly how you can find your dream job."

Chapter Three

Domhnall

I stand in the garden behind Jack and Autumn's house, arms crossed over my chest, watching the psychologist trimming bushes and flowers. Why am I doing this? Dinnae have a clue. Jack asked me two questions back in his office, then announced that we should go outdoors for the rest of our "session." Not that I wanted any such thing. A dram of whisky sounds more appealing, but Jack is a decent bloke, and I don't want to insult him.

But I am getting bloody sick of watching him fiddle with the greenery.

I'm also bloody sick of staring at the stone wall that surrounds the backyard. It's an attractive feature, but the more I look at it, the more I want to pound it into dust. That might be a sign I'm losing my mind.

No, Jack is the bampot. A sane man would not spend time fiddling with bushes and flowers. I can't deny the sundial intrigues me, though. If Jack weren't intent on shrinking my head, I might ask him about that. The bird bath isn't as fascinating.

"Are you planning to mow the lawn too?" I ask. "Or maybe sing a song for the squirrels?"

Jack stops trimming a bush and turns toward me. "You are an impatient sort, aren't you?"

"Aye."

"You don't like to lose either."

"That's hardly a secret. Everyone knows it."

Jack ambles over to me, still holding the strange little scissors he'd used to trim the bushes and the flowers on the trellises. At least he's holding the scissors with the sharp point down. "I was there in Oregon."

"Is that supposed to mean something to me? You went on holiday in America. Congratulations."

"No, Domhnall, that's not what I'm trying to get at. I've been too subtle, though, haven't I? Let me make it clear." He leans toward me and speaks in a soft yet forceful voice. "I was at Alex and Cat's wedding, which you crashed, and I saw the way you lost Jessica O'Connor and how you lost to Grey Dixon in the Highland games."

"Yes, I grew and changed and became a better person on the inside. That's what I'm meant to discover, aye? Well, now I've done it. Thank you for the lesson on trimming bushes, but it's time I say goodbye."

Jack grasps my arm just as I start to turn away. "We aren't done yet."

"Yes, we are. You asked me two questions, then dragged me out here. I've had enough."

"Do you want Fiona back or not?"

"Aye, of course I do."

"Well, then. Here's how you start." He offers me the strange scissors. "And it's called pruning, not trimming."

I stare at him for a moment, but if I'd wanted to intimidate him, I failed. Jack seems quite serene, though I sense a bit of mischief in his expression. I might as well go along with this nonsense. Sighing, I take the small implement. "What do I do with these scissors?"

"They're pruning shears." He grasps my upper arm again, leading me over to the pink flowers that cover one of the trellises. "These are climbing roses. Your job is to cut away the little bits that aren't growing well."

"What makes you think I give a toss about gardening?"

"Oh, I'm dead sure you don't give a toss. That's the point." He gives me a hard push, forcing me closer to the trellis. "You need to expand your horizons."

I groan and trudge up to the climbing roses, then start to root about to find sickly ones. Is that how pruning works? Jack didn't elaborate. Instead, he ambled over to the wooden bench several yards away and sat down. Now, he sits there watching me as if every minute move I make is fascinating and important. I go about my work, though I have no clue if I'm doing it right. Since Jack doesn't complain, I assume I haven't destroyed the roses. After about ten minutes, I decide I've completed my task.

Has it been only ten minutes? Or more than that? I don't have a watch to tell me the time.

I stride over to Jack and hand him the pruning shears. "It's done. May I go home now? Or do you mean to have me prune the whole garden?"

"You've done enough." He accepts the shears and pats my arm. "That was excellent, Domhnall. Once your therapy session is over, we'll go for a drive."

"What? I cannae do that. I have a job, ye know."

"Not on Saturday. You work on the weekdays only. Everyone knows that because Fiona told us."

My first impulse is to snarl and spout grumpy nonsense. But I dinnae do that anymore, not since I met Fiona. Anytime I feel the urge to act like a *tolla-thon*, I quash it. Behaving like an ersehole won't solve my problems.

Instead of snarling, I tell Jack, "Aye, I don't work on the weekends anymore, not since I became the general manager of the new Sterling Dalton Fitness Center location in Loch Fairbairn."

"That would be the newest branch of the company you and your American mate own."

"Aye, our second branch in Scotland. Callum's wife Kate is the assistant manager and senior therapist—for both physical and mental sorts of therapy. Her clinic merged with our company earlier this year."

"A great partnership, aye?" When I nod, Jack points to the bench. "Sit down, Domhnall. We need to have a serious conversation."

"I answered your two questions, and I went along with your barmy gardening experiment. That's enough."

He shakes his head. "Sit down."

That's the last thing I want to do. I'd much rather drive home as fast as I can, pull Fiona into my arms, and kiss her until she goes limp against me. But I think I might have finally decided Jack isn't a bampot after all. Maybe I should let him give it a go, though I'm still not convinced therapy will fix my problems.

I drop onto the bench. "I'm listening."

He chuckles. "That's not how therapy works. You speak, I listen. So, let's begin with those two questions I asked you earlier. Remind me of what they were."

"Do you have senile dementia? I told you my answers earlier."

"Tell me again. I'll get you started by asking those questions again." He looks directly into my eyes. "Do you love Fiona?"

"Yes."

"Do you love her enough to do anything, even humiliate yourself or give up something you want badly, to make her happy?"

"Yes."

Jack studies me for a moment. Then he leans in until I can see every line and speck of deeper color in his irises. "Now tell me the long version of that answer."

"Dinnae understand what you want."

"I want to know why you fell in love with Fiona."

So, it's going to be *that* kind of conversation. I spill my bloody guts to Jack, and somehow that will help me figure out how to make things right with Fiona. It sounds like rubbish. I wince and scratch the back of my head, avoiding Jack's gaze. "I fell for her because she wasn't intimidated by me. I could growl and snarl and curse at her all I wanted, but she would just smile."

"Was Jessica afraid of you?"

"No, of course not."

"How did she react when you snarled at her?"

"I never snarled at Jessica O'Connor."

Jack pulls away, so at least now he isn't staring into my eyes from millimeters away. But now he wears a slightly smug expression. "How many women have you snarled at, Domhnall?"

I begin to feel itchy all over, though I have no idea why. The urge to scratch becomes almost irresistible, but I fight it. That means I clench my teeth, which forces me to squeeze words out in a barely intelligible way.

Jack cups a hand over his ear. "What was that? I couldn't understand any of it. Try relaxing your jaw."

A sigh blusters out of me. "I said I have never snarled at any other women."

"Only Fiona?" When I nod, his smug smile stretches wider. "Ah, the truth is revealed at last."

"What truth? You're off your head."

Jack clamps a hand down on my shoulder. "You only snarl at the one you love."

"But I loved Jessica."

"Did you? Or had you convinced yourself that she was the one for you because you don't like to be alone?"

I jump up and fist my hands. "I am not afraid to be alone. Jessica never moved in with me, though I wanted her to. Said she needed to maintain her independence."

"And you didn't mind? You two were engaged, after all."

"Not every couple decides to live together before they're married."

But aye, the more Jack pushes me to talk about Jessica, the more I begin to wonder if she wasn't the only one who had reservations. Maybe I did too. Being a pigheaded *bod ceann*, I might have overlooked the signs. I cared for Jess, and

I wanted to marry her. But did I want that for the right reasons? After an hour with Jack, I've begun to question everything I thought I knew about myself.

Jack must be either a genius or a lunatic.

Right now, he's giving me another smug smile. "You are sensitive about the topic of Jessica, aren't you? Why is that?"

"Because she wouldn't move in with me."

"Hmm." Jack folds his arms over his chest again and tips his head to the side, his gaze focused on me. "How did you feel about Jessica's best friend?"

"Grey Dixon annoyed me."

Jack chuckles. "Annoyed you? I was there, remember? When Jessica and Grey realized how they felt for each other. You lost the woman you claimed to love, and you lost her to a Brit. A much-younger one. A computer geek. Grey is very clever, and he was accepted by the MacTaggart clan with great enthusiasm. You, on the other hand..."

"They hate me. Aye, we all know that. Fiona was the only MacTaggart who didn't think I was a complete ersehole, and I fucked it up with her. That's what you pushed me to say, as if it's a stunning revelation." I clap sarcastically. "What a bloody brilliant therapist you are."

"I'll accept the compliment, even though it was sarcastic." Jack once again tips his head to the side and studies me. "Why did you and Fiona move to Loch Fairbairn? You both had jobs in Inverness."

"She missed her family. But you already know that."

"You were willing to move to MacTaggart country to make her happy, but you won't share all of yourself with her. Why is it?"

When I open my mouth to respond, he throws a hand up to stop me.

But then he waits a moment, with his hand still raised, before he speaks. "We can explore that question later." Jack clasps my hand and gives it a brief shake. "Congratulations, Domhnall. You've survived your first therapy session and experienced a breakthrough."

"What breakthrough? You're off your head for sure."

"Calling me crazy is a positive sign. Now, get out of here. I want to spend the rest of the weekend with my wife and child, not a stubborn erse like you." He releases my hand, finally. "We'll pick this up another time."

I grumble as I stalk out of the backyard and out to the driveway. My pickup truck is parked along the street, so I climb in and head out, though I have no clue where I'm going. Home? Is Fiona there? She banished me. But I have nowhere else to go. Might as well see if she's home. If she is... I'm not sure that's a good thing. She seemed ready to batter me earlier.

Aye, I've hurt the lass badly. But I never meant to do it.

On the way home, I drive a bit too fast and take the corners a bit too steeply. Still, I manage to arrive in one piece. As I trot up the porch steps, I notice a dark shape in the corner. I halt and stare at the black rubbish bag. It's been tightly sealed, and a sheet of paper has been taped to it. The makeshift sign has two words scrawled on it.

Domhnall's rubbish.

Given the sharp slant to the letters on the paper, I know she must have still been fuming when she wrote that. When I slide my key into the lock on the front door, it turns easily. Well, at least she hasn't changed the locks—not yet. I go inside and instinctively walk down the hall into the bedroom. Her attempt to eradicate me seems to have included getting rid of my pillow too. It's probably inside that rubbish bag.

I go into the kitchen and grab a bottle of whisky and a glass, then shuffle into the living room to drop onto the sofa. *Mhac na galla.* How did everything go so wrong?

The distinctive sound of a key being inserted into a lock makes me jerk my head toward the front door. It swings inward, and Fiona walks inside. She freezes when she notices me.

I jump up with the whisky bottle still in my hand. "Fiona, I—We should talk. Please."

Her brows lift. "Domhnall Sterling is being polite? That's new."

"Never have I been rude to you." I wince. "Well, except for when we first met at Alex and Catriona's wedding. And I occasionally snarl at you, though I don't mean to do it. Can we talk? Please?"

I'm virtually begging. Me. Begging.

Fiona stares at me for a moment, then kicks the door shut. "All right. Let's talk."

Chapter Four

Fiona

I agreed to talk to Domhnall, but I'm still not sure that will have the effect he's hoping for. I won't fall into his arms and beg him to make love to me. *Oh, bloody hell.* Now I'm beginning to get aroused, all because of a casual thought that was meant to be sarcastic. I can't deny I've always had a weakness for Domhnall. I had a poke with him only a matter of days after we met, for heaven's sake. He might have impressive skills in the bedroom, but I will not fall for his tricks ever again.

No sex. Full stop.

As I shuffle into the living room, I drop my purse on the end table, and my attention wanders to the well-muscled man sitting on the sofa beside that table. His black T-shirt stretches taut over his chest and biceps. The way he has his knees spread draws my focus down to his groin and the bulge of his cock.

I stop and try to gather my wits. But my pulse quickens. I lick my lips without meaning to do it. My nipples tighten too, and a delicious tingle races over my skin.

Why can't I stop wanting this man?

Domhnall pats the sofa cushion beside him. "Sit down, *gràidh*, please."

I do sit down, but not beside him. Instead, I wedge myself into the corner of the sofa furthest from him. "Say whatever it is you wanted to tell me."

"We need to have a conversation, *leannan*. That doesn't work if you won't talk to me."

Every time he calls me "sweetheart" in Gaelic, I melt for him in ways that are not conducive to having a serious conversation. I wish I didn't become a puddle of warmth, but I can't stop it—especially when he speaks in that soft, deep tone. It's hot and sweet at the same time, and I unconsciously relax, slumping into the sofa cushions.

He turns toward me. "Will you talk to me now?"

"Aye."

Despite the fact he suggested it, he doesn't look like he wants to talk. Domhnall seems almost anxious about what I might say. When did I become frightening? I imagine it's not me, not really, but rather the fact that I kicked him out of the house. That means I should start things.

"You want to know why I tossed your belongings into a rubbish bag and dumped them on the porch." I wriggle a wee bit, suddenly uncomfortable on the plush sofa. "The truth is, this has been building for a while. You must realize that too. We haven't been getting on as well as we used to, and that's due in large part to one thing."

"What is it?"

"Every time I ask you about your past relationships, you tell me it's none of my concern."

"The past doesn't matter. But it's not true I never tell you anything about my previous relationships. You know all about Jessica and my ex-wife."

I can tell he honestly believes that, but I cannae let him get away with that claim. Time to burst his bubble. "You might believe that, Domhnall, but it's not true. I know only what you told me when we first met. Every time Jessica rebuffed you, like the grumpy sod you are, you retreated to whatever hideaway you could find. Back then, it was the woods that surrounded the nudist resort."

"Aye, and then you harassed me until I told you everything."

"That's half true. I did push you to talk about the situation, but you absolutely did not tell me everything."

He screws up his mouth and faces forward again, essentially cutting me out of his view, and keeps his arms barred over his chest. "That's bollocks. There's nothing else I can tell you."

Oh, aye, Domhnall Sterling is the stubbornest man on earth. Even my three brothers can't best him in that contest. But I was there when Domhnall and Grey Dixon literally battled over Jessica O'Connor. Domhnall lost. Worse, he cheated and was humiliated when Grey won the Highland games and his own trickery was exposed. I know how he cheated, but I've never gotten him to fully explain why he was so desperate to outdo Grey.

"You are the one who's full of rubbish, Domhnall. The day we met, you told me that you meant to convince Jessica she was making a terrible mistake because Grey was taking advantage of her." Since he won't look at me, I move onto the coffee table directly in front of him. "Why did you say that? Was it just macho posturing? Or did you honestly believe Grey was using Jess?"

He shrugs one shoulder.

Yes, he's definitely more stubborn than my brothers. And this was one of the reasons we had a row this morning that ended in me tossing his stubborn erse out the door. This time, I won't let him slither under my skin. "Did you honestly believe you knew Jessica better than Grey did? He'd been her best friend for years, long before you met her."

Domhnall says nothing for several seconds, his gaze now aimed at his own feet. "Maybe that was a lie I told myself. But I did want to win her back. That was always true."

"Why on earth was it so important for you to salvage a relationship that only you wanted?"

"You know why. I've only had two serious relationships in my life, and neither of them ended well. I dinnae like to lose."

He had been on the cusp of admitting something important, I could feel it. But then he reverted to the line I've heard too many times. *I dinnae like to lose.* That's an easy out, but I can't let him wriggle away from the truth anymore.

"Domhnall, please, I need to know the deeper reason."

"Then you want a different man. I have no deeper reasons for anything."

I slide off the coffee table to kneel between his legs. With my hands resting on his thighs, I try one more time to convey how much I need him to open up to me—all the way, no holding back. "I'm begging you, Domhnall, share everything with me. Why did you really try so hard to get Jessica back? Even after she and Grey became a couple?"

He shuts his eyes and exhales a long breath. "You were right to send me away, Fiona. I can't give you what you want or need, and especially not what you deserve."

Domhnall pushes my hands away and steps over me to head for the front door. I trot after him, barely catching up before he swings the door open. He grips the knob so tightly that his hand shakes faintly.

I reach for him.

He shrugs away from me. "Jack was wrong. I haven't experienced a breakthrough. That was a mirage, and now I need to accept the truth. You deserve a better man than I am."

"That's for me to decide, not you."

"No, it's an indisputable fact. Everything your family thought about me when I first me them is true."

He yanks the door open wide and stalks onto the porch, slamming the door behind him.

I stand here staring at knob, unable to move, struggling to understand why he always pulls back into himself whenever he's inches away from divulging the truth. I responded out of fear and anguish this morning. That had been a mistake. I shouldn't have booted him out of the house. But most of all, I should never have told him it was over between us.

Should I give up on him? I don't want to do that. But we can't go on like this much longer. And after what he just said… I rip the door open and sprint outside, determined to race up to Domhnall's pickup truck. He just started the engine, which means I have seconds to get his attention and try one last time to convince him to go inside and spill his ruddy guts to me.

But I halt halfway across the lawn, suddenly frozen, unable to think of a single word I might speak to change his mind. I've said it all before.

The truck surges forward, then stops. I can see him inside the vehicle, staring at me with a hard expression. As if I've never seen that before.

I march up to the passenger door and bend over to peer through the glass at him. "Roll down the window, Domhnall."

His expression grows even harder, but I still am not fazed by his behavior. It's fear, not anger. At last, he rolls the window down. "What the bloody hell do ye want from me, Fiona?"

"You know what. I want the truth. You know everything about me, but I still don't know enough about you."

He rolls his eyes, and his tone turns sarcastic. "Oh, aye, the saintly Fiona MacTaggart never keeps a secret. That's rubbish, and you know it. If ye want me to tell you all my secrets, best be ready to reciprocate."

I gnaw on my bottom lip while I consider his demand. Maybe I do have one secret, but it's a wee pebble compared to the mountain of mysteries that Domhnall keeps hidden inside himself. I've waffled about our relationship for two years, but even more so lately. My heart keeps pushing me to forgive him and try to work things out, but I cannot do that anymore.

Here, in this moment, I've made my final decision.

"All right, Domhnall, have it your way. We're done, for good. Get your bag of rubbish off my porch and go." Technically, he owns the house. It's his name on the deed. But that's beside the point. "If you knock on the door, I'll ring the police station. I'm sure the constables will be happy to lock you up in the Loch Fairbairn police station for me. I dated two of them, after all."

Domhnall stares me again, this time with his gaze narrowed. "Then why dinnae ye go to the station now and pick your next boyfriend."

He rolls the window up and drives away.

Well, at least he didn't squeal the tires.

Are we both behaving like children? Aye, we are. That's one more reason why we should never have become a couple—and why I shouldn't take him back. We bring out the worst in each other.

It's over, for good.

Maybe I have said that before, more than once, but I mean it this time. I swear I do.

Across the street, I see my cousin Errol Murdoch and his wife Ashley coming out of their house, heading this way. They hold hands as they cross the street. Domhnall and I live in the house Ashley had leased when she was trying to convince Errol to go on a wild expedition with her in the Grand Canyon. I like having family just across the way. We bought this property for that reason.

Today, I wish we'd never done that. I should have chosen a home in the back of beyond, like my brother Rory. Why? Because I know Errol and Ashley must have seen my argument with Domhnall, and now they want to commiserate with me.

Bod an Donais.

Since invoking the devil's penis won't stave off the inevitable, I straighten my posture and my clothes, then force myself to smile as Errol and Ashley approach me.

Ashley pulls me into a hug. "I'm so sorry you and Domhnall had a fight."

"Could you hear what we said?"

"No, of course not. We were inside the house."

Errol nods. "Aye, but we could see you two. That was quite the row, by the looks of it."

"I don't want to talk about that *ruinnse*. We are over."

Ashley sidles up to Errol and speaks in a stage whisper. "What did she just call Domhnall? Something uncomplimentary, that's all I could tell."

"She called him a monumental prick."

"I see." Ashley smirks. "Does he really have a monumental—"

Errol slaps a hand over her mouth. "Afraid my wife can't speak right now. She's developed a sudden, acute case of laryngitis. It will pass in a moment—after we've changed the topic of conversation."

Ashley peels his hand away from her mouth. "Very funny, Errol."

The answer to Ashley's question is yes, Domhnall Sterling has an impressive cock. Not that I will ever admit that out loud.

"I'm not in the mood to talk about Domhnall," I say. "So, if that's the only reason you dashed over here..."

Errol whispers something to Ashley, and she nods. Then he clears his throat. "No, we had another reason besides making sure you're all right. We had thought to hold off sharing this news, but you seem like you need to get out of the house for a wee bit. Aye?"

"Definitely. But if this involves any sort of meddling meant to save my relationship with the *ruinnse*, I'm not interested."

"No meddling yet." Errol grins. "You want a new job, and we've arranged something for you that we think you'll like. But we aren't quite ready to reveal the surprise."

Perfect. Another secret.

Chapter Five

Domhnall

After leaving Fiona, I drive...nowhere. What am I meant to do now? The bloody woman won't give up her quest to pry all my secrets out of me. She claims she has told me absolutely everything about her past, and I have no reason to doubt that. But my past is nothing I want to share with her or anyone. My ex-wife never cared that I didn't tell her about things that happened before we were married.

Of course, Sophie engaged in an affair with another man for most of the time we were married, though I only found out near the end. I know that experience changed me. I'd only been with Sophie and Jessica until the day when Fiona suggested I should try kissing someone else. Then she pressed her mouth to mine.

And everything changed.

Until I fucked it all up.

I drive without any destination in mind, meandering down the streets of Loch Fairbairn until I finally turn onto the trunk road. What will I do now? I'm literally homeless.

Up ahead, I spot the half-finished excavation site Ian MacTaggart and Alex Thorne had dug up a few months ago after ground-penetrating radar revealed something under the surface. For reasons I cannot explain, I pull over in the small, makeshift car park and get out to amble over to the single standing stone. It lies within a ditch, since it had been buried until recently. Within the trench surrounding the stone, which would tower high above my head if I leaped into the trench, lie the half-buried remains of a cairn. Apparently, Alex and Ian haven't got round to finishing the excavation.

I have no idea why I'm standing here, staring down at the ancient site. Maybe I'm feeling rather old myself, though I'm hardly ancient. For the third time, a woman I love has booted me out of her life. The problem is me, obviously.

The sound of a car coming up the road behind me interrupts my contemplation. I don't bother to turn and look. My pickup truck is parked off the road, so it's not in anyone's way. But then I hear the oncoming car slowing down.

If I ignore the erse, maybe they'll go away.

A hand claps down on my shoulder. "Ah, there you are. I should have known a Scot who lost his woman would try to top himself in an ancient cairn. It's incredibly obvious."

Bloody hell. I know that voice, and it's not Iain. "Away and take your face for a shite, Alex."

He chuckles. "Yes, I had a feeling that might be your response."

"Shouldn't you have someone else with you? Excavating doesn't sound like a one-person job."

"It isn't. But I am not here to excavate anything. I saw you brooding alongside the road and thought I'd watch the festivities as you end your mortal existence." He comes up alongside me and leans forward to look into the giant hole in the ground. "Hmm, I don't think it's quite deep enough to kill you. Shall I give you a good push? Maybe you'll crack your skull on the standing stone."

"Falbh dàirich fhein."

"Fucking myself isn't as fulfilling as you might think." He turns in my direction, studying me intently. "You're strangely vigorous for a suicidal man."

"I am not suicidal."

"Aren't you?" Alex crosses his arms over his chest and gazes into the excavation pit again. "Well then, why are we gazing into the abyss?"

"Because Jack rang you and suggested you should track me down. Aye?"

Alex puckers his lips, then sighs. "Yes, all right. Jack sent me to find you, and Kirsty spotted your pickup truck heading down the street where her shop is located. I simply followed your trail."

"Mhac na galla. You lot are like living GPS units."

"Indeed we are. With so many MacTaggarts in the Highlands, no one can escape from them."

I glance at him sideways and smirk. "So that's why you married Catriona. The MacTaggarts held you captive."

Fiona hadn't done anything of the sort to me. Does that mean she was right to break up with me? I have never made her feel so desperate to keep me that she would resort to abduction.

I'm turning as barmy as the MacTaggarts and their in-laws.

Alex claps a hand on my shoulder again, this time squeezing a wee bit. "Listen carefully. You have two options in this situation—give in or fight."

"I can't fight when Fiona won't speak to me."

"That's not what I meant." He pulls out his mobile and dials a number. "Yes, pet, we are indeed ready. Send in the hounds."

He ends the call.

What hounds? Living with a MacTaggart must have softened his mind so much that it turned to pulp.

"Thank you for the bizarre and unhelpful advice, Alex. But I'm leaving now. Must be a hotel room available somewhere in the Highlands."

I pivot on my heels and march toward my truck.

Alex chuckles.

That Brit is the barmiest of the barmy.

I climb into my truck and shove the key into the ignition. When I turn it, nothing happens. I try five more times, but still, nothing happens. My bloody pickup truck is broken. Aye, this day just keeps getting better. Maybe next, an asteroid will crash down on my vehicle, crushing me to bits.

Alex walks up beside the driver's window and knocks on it.

I roll down the window. "What now? My sodding truck is dead. I need to ring someone to tow it back to…Dinnae know where."

"No need for a tow." He dangles a cable in my face. "I removed the battery cable."

"You did what? How in the world—I didn't hear you open the bonnet."

"Of course not." He drops the cable on my lap and pats my cheek. "Former grifter, remember? If I could pick someone's pocket without them noticing, I can most assuredly remove your battery cable without rousing your suspicions."

"But—That's not poss—" I give up and smack my palms on the steering wheel. *"An Diabhal fhéin."*

"If only it were the devil who tricked you. Alas, it was merely the British Bastard." He straightens and holds a hand over his eyes like a visor, squinting as if he sees something. Then he waves his hand repeatedly as the sound of tires crunching on gravel draws nearer and finally stops. "Hurry it up, gents. Domhnall might nosedive into the excavation pit if you take too long."

"Dinnae worry. We won't let him get away."

That sounded like…Munro MacTaggart. He hates all this meddling rubbish as much as I do. But he's helping Alex and whoever else is conspiring with him.

Alex pulls my door open. "Your valet awaits, Mr. Sterling."

Since I clearly have no choice, I heave myself out of the truck and turn to face my captors. Munro has been joined by the American Gavin Douglas, husband of the Three Macs' youngest sister Jamie, as well as another man I don't recognize. "Who the fuck is that laddie?"

"Thane Buchanan."

"Another cousin with a MacTaggart mother, eh?"

"No. He's a Buchanan through and through."

I arch one brow. "I thought your cult only involved MacTaggarts and their American wives and husbands."

"You are still so naive about the MacTaggart clan. No matter. We shall have you fully indoctrinated soon enough." He shoves two fingers into his mouth and whistles with such piercing volume that I wince. "Get a move on, would you? Before the prisoner decides to do a runner."

As I walk past Thane Buchanan, he eyes me with a strange expression, something between curiosity and disdain. Or I might be off my head now, thanks to the MacTaggart clan's bloody annoying antics.

When we reach the other car, Munro is leaning against it while Gavin stands tall and straight like the soldier he used to be.

Munro shakes his head. "Ye didn't heed my advice, eh?"

"You told me to be unstoppable. That's vague, annoying nonsense."

The Wild Man eyes me up and down, then shakes his head again. "Having big muscles doesn't make you clever or powerful. Until you accept that, you'll never figure out how to stop Fiona from pushing you away."

"She wants things I can't give her." Why am I having this conversation with Munro? Here on the roadside? It's ridiculous. "My relationship with Fiona is no one else's business."

Gavin steps up to me, wearing his best military-man glare. "When you mess with one of our women, we don't take it kindly. Breaking Fiona's heart was your first mistake. Your second was assuming we would wait before we started the reeducation of Domhnall Sterling. And your third mistake…"

"Maybe we shouldn't tell him that bit yet," the British Bastard says. "It would ruin the surprise."

Gavin aims his hard stare at Alex. "You interrupted me, asshat. And you don't know half as much as you think."

Alex waves his hand in a dismissive gesture. "Go on, then, if you must. Americans are so ostentatious."

Gavin rolls his eyes again and faces me. "Your third mistake was to assume we don't want you and Fiona to get back together."

"For the last time," I say through gritted teeth, "my relationship with Fiona is none of your bloody business."

Munro pushes away from the car to stand beside Gavin. "You made it our business when you became involved with Fiona. That gives us the right to do whatever we please to rectify the situation. And by 'rectify,' I mean we will batter you in every way imaginable."

Gavin smirks. "He means that metaphorically."

"No, I don't. But we'll start with the less dangerous option." Munro reaches through the open window of the car and pulls out a full roll of duct tape. "Mouth and wrists, for certain. If ye struggle too much, it'll be ankles too."

Alex taps his finger on his chin. "Hmm, perhaps we should blindfold him as well."

These men are harassing me. They might have once tied Owen Metzger to a chair on the green at Dùndubhan, but they know they cannae pull that bollocks on me. I helped restrain the laddie, after all. Well, it's more accurate to say that I stopped him from running away—by lashing my arms around his midsection. I'd been working with Munro at the time, during the mad series of events the MacTaggarts and their British mates had concocted to help Owen and his lass, Poppy Goodburn.

If these three think they can run the same con on me, they're dead wrong.

Gavin throws his head back and shakes it at the sky. "Honestly, you European guys are such divas."

"European!" Alex and Munro balk at the same time, their disgust evident on their faces. Strangely, Thane has no reaction to that statement.

Munro scowls at Gavin. "I am Scottish, ye *cacan*."

"And I am the British Bastard," Alex declares. "That means I'm from England, not Europe. Glance at a map now and then, Gavin."

The American shrugs. "Scottish, British, European. What's the diff?"

"Haud yer wheesht!" I shout. "If you lasses are done squabbling, why don't you go back to the schoolhouse and play with your baby dolls?"

Gavin raises his hands. "The European guys started it."

While they harass each other more about nationalities, I suddenly realize I have no choice. A man with no home and no woman has nothing. So, I march up to the car and climb into the backseat.

The others don't notice for several seconds.

Abruptly, they freeze and swivel their heads toward the car. Several sets of eyebrows shoot up in unison.

Gavin points at me. "Did he surrender without even arguing about it?"

Alex appears completely bemused. "Yes, I believe he did."

"Who gives a toss," Munro growls. "Gavin and Thane, get in the car. Alex will drive Domhnall's truck."

Munro gets into the driver's seat, while Gavin takes the front passenger seat. They've left me alone in the back, not that I care. But I don't stay alone for long. Thane Buchanan climbs into the backseat and casts me another odd look, then faces the front and ignores me.

As we're rolling down the road, Munro watches me in the rearview mirror. "You would do well to start heeding my advice, laddie. To be unstoppable means not running away and confronting your problems head-on, but you seem to be having trouble with the concept."

"Vague proclamations are not helpful."

"Aye, but you gave up so easily."

Gavin twists around in his seat to look at me. "Don't worry, Domhnall. We've got a solution all worked out for you."

I know how this lot comes up with "solutions." Since I have no idea what to do with myself now, I might as well go along with their insanity. They will, no doubt, drag me out to the most remote location in in this area, namely the castle of Dùndubhan. But then Munro drives past the turn that would take us there.

"Where are you going, Munro?" I point out the window. "Dùndubhan is that way."

Gavin looks at me over the back of his seat. "What made you think we're going there? You, pal, have to earn Dùndubhan."

Whatever that means, I have a feeling I'll wish I'd jumped into that excavation pit after all.

Chapter Six

Fiona

I have been sitting on the sofa staring at a horrible TV series for more than an hour. The story might not be to my liking, but that isn't why I keep staring at the screen. I've spent all this time trying not to think about Domhnall, but my thoughts keep circling back to the topic of that *bod ceann*. I haven't come up with any answers to the many questions his behavior brings up.

Should we not have moved to Loch Fairbairn?

He had been running Sterling Dalton Fitness with his partner, Mick Dalton, since before I met Domhnall. But after we became a couple, Domhnall moved from America back to Scotland to start a new branch of the company, all to make me happy. We lived in Inverness for a while, but I missed my family. He knew how close I was with my sisters and brothers, my cousins too, so he sacrificed what he wanted for me. And he created another branch of Sterling Dalton Fitness in Loch Fairbairn just for me too.

Maybe I've been the one in the wrong. But no, his secrets have split us apart, not the fact that we relocated.

I've just shut off the television when the doorbell rings.

My heart beats faster, and I feel a ridiculous flutter in my tummy as I rush to the door and swing it open.

The man who grins at me is not Domhnall. "Fiona, darling, how splendid it is to see you."

I gawp at him for a moment, unable to make sense of what I see and hear. Then I splutter and finally speak. "Easton Yates? What are you doing here?"

The Brit's grin widens more. "To see you, pet. Why else would I come all this way?"

"I have no bloody idea." I shake my head slowly. "Ye cannae just show up on my doorstep and…do whatever you're doing. I haven't seen or heard from you for two decades."

"Yes, I know that." He lays a hand on the door and pushes gently. "Let me in, Fiona. We need to talk."

Now that my shock is waning, I begin to grow suspicious. "After all these years, why should I want to see you? And how did you even find out where I live?"

"Your name and address are in the phone book, love."

"No, they are not." I told him the truth. Domhnall had bought our house on his own since his credit is better than mine. My dress shop had failed. I filed for bankruptcy after that. So, the only name in the phone book for this address would be Domhnall's.

Whatever this man wants, I don't care. "Goodbye, Easton."

I try to shut the door, but he lodges his boot in the jamb to stop me. "We *will* have a conversation, Fiona."

"Like hell we will."

I kick him in the shin, and when he stumbles backward, I slam the door and lock it.

"Open the door, Fiona. Don't behave like a child."

No, I will not respond. I can't understand why he's here or how he found out where I live. But that doesn't matter because I will never speak to him or let him inside my home.

I push away from the door as a realization hits me. Our home. That's what it used to be.

Easton starts whistling casually, as if he's having a wonderful time harassing me. "Come out and play, Fiona darling."

"Leave now, or I'll ring the police."

"Why are you so afraid of a little conversation? Perhaps you think you can't resist me."

I snort. "In your dreams. Go away right now, or I'll ring my brothers. They don't take kindly to men who harass women."

Why do I need to ask my brothers for help? Am I so pitiful that I can't handle a *tolla-thon* like Easton Yates? I used to sleep with the man, for pity's sake. Surely I can get rid of him on my own.

I turn around and pull the door open. "What do you really want, Easton? No malarkey about wanting to talk. Tell me the truth, or you'll regret it."

"Because your brothers will…do what, precisely?"

"They won't need to do anything. I'll get rid of you myself."

He chuckles. "That's adorable, Fee. You think you're a superhero."

"I hate being called Fee. You know that."

"Women always say the opposite of what they really want." He thrusts his arm out to pat my erse before I realize what he's about. "But I know all your true likes and dislikes."

I huff. "You know nothing."

When he reaches for my erse again, I grab his hand, bending it backward from the wrist until he winces.

Easton wrenches free of my grasp. "That wasn't very nice, Fiona."

"You aren't behaving nicely either. What happened to you? When we were dating, you always said please and 'thank you,' and you pulled chairs out for me. Now, you're acting like a right bastard."

He shrugs. "I'm older and wiser."

"What does that mean? A wise man wouldn't harass me."

"Maybe I want to reminisce about our time together, all those years ago."

I can't tell if he's having me on, or if he genuinely wants to reminisce. His behavior so far suggests that he only wants to torment me. None of this makes any sense.

Two figures emerge from the house opposite mine and jog across the street toward my yard.

I point past Easton's shoulder. "Best have a look. My reinforcements have arrived."

And I hadn't even rung Errol and Ashley. Maybe they're psychic. Or maybe I'd been shouting more loudly than I realized.

Easton glances over his shoulder. "Who are those two?"

"My cousin and his wife."

Ashley and Errol hop onto the porch. Errol bars his arms over his chest and does his best to seem menacing, though it's not in his nature. He achieves the effect rather well, though. "Who is this *bod ceann* who's harassing you, Fiona? Should I batter him?"

"Thank you, but no. He was just leaving."

Easton turns halfway, so he can see all of us. "Well, I can see I'm not welcome right now. Might as well be on my way. If you want to talk, Fiona, just ring me at the Loch Fairbairn Arms, Room 130."

He hops down the steps and whistles again as he dances his way back to his car. Within a moment, he has driven away.

Errol squints at the receding vision of Easton's car. "How did he get a room at the Loch Fairbairn Arms? It's been booked up for two weeks."

Two weeks? Easton couldn't have arranged his accommodations that far in advance. Well, he could. But why would he do that? Planning ahead to come to my town and pester me? It makes no sense. I don't care about whatever Easton is playing at, except for how it affects my life.

He's cocking it up. That's how his sudden appearance has affected me.

Ashley grasps my arm. "Fiona, are you okay? You look like you've fallen into a trance."

"What? Oh, no, I'm fine. Just can't understand what Easton wants."

She leans in close to whisper, "If you want to tell us about that guy, we'll keep it on the down low until you're ready to share it with everyone."

"No need for secrecy. I'm sure every MacTaggart in the Highlands has already heard that a British scunner came to my house." I hug myself as a realization makes every hair on my arms and at my nape stiffen. "How did Easton find me? I dinnae like this situation at all."

"Do you worry he might harm you physically?" Errol asks. "If so, we have plenty of strong, angry men who will batter the scunner on your behalf."

"I think I'd rather start with staying somewhere else for a wee while. Maybe Easton will give up if he can't find me."

Ashley gives my arm a light squeeze. "Who is this Easton guy?"

"Never mind that for the moment," Errol says. "First, we need to get Fiona away from here. Someplace that British *cacan* would never think to look."

"Dùndubhan?" Ashley suggests.

Errol shakes his head. "Too many people know about Dùndubhan. It is a museum now, in addition to a bed-and-breakfast."

"Right. I forgot about that for a second."

We all stand here for a minute or two, each of us trying to come up with a solution to my housing problem.

Finally, Ashley gives me a sheepish look. "Well, one option would be to have Domhnall move back in with you."

Errol shakes his head, and his expression turns devious. "Oh, no. I have a much better idea." He slants toward me, his voice hushed. "How do ye feel about World War II era planes?"

"I hope you're not suggesting I should fly around in your decrepit DC-3 for the rest of my life."

"No, but you might need to get used to hearing it taking off and landing." He straightens and nods once. "Aye, you should stay with Torcall. He's a crusty old coot, but he has a heart of gold. And I guarantee Torcall Murdoch will never let any man harass you. He also has a very nicely decorated house for an old bachelor."

I'd met Errol's great-uncle a few times, and he is quite a character. Staying with him for a few days or even a week seems like the best option. Hopefully, Easton will get bored and go home. "I thought Torcall was married. But you called him a bachelor."

"He used to be married, but his wife ran off with a chancer who flies charters from the Glencoe airfield. They moved to South America, last I heard. Torcall filed for divorced as soon as was legally permissible."

"Is that why he lives out in the middle of nowhere?"

"Aye. But dinnae worry, Torcall isn't a rabid grizzly bear—most of the time."

Maybe that's what I need. A rabid grizzly bear of a man who will stop Easton from harassing me at any cost. I feel oddly better just knowing Torcall is a tough man.

Domhnall used to make feel that way. I thought of him as my knight in shining armor, and I still feel that way about him, though I wish I didn't.

Ashley and Errol insist that I should leave right away, so I gather up everything I might need for a week's stay at Torcall's house. As I walk out the front door, I pause and study the living room, the only part of the house I can see from this vantage. A lump forms in my throat. Tears threaten to gather in my eyes, making them sting. Until this morning, I had shared this home with the man I loved, but now everything has fallen apart.

Errol slings an arm around me. "You'll be back soon, *gràidh*. Domhnall will come to his senses, and you two will be right as rain again."

I pray he's right about that, though I should curse at the prospect.

Shutting the door, I follow Ashley and Errol out to their car across the street. Ashley insists I should sit up front with Errol, and I'm too jeeked and shell-shocked to argue. But as we start down the road, I suddenly remember something I'd heard about Ashley.

I twist my torso to look at her around the back of my seat. "Don't you get motion sickness? You should be up here. I don't suffer from that problem."

"Oh, I'm fine. After our adventure in the Grand Canyon, I was cured of my motion sickness. Haven't felt a twinge since."

Errol grins. "There's nothing like almost drowning in the Colorado River to get you over that wee problem. You're as barmy as I am now."

I face the front again and try as hard as I can not to think about Domhnall or Easton. Until Ashley brings up the latter.

"So, Fiona, are you going to clue us in on the whole Easton situation? It's fine if you don't want to do that yet."

I exhale a deep sigh. "Might as well put it in the grapevine now and get it over with. I met Easton Yates when I was away at university, and we were a couple for the better part of three years."

Errol glances at me sideways. "This is the first I've heard of you having a boyfriend while you were away. You must have sworn your sisters to secrecy, eh?"

"No. I never told anyone about Easton."

Ashley leans forward to peek at me around the back of my seat. "Why did you hide your relationship?"

I squirm in my seat and avoid meeting her gaze. "I was afraid my family wouldn't approve, since Easton is British. This was before Catriona went away to grad school and secretly lived with Alex Thorne for two years. No one would have cared, but I was young and naive and completely smitten. The secrecy felt romantic and sexy."

Neither Errol or Ashley says anything for a moment that seems like an eternity. At last, I can't stand the silence any longer. Time to blurt it out.

"Easton Yates is my former fiancé."

Chapter Seven

Domhnall

*A*fter a while, we turn off the paved roads and head down a long gravel two-track that takes us deeper into the woods. The trees become a canopy over our heads, blocking out most of the sunlight. But I'm not interested in the scenery. I want to know what the bloody hell these lunatics are doing, dragging me out into the back of beyond with no explanations.

I'm unlikely to get any answers from these three.

"We're almost there," Gavin announces. "No point in trying to make a break for it once we stop. With three ex-military men in the car, you won't stand a chance."

Four ex-military men. But I've never told anyone but Fiona about my past, not even my ex-wife. The third veteran must be Thane.

I glance at the man sitting beside me. Thane Buchanan has not spoken a word since I first saw him, and I can't figure out why he's here. The man seems older than Gavin and perhaps Munro too. I've never been skilled at deducing a person's age simply by looking at them. But Thane has faint wrinkles around his eyes, and that suggests he's probably in his forties, at least.

"How do you know Fiona?" I ask him.

Thane still says nothing. He acts as if he didn't hear me.

I lean forward, poking my head between the front seats. "Is your silent friend hearing impaired?"

Munro chuckles. "No, laddie. Be glad for the silence. Once he starts to talk, you'll know you're in trouble."

"Enough with the mysterious bollocks. Tell me who Thane is and why he's here helping you lot kidnap me."

"Mysterious bollocks, eh? Dinnae think Thane appreciates being accused of peddling that rubbish."

"*Falbh dàirich fhein*, Munro." Aye, I just told him to go fuck himself.

A hand clamps down on my shoulder from behind, and I'm slammed backward into the seat. Thane shakes his head. "Fiona is a wonderful woman, and I dinnae take kindly to anyone hurting her. We know what you're after, but you'll need to prove yourself first."

He releases my shoulder and faces forward.

The mystery man finally spoke. But I still have no idea who he really is. I doubt he'll answer any questions to explain himself, so I slump into my seat. Thane is right about one thing, though. Fiona is a wonderful woman.

Finally, Munro slows the car down as he turns onto an even narrower two-track. The woods open up to reveal a large, grassy clearing with a small house positioned at one end. Not far from the house, Errol's DC-3 sits there waiting for its barmy owner to arrive. Errol calls the plane Marilyn. Only a man who's off his head would name a DC-3.

Munro parks near the front door of the house and blares the horn in three sharp bursts, holding the last one for several seconds.

The front door of the house bursts open, and Torcall Murdoch trots out. I have no idea how old Torcall is, but he looks like a stereotypical grizzled mountain man, with wild gray hair and a bushy gray beard.

Munro and Gavin jump out of the car to greet Torcall. But when I attempt to exit the vehicle, Thane grasps my shoulder again and shakes his head without even glancing at me. The man is starting to remind me of the spies I'd met in the army. But even Logan MacTaggart, a former army intelligence officer, doesn't behave the way Thane does.

Munro, Gavin, and Torcall are laughing and chatting, but I can't understand their words. The car windows make it difficult to hear them.

Finally, Munro opens the rear door on Thane's side.

My silent seat mate keeps hold of my shoulder as he slides out of the car, dragging me out with him. I have to scramble across the seat to keep from being dumped out on my erse. I could have fought him, but that seemed like the wrong thing to do right now. Besides, I'm curious about what these men have in mind for me. Torcall doesn't seem like the sort of man who could help me win Fiona back.

Once I've regained my footing, after being dragged out of the car, Torcall winks at me. "Good luck, laddie. Might want to start praying."

He climbs into the front passenger seat of the car.

Gavin and Munro escort me to the door of the house while Thane simply stands beside the vehicle watching us. Munro knocks on the door but doesn't wait for whoever might be waiting inside to open it. He walks right in. Gavin and I follow. I'm led into the living room, a small but clean space, which surprised me because I'd assumed a grizzled mountain man would have a cluttered house that hasn't been cleaned in months.

We all stop near the sofa.

Gavin and Munro exchange glances I can't decipher. Then Gavin says, "Good luck, bro."

He trots out of the house.

Munro smirks at me, then shouts toward the hallway, "You can come out now!"

He rushes outside, and within seconds, I hear the car driving away.

What the bloody hell? They left me here alone in Torcall's house? I rub my eyes and sigh. Those barmy men.

"Domhnall? What are you doing here?"

I jerk and lower my hand from my face, gaping at the woman who stands a few yards away. "Fiona? What are *you* doing here?"

"Errol and Ashley brought me. They said it's part of my therapy, though I haven't had any sort of psychological counseling. They're off their heads."

"Aye. They kidnapped me, and someone called Thane tried to unnerve me by not speaking."

"Thane Buchanan?"

I nod.

She lifts her brows. "Cannae believe they brought him in on this ridiculous meddling scheme."

"Have you slept with Thane?"

Now she scowls at me. "What business is that of yours? We aren't a couple anymore, and my past has nothing to do with you."

"That means yes." And now I want to race after that car so I can haul Thane out of it and give him a right thrashing.

She crosses her arms over chest. "My life is none of your concern anymore."

How can the lass tell me that? I would do anything for her. Wouldn't I?

Fiona stalks past me and yanks the front door open. "Get out, Domhnall."

"Do you have a car? I don't, and it's too far to walk back to Loch Fairbairn."

"Then sleep with Marilyn."

"I am not spending the night in Errol's plane. There's no bed, not even a cushion to lie on."

She throws an arm out to indicate the doorway. "I don't care. Leave. Now. You can always sleep on the grass."

The pigheaded woman will not relent. But I suppose this is the sort of situation Munro had meant when he told me to be unstoppable. That means I can't let Fiona chase me away. But for the moment, I'll make a strategic withdrawal to consider a new plan of attack.

I approach the door but pause there.

Fiona lifts her chin. She must not realize that her defiance always makes me want to have a poke with her. Every time we argued, even about trivial things, I would get so randy that I had to seduce her. She never complained about that. Fiona loved it, which I know because she was never quiet while we shagged. And when she came...

"Get out, Domhnall. Now."

"All right, I will. But first..." I sling an arm around her waist and tug her into my body. Then I lift her up just enough that our faces are level. "Before I go, answer one question for me."

"What is it?"

I cup her erse with my free hand, making her suck in a wee breath. "Do ye want to fuck right here, right now?"

She compresses her lips and blows a breath out through her nostrils. But she doesn't answer my question.

"Best find out on my own, then." I give her erse a light squeeze as I slide my other hand up her back to grasp the nape of her neck. "I swear I can already smell your cream. And your nipples are stiff. I can feel that."

I rock my hips forward, rubbing my erection against her belly.

Fiona gasps.

Bod an Donais. I need to rip her clothes off and thrust inside her warm, slick sheath. We haven't had a poke for weeks now. To live with her and sleep with her but not make love to her... That's the definition of torture. But I shouldn't seduce her, not when we have so many things we should talk about first. I dinnae want to do that, which means no sex.

Fiona's lips have turned a bonnie shade of rose. I'd wager her nipples are the same color.

"Stop thinking about sex, Domhnall. You need to leave the house."

"Is that what you really want?" I grasp her hips and pull her into me, grinding my cock into her belly. When she sucks in a wee, sharp breath, I know we both want the same thing. "Stop denying that ye want me, *gràidh.* Just say the word, and I'll strip us both in five seconds flat."

The stubborn lass maintains her mulish expression even while she presses her tits to my chest and fists her hands in my shirt. She's breathing hard too, and her eyes have darkened. "I want you, Domhnall."

I can't hold back my smirk. "I know that."

Her gazes narrows. Her lips pucker.

And she knees me in the groin.

I grunt and stumble backward, doubled over as I speak through gritted teeth. "What the bloody hell did ye do that for?"

She stumbles backward two steps. "It was the only way I could stop you from seducing me. We both know I can't resist you when you're trying to seduce me. That's my weakness, but I won't give in this time."

"Were ye trying to literally bust my balls?"

"No. I'm sorry for kneeing you like that, but I had to break the spell."

I straighten and adjust my dokey, wincing a wee bit. "Aye, the spell is broken now."

She opens the door and nods toward it. "Good night, Domhnall."

"Good night? It's daytime, ye barmy lass."

"If you mean that the sun is still up, then you're right. But according to astronomy, it's now civil twilight." She lifts her chin. "Errol told me about the three stages of twilight."

Errol had no idea, I'm sure, that Fiona might use that information as an excuse to boot me out of the house. But I'm too jeeked to argue with her anymore. This has been a trying day, to say the least. So, I walk out onto the porch. Before I can say goodbye, or say anything at all, she shuts the door.

Well, at least she didn't slam it in my face this time.

I trudge out to the dilapidated DC-3 that Errol calls "Marilyn" and climb the cramped steps that lead up to the door on the side of the plane. After a moment of struggling, I finally get the door open and climb inside. I decide to leave the hatch open so I can get some air in here. I have limited options for sleeping. The cockpit is rather cramped, and I'm a large man. I cannae imagine how Errol squeezes himself in there, or how Magnus managed that feat.

No, I won't try to sleep in the cockpit.

But I do find a blanket stuffed into some sort of cubbyhole. It looks relatively clean, so I take that and wander back into the cargo area. I have never set foot in "Marilyn" before today, and I reckon I expected to find cargo in the cargo hold. But no, there's nothing in here. Just ratcheting straps attached to what look like metal tracks that run the length of the hold. Small, round windows allow some light to penetrate the space. I also find several sling-like seats attached to one wall.

Aye, this looks like a luxurious place to spend the night.

I lay my blanket down on the floor, between two of the metal tracks, and then settle in on top of it. Lying on my back, I stare up at the ceiling with my hands clasped over my belly. Noises from outside filter inside, but that doesn't fash me. It's just wildlife.

Then I hear a soft humming sound. Must be the wind. But the sound grows louder, seeming to approach the plane. I must be imagining it. When

I glance out the door, I can't see anything, though the humming swiftly grows louder as if the source is racing toward me.

Suddenly, I feel the pricking of something biting my arm.

What the bloody hell? I spring upright as more spots on my arms begin to sting from being bitten. That humming sound surrounds me, and abruptly, I realize what it is.

Fucking midges. The bane of the Highlands.

"Ah, *iasg is feòil!*" I leap up and stagger toward the open hatch, then try to climb down it but trip on the second step. As I leap down onto the ground, striking with a *whump*, I hear those bloody midges swarming toward me again. "*Mhac na galla!*"

I scramble to my feet and sprint for the house. To hell with what Fiona wants. I am not going to sacrifice my flesh simply because she's in a fankle. The lass will have to accept that I'm sleeping in the house tonight. Fortunately, she didn't lock the door. I tear it open and leap inside, slamming the door behind me. I don't think any midges made it inside. I'd run as fast as an Olympic sprinter.

As I sag against the door, I release a long, groaning sigh. The I shut my eyes and slump down further until my erse meets the floor.

"Domhnall! What happened?"

I crack one eye open. "Midges."

She bites her upper lip. "How badly did you get bitten?"

"Think I escaped before those wee beasties could eat me alive."

Fiona switches the overhead light on, then kneels in front of me. Her gaze travels over all my exposed skin. "Looks like it isn't too awful. I've seen worse. But I should put some calamine lotion on your bites. Go into the bedroom, and I'll get what you need."

"Thank you, *mo leannan.*"

But how long will she let me stay in this house?

Chapter Eight

Domhnall called me his sweetheart, but that won't change my mind about him. Aye, I feel bad for him thanks to those midges. That's the only reason I follow the *tolla-thon* down the hallway. I veer into the bathroom as he goes into the bedroom. Did he get bitten up on purpose to make me feel sorry for him? No, that's ridiculous. Domhnall is many things, not all of them good, but he is never nefarious. Besides, he seems genuinely miserable after his encounter with midges. It might be a male-pride issue rather than physical strife.

Domhnall has an overabundance of male pride. Or at least he used to.

Once I've combed through the contents of the bathroom closet to find the calamine lotion, I hurry into the bedroom.

And I freeze.

Why? Because Domhnall is lying on the bed, naked, stretched out with his hands clasped under his head, seeming supremely relaxed. I'm glad he's feeling better, but he didn't need to undress. All his midge bites are on his arms and throat, and he doesn't have many of them, anyway. What captures my attention is not the sparse red spots on his skin. No, I can't tear my gaze away from his body. My focus travels down every inch of him, from his impressive biceps and the defined muscles on his torso to those powerful thighs that I've felt flexing when we made love.

But the part of him that entrances me the most is his cock.

As I admire that part of him, I grow warm and tingly. The hairs at my nape and on my arms lift and make my flesh sensitive, so much so that I think if his little toe brushed against my hand that I might come.

"Stop looking at me that way, Fiona. Unless you're wanting me to take you right here, right now."

"That's inappropriate. We broke up."

"No, you threw me out of our house. But ye never said you were breaking up with me."

"Yes, I did. 'We are over,' that's what I said."

"But you're going along with your family's barmy scheme to get us back together."

Oh, bollocks. He's right about that. I have gone along with it, and I can't explain why. Maybe I do still love him, but that will fade away eventually. He hurt me too badly for me to forgive him.

But maybe I could… No, I will not give in to my lust for him. He's counting on that, and I refuse to give him the satisfaction of being right. No more waffling. No more melting for him.

Domhnall slides a hand down the center of his torso, languorously, deliberately, until he reaches his groin. Then he bends his knees just enough that he can tip his legs to the side and make room between his thighs. He shifts his hand down to clasp his cock and stroke it with sensual leisure. "Ye want me, *mo leannan.* Let's relieve the tension between us, then you can tell me to bugger off."

The sexual tension in this room has become overwhelming. I never could resist this man. I had a poke with him just days after we met. We had slipped into the guest house at the nudist resort and sneaked into the kitchen. He took me on the countertop. I can still remember every sensation, as he pulled my erse forward to get a better angle, then thrust into me with power and delicacy, two things that seem contradictory. But with Domhnall, it made sense.

"Ah, *gràidh,* ye want me inside you. So just give in and do it."

The deep, rough tone of his voice makes my clit pulse. Domhnall could seduce a nun into having wild, wicked sex with him. And I don't know for how long I can resist the lust he inspires in me. It's like a tidal wave of desire rushing toward me, rising higher and higher until I can't breathe anymore.

He releases his now-hard cock and lets it bounce between his spread legs. While he skates his palms up and down his inner thighs, he gazes at me with the hottest, most devilish, most irresistible smile I've ever seen—even from him. "I'll talk dirty to you, *gràidh,* and you can be in control."

Oh, aye, he is *an Diabhal fhéin*—the devil himself—luring me down into the abyss of erotic pleasure.

He lifts his arms to grasp the headboard rails and hoists his hips just enough to ensure I'm staring at his cock again. "You can even tie me up, *mo leannan.* I'll be at your mercy."

It can't be a coincidence that the devil shares his first name with the man who's determined to seduce me tonight. Domhnall Sterling is every bit as wicked as *Dòmhnall Dubh,* Black Donald, the devil himself.

His lips curve into a carnal grin. *"Is iomadh rud a nì dithis dheònach,* Fiona."

Aye, we can do many things together. All night. Until we're both slicked with sweat and struggling to catch our breath. To take control of him… A shiver of delight rushes through me at the mere thought of doing that.

I strip off my nightgown and climb onto the bed. As I crawl between his legs, aiming for his cock, he groans deeply. That sound makes my breath catch. When I lie down with my head hovering over his hard length, he sucks in a breath and grips the headboard rails more tightly. I take hold of the base of his erection, then drag my tongue over the crown.

He jerks and gasps.

Aye, I'm liking this game. Me in charge of Domhnall. I can have my way with him for as long as I want. It won't change the fact that I threw him out of the house, and I won't take him back unless he shares everything with me. But we can have a bloody good time tonight.

I curl my lips over my front teeth and let my mouth descend on his cock. His body has always fascinated me, but he would never let me go down on him in this way. Now, he lies there watching me do it. I notice the veins that run through his cock, and the velvety texture of his skin. A soft moan whispers from my lips as I begin to pump him with my mouth and my hand. With my other hand, I stroke his inner thigh and then move higher to skim my palms over his lower belly.

"Fuck, Fiona, you're killing me."

My lips tighten into a smile even while I keep sucking and licking and pumping him. The swollen length of his cock nudges the back of my throat, but I dinnae care. He arches his back and lets out a strangled cry. The sensual curve of his spine and all those flexing muscles only distract me for a moment, then I increase the pace and the strength of my sucking until he splutters and his hips lift off the mattress.

Aye, he's ready to come. I could push him over the edge in a heartbeat.

But instead, I rise to my knees and wipe my mouth with the back of my hand. "Mm, ye taste so delicious."

"Ye didn't make me come."

"I know." I lick my lips, gazing down at his incredible body. "Mm, I want to do wicked things to you, *mo gaoloch.*"

"Then do it."

I lean back, holding myself up with my straight arms, and shimmy forward until his cock nudges my mound. Then I wriggle until I get his length nestled between my thighs and shimmy forward again, sliding his erection inside me as far as it can go. I can't stop myself from moaning. To have him inside me again, after such a long time without sex, feels better than anything. Now that I have my feet planted on the mattress at either side of his hips, we're ready to go.

"Fuck me, Domhnall. Stay in this position and do it. I know you have the strength and stamina to make us both come this way."

He lets out a deep, hungry groan.

And then he starts thrusting, taking it slowly while we both adjust to this unfamiliar position. Oh God, this feels incredible. I rock my hips while he keeps thrusting, and soon, we're both making wild noises as our pace accelerates and the bed begins to creak. I throw my head back, my mouth gaping, as I shout his name and fist my hands in the sheets.

Domhnall releases his hold on the headboard rails and sets his elbows on the mattress, then pushes up, straightening his arms to give him more leverage. He bucks his hips, pounding his cock into me, and my heart beats so hard and fast that I feel a wee bit lightheaded, but I won't tell him to stop. I need him to finish us both off. But I suddenly realize I don't want to do that, not yet.

So, I grasp his knees and hoist myself off his *slat*. Now kneeling above him, I fight to pull in full breaths. My body is on fire, and the need to come throbs inside me, and yet I know I can drive us both even wilder by shifting into a different position.

"Bloody hell, Fiona," Domhnall snarls. "Are ye trying to drive me mad?"

I nod, since I still can't summon my voice.

He reaches for me, but I slide off the foot of the bed, landing on my feet. My legs are a wee bit shaky. When he scoots up to the foot of the bed and reaches for me again, I plant one foot on his chest and shove him backward. He willingly flops down on the mattress with his glorious cock waving. The rosy tip has a single bead of moisture poised atop it.

Domhnall groans. "I'm begging ye, *mo leannan*, dinnae stop now."

"I haven't stopped. But I need to get a few things." I hold up a hand when he seems about to sit up. "Stay right there, Domhnall, and close your eyes. If you peek, I'll go into the bathroom and finish myself off without you."

Domhnall Sterling, the stubbornest, most rugged man I've ever met, obeys my command. He relaxes and shuts his eyes. His lips curl into a soft wee smile.

I hurry to the closet, yanking the folding doors open, and root about until I locate the two items I need. Then I return to the bed and tie my favorite silk scarf around his head to blindfold him. I'm still not done yet, though. Next, I trot over to the little table by the window and drag it to the foot of the bed. In the process, I move his legs aside. But once I've positioned the table where I want it, I set his feet on that surface.

What I'm about to do to him, I've never tried before. It's another first for us, I'm sure. "Sit up, Domhnall, but dinnae remove the blindfold. And keep your feet on the table."

He does exactly what I said. Maybe there is hope for us after all.

No, that's just my hormones talking.

I turn around and climb onto his lap, guiding his cock into my opening until it's fully seated inside me. My high heels give me more leverage, and I know he'll lose his mind when he sees me in them while we're doing this. But first, I want to leave him guessing for a while.

Grasping his knees, I bend forward and begin to ride him.

He sucks in a sharp breath and takes hold of my hips while he rolls his own in time with my movements. Our gasps and grunts and groans fill the room, and I no longer want to keep him blindfolded. So, I reach behind me to undo the knot, letting the scarf tumble to the floor.

Domhnall leans his head over my shoulder to stare at my high heels. "*Bod an Donais.* I love those shoes."

He shoves one hand between my thighs to rub my folds and mercilessly grind his thumb into my clit.

I can feel the orgasm rising inside me. The tension builds and builds while my breaths shorten and my nails dig into his thighs. "Domhnall, please, make me come."

Almost there. On the edge. Teetering so close to the precipice…

Domhnall stands up and tosses me onto the bed, on my back. I bounce a few times while he just stares at me, his chest heaving. "Not yet, *m'eudail,* not yet. I haven't had my turn."

Chapter Nine

Domhnall

What can I do to Fiona that she hasn't already done to me? My cock wants me to finish us both off, but I dinnae want her to feel cheated. She clearly means to drag this out for as long as possible, and I never want to leave her less than satisfied. As a couple, we had never done anything this unusual or adventurous. Is that what she wanted? More excitement in the bedroom? I still have no idea what Fiona wants from me, other than information about my past.

No, I can't tell her about that. It's irrelevant, anyway.

Or I might be deluding myself, and it is relevant.

Bloody hell. I cannae think straight with my dokey about to explode and Fiona lying there spread out on the bed, wriggling about like she might come at any second.

She has never looked more beautiful.

Fiona gets on her hands and knees to crawl closer to me. Her focus remains locked on my erection. "You wanted to have your turn, but you haven't done anything yet. I'm on the edge, Domhnall. If you don't do something soon, I might take care of things on my own."

I clench my fists, desperately trying not to let her push me over the edge. Why am I trying to hold off the inevitable? Dinnae remember anymore. While she wriggles her erse, I absently stroke my cock.

She rises to her knees and waddles up to me. The lass places her wee hands on my chest and drags them down to my waist.

I need to devour her *brillean* until she comes, then thrust into her *cìrean coilich* so hard that she'll go off again while my *slat* is buried deep inside her body. It's been too bloody long since I felt her *péiteag* wrapped around me.

The lass cups her tits with her own hands, massaging them as if she's trying to push me to the breaking point. Her tactic works.

I grasp her thighs and flip the lass onto her back. She lets out a sharp yelp. I take hold of her hips and pull her snugly against me while I guide my length into her sheath. She feels hotter and slicker than ever, and her cream lubricates my cock, the scent of it driving me half mad. Then I begin to thrust while still holding on to her hips. Her legs dangle in the air. Her tits bounce with every powerful thrust, and I grunt and groan, so desperately relieved to be fucking her that I can't think about anything else. She fists her hands in the sheets and bites down on her bottom lip.

"Harder, Domhnall, please."

Then she tightens her inner muscles around me.

"Ah! Fiona, ye vixen, dinnae do that."

She does it again.

I slap my hands onto the bed and begin fucking her so hard and fast that even I cannae believe what I'm doing. She cries out over and over as the sounds of her pleasure fill the room. The pressure mounts inside me, like a ratcheting mechanism tightening more and more until it feels like my entire body might explode. I throw my head back, teetering on the edge, so close to it that the slightest thing might set me off.

Until a thought bursts into my mind. I'm not using a condom.

That one rational realization has broken through my desperate need to erupt inside her body. Since I cannot stop, I rub Fiona's clit like a maniac, pushing her over the edge. I keep on rubbing that nub while I withdraw my cock and pump it with one hand. Fiona shouts as her body pulls in on itself, and I know she's hit her peak. Still, I keep working her clit while the jet of my release sprays over her belly. Once I'm done, I can't do anything except tip my head back, shut my eyes, and let out a groan that's so deep I can feel it I my chest.

Speaking is out of the question. My breaths come in short, sharp gasps.

Fiona lies beneath me, seeming dazed. Her lids drift shut.

"Are ye all right, lass?"

She peels her lids open. "Aye, I'm fine. Domhnall, that was…"

"I know."

Fiona lays the back of her hand on her cheek and exhales a satisfied breath. "Breakup sex is bloody fantastic."

Breakup sex? No, this was a renewal of our relationship. That's how it felt to me. But apparently, Fiona disagrees.

I carry her into the bathroom and turn on the shower, then set her down inside the stall. She doesn't complain while I wash off her belly and proceed to bathe us both. The lass just leans against the wall with a blissful smile on her lips. She even closes her eyes. After the poke we just enjoyed, I could lie down and go to sleep right here in the shower, so she must be exhausted too.

After cleaning ourselves up, I carry her back to the bed and lay her down there, pulling the covers over her. Then I gather our clothes and set them in neat stacks on the dresser before I crawl into bed with Fiona. She is asleep now, with that sweet smile still curling her mouth. I nestle against her backside cautiously, so I won't disturb the lass.

What will happen when she wakes up in the morning? I won't worry about that right now.

I didn't even notice when I fell asleep, because the next thing I know, the sun is shining into the bedroom and birds are singing outside. At some point, I had rolled onto my back. Fiona now lies sprawled over me with her hand uncomfortably close to my groin. I can feel my cock swelling already. Aye, that happens on most mornings. But to wake up with her soft, warm body on top of mine makes me want to shag her again.

But mostly, it makes me need to hold her forever.

Fiona yawns and stretches with her eyes still closed. She wriggles on top of me but still seems unaware of the fact that I'm lying beneath her. Then she sighs with deep satisfaction and wriggles again. Her hand bumps into my growing erection.

She freezes. The lass opens one eye, glancing round the room, then opens the other eye. She sets her hands on my chest and pushes up onto her straight arms to gaze down at me with a mixture of confusion and consternation. "Why are you still here?"

"Because we had sex and then fell asleep. That's what people do."

"No, ye *cacan*. Why are you still here? We aren't a couple anymore."

"We made up last night."

She slides off my body and sits cross-legged beside me. "Go home, Domhnall. We had our breakup sex, and it's over."

Bloody hell. She still hasn't given up on the breakup-sex idea. "We love each other, *mo leannan*. That means we should be together."

She folds her arms over her chest. "Are you going to tell me about all those things you refused to talk about before?"

I don't want to lie to her, which means she won't be happy with my answer. "No, I will never talk about those things. They're irrelevant."

"Then we have nothing else to say to each other." She hops off the bed and begins to search for something. "Where are my clothes?"

I point toward the small piles that I left on the dresser. "Right there."

Fiona's brows wrinkle as her gaze shifts to the dresser. She glances at me sideways, then approaches the dresser as if she expects a demonic doll to leap out of it and strangle her. The lass carefully picks up her stack of clothes and stares at it with the same uncertain expression.

Finally, she looks at me. "You folded my clothes?"

"Aye."

"I have never seen you do chores. I always take care of the laundry, and I didn't think you knew how to fold anything except maybe a piece of paper."

"Now that you know I can fold clothes, I should show you my skills at doing the laundry."

Her eyes widen, though only for a second. "Laundry skills? Have you ever looked at a washing machine? It has all sorts of settings and buttons."

"Of course I've seen a washing machine. But you always did the housework, so I assumed you didn't want me to do that. It's a woman's job, isn't it?"

"A woman's job?" She marches up to the bed, on the side where I'm still lying down. "You never had any inclination to do chores. If you had wanted to be helpful, you would have done it." She squints at me. "It's no wonder we didn't work out."

I'm beginning to feel annoyed now too, and I spring off the bed to stand inches away from her. "Are you implying I'm a sexist? I'll gladly do the laundry three times a day if that's what it takes to convince you I dinnae want to break up."

"You aren't a sexist." She stabs a finger into my chest. "You're a lazy *bod ceann*."

"How can you call me lazy? I run a fitness center, for pity's sake. That means I work out regularly, and I offer training sessions in the gym and outdoors."

"And ye worked so much we hardly saw each other."

We both freeze. Our gazes remain locked, but neither of us knows what to say next. She thinks I work too much? Why didn't Fiona tell me that sooner? And I am not lazy. Where did she get such a ridiculous idea? I think she might have just opened up a door for me, a wee bit, without realizing it.

Her breasts heave. Her lips pucker. And *bod an Donais*, I want to shag her again.

But I won't do that. Instead, I take two slow, deep breaths to calm myself. Then I grasp her upper arms, bending my knees until our eyes meet. "I will do all the housework and the yard work and anything else you want."

"That's not the point. Domhnall."

"What is the point? I don't understand."

She closes her eyes and sighs, then looks at me. "We just aren't a good fit for each other. I'm sorry, Domhnall. We are over."

Fiona kisses my cheek and rushes into the bathroom with her clothes.

My shoulders slump. I bow my head and blow out a breath. Am I giving up? No, I cannae do that. Fiona is the only one for me, and vice versa. I know that, and she knows it too, otherwise she wouldn't have bothered with "breakup sex." But we are not over yet, not by a long shot.

Be unstoppable. That's what Munro told me, and he's right.

I get dressed and head for the kitchen. I can hear the shower running, so I have time to enact the first phase of my plan. Fiona feels like I haven't helped out enough at home. All right, then. I will cook her a fine meal and do some chores too. This isn't our house, but by cleaning up Torcall's kitchen, I can show the lass that I don't mind doing housework.

Aye, that will do the trick. Won't it?

Of course it will. Probably.

Mhac na galla. That isn't the way to win her back. Fiona wants to know about my past, but I can't give her that. Technically, I could. I'm capable of speaking the words, but my mind refuses to let me. This is all I can do, for now.

By the time I've finished my self-appointed tasks, Fiona walks into the kitchen and stops dead. Her gaze is nailed to me. "You shouldn't still be here. We broke up, ye eejit. How many times do I need to tell you that before you accept the truth?"

"You said we broke up, but I disagree. That means we are still a couple." I spread my arms. "Look at what I've done for you."

She gives the kitchen a cursory examination and shrugs. "You cleaned up. I appreciate that, but it doesn't change anything."

"I cooked for you too."

"Do you want a medal for that? It still changes nothing." She wraps her arms around herself. "You know what you need to do to make things right, but you refuse to do it. There's nothing else to say."

Of course my grand gesture didn't work. I'm a bloody eejit.

Fiona eyes the two plates of food, then picks one up and hands it to me. "Take this outside. I need to be alone."

"The midges might eat me alive."

"I doubt that. The sun is up, and midges prefer to come out at dawn and dusk."

She thrusts the plate at me.

A strategic withdrawal seems like my only option for the moment, so I take the plate and head for the front door. I've just reached it when Fiona rushes up to shove a glass of milk at me.

"Your forgot this, Domhnall."

"The milk was for you."

She thrusts the carton at me again, making it slosh, though it doesn't spill out.

Fiona MacTaggart is the stubbornest woman on earth.

I take the glass and head outdoors. Though I glance back once, she has already shut the door. The lass probably locked it too. I sneak over to the window and peer inside. I can see into the kitchen just enough to know she's having her breakfast at the island.

I twist the knob, but it won't move.

She *did* lock the door. That must mean she wants me back. Why else would she need to keep me out? She's afraid she can't resist me.

Aye, sounding like an arrogant bastard will make Fiona change her mind.

I stride out to Errol's plane and drop onto the ground on my erse, leaning against the steps that lead into the decrepit contraption. I keep watching the house while I eat. I'm not waiting for Fiona to rush out here and beg me to take her back. No, she's too stubborn for that. Arguing with her does no good. We're both too bloody-minded to give in, even if we know we're wrong. We've both made mistakes, though mine are worse and the cause of our troubles.

Thankfully, I don't encounter any midges this morning.

I watch the sun rising over Torcall's house and get a wee bit distracted from my surveillance of the cottage when a fox trots past the nose of the DC-3. Then the crunching of tires on gravel seizes all my attention. Someone is approaching the property. Fiona's barmy family wouldn't come to take me away yet. That wouldn't fit with their scheme to force us into spending time together, alone, in a remote cottage.

After a brief moment of indecision, I set down my nearly empty plate of food and duck under the DC-3. I'll get leg cramps if I do this for too long, but I doubt whoever is coming up the drive will make me wait. The shadows under the left wing provide just enough cover.

The crunching noise grows louder, and a beige four-door vehicle rolls into view. I can just make out the silhouette of the individual inside the car, and I can also tell that person is alone—unless more people are hiding in the trunk or the backseat. That seems unlikely. Who is the driver? A friend of Torcall? No, that also seems unlikely.

The driver parks near the house.

I creep a little closer while remaining in the shadows.

As the engine shuts off, the driver climbs out and stretches his entire body. He yawns too and smiles as if he's very satisfied with his current situation. He won't feel like that for long. Time to find out who that man is. He's too young to be a friend of Torcall. I've heard that Errol's great-uncle enjoys his hermit lifestyle, which means no guests.

The newcomer wears posh clothes, not that I'm an expert on fashion. I'd wager this *cacan* cares a lot about his appearance.

I scuttle forward more, still crouching.

The cottage door swings open, and Fiona stalks out to greet the new-comer. She scowls at him.

Not happy to see the *cacan*. Good. But she seems to know him.

My jaw tenses, and so do my fists.

Fiona sets her hands on her hips. "What in the world are you doing here, Easton?"

She *does* know him. A genuine growl rumbles out of me, and I can't stop myself.

I charge at the *cacan*.

Chapter Ten

Fiona

Footfalls pound behind me, and Easton's expression shifts from smugness to total bafflement. I whirl around to see what snarling wild beast is rushing toward us. But it takes me a moment to understand what I'm seeing. Is that Domhnall? Charging at us? What on earth is that pigheaded man doing now? Before I can react to intervene, it's too late.

Domhnall tackles Easton to the ground.

My mouth gapes. I can't speak. My mind seems to have gone blank. The wild animal is my ex-boyfriend, and the victim of his assault is my ex-fiancé.

"Who is the *bod ceann*?" Domhnall asks. "You know this *cacan*, but ye haven't introduced him to me yet."

"This is Easton Yates, my ex-fiancé."

Easton lets out a hoarse cry as he tries to shove Domhnall off his body. But he doesn't stand a chance. Domhnall Sterling was an alternate on the UK Olympic wrestling team back in the day as well as a boxer. He won several amateur bouts. If I don't stop this, he might pummel Easton to a pulp. Maybe I might sort of like that. Just thinking about it makes me tingle in the most inappropriate ways. Though women don't usually like to admit it, most of us get aroused when a man fights for us.

But this display of masculine strength won't solve any of our problems—not my issues with Domhnall or Easton's bloody annoying attempt to do…something. I still haven't figured out his motives.

"Stop!" I shout. "Let go of him, Domhnall!"

The men ignore me. Well, they probably can't hear me, what with all their rolling about while grunting and snarling at each other.

I ignore another tingle that sweeps over me. All right, maybe I don't try that hard to ignore it. But I need to get their attention, and shouting did no good. Time to try Emery's tactic.

Shoving two fingers into my mouth, I let out a sharp, ear-piercing whistle.

The men freeze. With their bodies still entangled, they both turn their heads to gawp at me.

I remove my fingers from my mouth. "Stop this nonsense at once. I am not impressed by your juvenile display. Domhnall, let go of him. Easton, get back in your car and leave."

Domhnall disentangles himself from Easton and even offers the British *bod ceann* a hand to get up. Easton lifts his chin and clambers to his feet on his own. He takes a step toward me but stumbles and crashes into Domhnall, who simply aims his tough-guy stare at Easton. My former fiancé backs away and brushes off his clothes. Then he opens his mouth.

I raise one finger. "Haud yer wheesht. I have nothing to say to you, so get in your car and leave."

"Can't do that, pet."

"Are you stalking me? No one would have told you where I am, so you must have been tracking me somehow."

"Oh, yes, I'm suddenly a computer wizard. You're being ridiculous, darling."

I stab my finger into his chest. "Tell me how you found me, Easton, or else I'll ring for the police."

"Don't be melodramatic, pet. I was going to share my clever method for finding you, but you keep cutting me off." He leans against the car, one arm casually resting on the roof. "It's quite simple, really. I visited a charming café in that village where you live. By sheer coincidence, I happened to be seated next to a couple who were talking about you. I believe their names are Kate and Callum. She's American, and he is—"

"My cousin. That's who he is. But I dinnae believe for one moment that you just happened to hear them saying that I've come to this remote homestead."

"No, it didn't quite happen like that." He tries for a sheepish grin that I'm sure he thinks is disarming, but it only annoys me more. "I followed that couple when they left the café. They went into something called a 'metaphysical shop'—the name of the place was unpronounceable—and I trailed after them. That's when I overheard Kate and Callum talking to the shop owner about you. They seemed rather pleased to hear that you and your brutish lover had been stranded here on purpose."

Should I believe his tale of coincidence and eavesdropping? I'll need to ring Kirsty and Kate to find out the truth. But I don't have time for that right now. Somehow, I must convince Domhnall and Easton to leave and let me be. There's probably a greater chance of a hurricane hitting Loch Fairbairn.

"You spied on the MacTaggarts?" Domhnall says with his teeth gritted. "And you came here to harass Fiona too. Oh aye, you deserve a right good skelping, and I'm the man to give it to you."

"No one will be skelped," I tell him. "You two can ride away in Easton's car. Go on, do it. Leave."

I wave my hands in a shooing gesture.

Easton smirks. "I have the keys. No one is leaving this place until I decide to go."

Domhnall pulls his arm back and fists his hand tightly. "You'll be begging to leave, ye *cacan*, once I'm done battering you."

Easton raises his fists and dances about in what he must think is a boxing stance, but he clearly knows nothing about the sport. "Come on, you tosser, let's go at it again and see who wins. Your girlfriend stopped you the first time, which means you aren't as tough as you pretend to be."

No, it means Domhnall is a gentleman at heart, underneath all the bluster and the snarling. If only I could crack his shell open... But no, he won't let me do that, and I'm at a loss for how to make him talk to me without scaring him away.

Kicking him out of the house probably didn't help.

Domhnall backs away while holding his hands palms up and crooking his fingers in the "come this way" gesture.

Easton saunters after him—while smirking, of course.

The testosterone in this clearing could smother all the wildlife.

Domhnall halts halfway to the airplane and assumes a boxing posture with his legs spread in the wide stance that will help him deliver harder punches. He raises his fists. Easton attempts the same stance while dancing on his toes and waving his fists about like a bloody eejit. Honestly, he has no idea what he's doing. His tongue pokes out between his lips too. *Ugh.* He looks like a preening moron, while Domhnall presents himself as manly and strong.

I stay well away from the two men and observe while hugging myself. I hope neither of them gets injured. But Easton seems determined to draw blood, though I doubt he knows how to fight properly. Should I warn Easton that Domhnall took up boxing a few years ago? He became very proficient at the sport too and even won an amateur match.

Domhnall's eyes narrow to slits. His expression hardens, and his determination shows on his face. He wants to destroy my former fiancé, but he has no idea Easton has never fought before, not like this. Punching a drunk ersehole outside a night club hardly counts. Domhnall is not stupid, though, so he must at least suspect Easton is faking it.

I leap between the two men, throwing my arms out to plant a hand on each of their chests. "Stop this. Fighting won't change anything. I don't want either of you, so it's pointless, anyway. Back away now and give up this childish argument."

Domhnall's brows lift. "Argument? No, this is a battle to the death, and your honor is at stake."

"You've got that the wrong way round. *Your* honor is at stake, but I don't care about that macho rubbish."

"Move away, Fiona. This is between me and the *cacan*."

"Like hell it is." I smack his chest while keeping my other hand on Easton. "If you're fighting over me, then it is my business too. Does either of you care how I feel about it? No, you don't."

Easton smirks.

I smack his chest hard, making him wince.

Now Domhnall smirks.

How can I get rid of them? Only one idea occurs to me, but they'll balk at it. Why should I give a toss about their feelings? They aren't interested in mine. So, I back away and wave toward the vehicle. "Get in the car. Both of you. Drive away before I ring the police."

Neither man moves. They just go on glaring at each other.

I set my hands on my hips. "Last chance. Go away, both of you."

They still don't move.

"Fine, then." I stomp back into the house and retrieve my purse, then stalk back outside. I had noticed, when Easton arrived, that he had set his keys on the dashboard of the car he hired. So, I march straight to the driver's door, brushing past Easton, and yank the door open.

"What are ye doing, ye daft lass?" Domhnall asks. "That isn't your car."

Easton huffs. "No, it's mine. Are you completely off your rocker, Fiona?"

I climb into the driver's seat and shut the door, then snatch up the keys and punch the button on the fob that locks the doors. While the men gape at me, I shove the key into the ignition and twist. The engine comes to life, but those two eejits keep staring at me in disbelief. Well, I guess they assume I won't actually drive away.

They underestimate me, and they will regret it.

I shift the car into reverse and ram my foot down on the gas pedal. As I yank the wheel, the car spins around, and I take off down the drive with gravel spraying up at either side of the vehicle, ticking on the exterior. In the side mirror, I can see both men. Easton simply stands there with his hands on his hips.

But Domhnall runs after me.

My throat tightens as I watch him in the rearview mirror, and my eyes begin to sting with the start of tears. Domhnall cares enough to chase me. But will he ever open up to me about his past? Maybe I need to come up with a plan of my own, rather than waiting for him to give in. That means I should talk to my sisters and the American Wives Club.

Oh, aye, Domhnall will love that. If he finds out. He doesn't need to know, since secrecy is vital in a meddling plan. Yes, I mean to meddle in my own life.

Finally, I can't see the house or the driveway anymore. They have dwindled out of sight. I probably shouldn't have left Domhnall and Easton stranded at Torcall's homestead, but drastic action seemed appropriate. They will either kill each other or make peace. I still have no idea what Easton wants from me, and I don't care.

Up ahead, I see a vehicle coming this way, roaring up the road. The dust cloud surrounding it makes identifying the car virtually impossible. But as I draw closer to the vehicle, it slows down, diminishing the dust cloud.

And I recognize the driver. It's Torcall.

I press down on the brake pedal to slow this car to a halt just as Torcall's pickup truck stops alongside me.

He rolls down his window and grins at me. "Fiona, lass, how is it going? And where did you get a car? We made sure you had no transportation."

"Aye, but none of you took into account what a stubborn ersehole Easton Yates is. He turned up in a car he hired—this one."

"You stole his car?" Torcall laughs heartily. "You're a wonderful lass. That was a brilliant idea."

"Not sure it is brilliant. Domhnall and Easton wanted to batter each other." I chew on the inside of my cheek. "I'm worried they might hurt each other."

"Oh, I doubt they'll do much damage. But I've come to check on you and Domhnall, so I can take care of that interloper too." He smirks and wags his eyebrows. "How was last night? There's nothing like an evening in a private cabin to spice things up."

Oh, good heavens. I do not want to discuss my sex life with Torcall Murdoch. "Maybe I should go back there and—"

"Nonsense, lass. Let me handle it. Murdochs know how to break up a fight."

"But I should at least return Easton's car."

"Tosh. Sounds like he deserved to be stranded." Torcall winks at me. "Leave it all to me, Fiona. Go on now, lovey, follow the road wherever it leads you."

I start the car rolling again while Torcall's pickup truck grows smaller and smaller in the rearview mirror. Torcall might not be my relative, but he has the same attitudes and wry, wicked sense of humor as my brothers and my cousins. Maybe he is the right one to sort out Domhnall and Easton.

Though I head for Loch Fairbairn, I decide against going back to the house I had shared with Domhnall until, um, yesterday. Instead, I drive straight to my sister Catriona's house, where she and Alex and their wee bairn live. I haven't seen my niece in a couple of weeks. That means this won't be just a "Fiona is a pitiful lass who needs gobs of help with her personal life" sort of visit. No, I'll get to hold my niece and coo and babble to her like a bampot.

The oldest sister should have a baby first. But my youngest sister got married and had a child before I did. Jamie might have been first, but Catriona was second. I still haven't even found a stable, long-term relationship.

Mhac na galla. I'm a failure, aren't I?

As I pull into the driveway of Cat and Alex's house, I force myself to shake off that depressing thought. I won't have my family thinking I'm a pathetic lump who can't even keep a boyfriend. Besides, I'm too old to have children now. I waited too long.

I park Easton's hired car along the road in front of Alex and Cat's home. Their two cars take up the driveway. I paste on a smile that I don't feel and march up to the door to ring the bell. The door opens within a few seconds.

Catriona smiles brightly. "Fiona, what a lovely surprise to see you today."

"Aye, it's lovely to see you too. I hope I'm not intruding on your family time with Alex and Maisie."

"Oh, tosh." She waves a hand dismissively. "Come in, Fiona. We're always happy to see you, and our family time includes you."

"Thank you, Cat."

She leads me into the living room, where Alex is sitting cross-legged on the floor with little Maisie. The wee bairn is playing with blocks. Her father picks her up and kisses her forehead, then babbles to her in baby talk for a moment. Finally, he lays her down on the wee blanket and blows raspberries on her tummy through her adorable pink onesie.

The first time I'd met Alex, I'd thought he was a flaming ersehole—because he *was* one back then. Catriona never gave up on him, though, and they're blissfully contented these days. It's hard to believe the man she used to despise, the one she called the British Bastard and the Limey Louse, has become one of my favorite people in the world. He honestly does feel like a brother to me.

Alex notices me and Catriona hovering just inside the living room threshold. Instead of seeming embarrassed, though, he smirks and proceeds to speak more words in a silly voice. "Do you see your auntie there, Maisie? Fiona needs a hug and a kiss, doesn't she?"

The baby giggles.

Oh, my word. She is the most adorable bairn I've ever seen. Maisie has Cat's pale blue eyes and Alex's angelic features. Will the wee bairn become as devilish as her father? Or as feisty as her mother? Maybe she'll be all of that and more.

Alex rises and carries little Maisie over to me. "Here you are, pet. Looks like you need a good cuddle. I hear Domhnall is giving you plenty of trouble these days."

I accept the precious package he offers me and hold Maisie close. She touches my nose and giggles. I can't help grinning in return.

"Oh, Alex, dinnae ask her about Domhnall," Catriona says. "Let Fiona relax for a while before you interrogate her."

"I do not interrogate anyone. My methods are subtler and far more elegant."

My smile is no longer forced. A few minutes with my family has reinvigorated me.

We all sit down on the sofa together, and I keep Maisie on my lap.

Alex hooks one ankle over the other knee and turns partway toward me. Then he rests his arm on the sofa's back. "So, Fiona, let's talk about your new career."

Chapter Eleven

Domhnall

Easton Yates and I have been circling each other for a while. Neither of us wants to cede the house to the other, which means neither of us goes inside. We stand on opposite sides of the drive, sizing each other up. How long can we go on like this? Until the *bod ceann* gives up and starts walking down the road out of my sight. One of us needs to surrender, and it won't be me.

I learned his last name because the eejit seemed to think it would impress me. "I am Easton Yates, you sodding Scottish lout!" he had shouted at me. What a stupid piece of shite.

A grumbling sound distracts us from glowering at each other.

We both lower our fists and turn to see who's coming. I recognize that pickup truck. It belongs to Torcall Murdoch, who is even barmier than his great-nephew, Errol. The ramshackle vehicle goes with the dilapidated airplane. Like uncle, like nephew.

Torcall brakes hard, which sends bits of gravel flying up. One piece hits Easton in the shoulder, and he cries out. A larger bit whacks into me, but I don't cry like a wee bairn about it.

When Torcall climbs out and slams his pickup's door shut, Easton jumps.

How on earth could Fiona ever have loved this *cacan* enough to become engaged to him? He must have drugged and brainwashed her.

Torcall halts between me and the *cacan*. "I dinnae see any blood. That means ye haven't fought yet. Well, go on. Get it over with."

I stare at him. "Get what over with?"

"The bloodbath. You want this British scunner gone, so get rid of him."

"Why are you encouraging me to batter him?"

Torcall shrugs. "Why not?"

Aye, he is definitely barmier than his great-nephew.

"I'll count down from five," Torcall says, "and then you two will fight. Five, four—"

Easton splutters. "This is insanity. What is wrong with you? Are all Scots utter brutes who settle their disagreements with violence? You lot really are savages."

I glance at Torcall.

He shrugs.

And I raise my fists. "Are ye ready to fight? Or do ye plan on complaining until the midges start eating your flesh?"

"Oh, please. Midges aren't flesh eaters."

"Haud yer wheesht!" Torcall roars. "The countdown will begin again. Four, three, two, one—kill!"

I dance around Easton, waiting for him to throw the first punch, but he just keeps moving further away while I follow him. When he finally punches, he misses me altogether and loses his balance. The moron scrambles to his feet and raises his fists again. His eyes are wild, and his face is covered with a sheen of sweat. I could easily punch him hard enough to make him pass out. But there's no percentage in besting a weakling.

With a groan, I stop and lower my hands. "Enough. I do not box with blokes who have no idea what they're doing."

"Are you forfeiting?"

"No. I'm canceling the bout."

"Scots are cowards, eh? No wonder Fiona threw you over."

Torcall takes hold of Easton's nose and twists. The *cacan* cries out. Torcall ignores his pain and drags the Brit toward the pickup truck by his nose and yanks open the passenger door. "Get in."

Easton scrambles to get in the vehicle.

Torcall shuts the door and, as he walks round to the driver's side, he winks and smirks at me.

"What about me?" I ask. "I don't have a car."

"You're a strong laddie. Walk to Loch Fairbairn."

"It's twenty miles away."

Torcall shrugs, then gets into the truck. And he drives away.

If I weren't so tired, I might have thought to leap into the bed of the pickup truck. As it stands, I'm stranded out here alone. If I knew how to fly a decrepit plane, I could get myself to the Glencoe airfield and hire a car there or call someone to pick me up. I don't know how to fly this type of aircraft, though.

How do I pass the time while I wait for inspiration or someone to rescue me? I shuffle into the house to drink Torcall's whisky and eat his food. I'm surprised to learn he has a large stash of chocolate truffles. I never would have guessed Torcall has a sweet tooth, since he's one of the gruffest, least sweet men I've ever met. He won't mind if I eat his sweets. The man has an entire cupboard shelf stuffed full of them.

After eighteen minutes of sitting slumped on the kitchen floor eating and drinking, I've had enough. Time to call for help. I pull out my mobile, but there's no signal here. I go outside. Still no signal. I return to the kitchen and grab the corded phone that's attached to the wall beside the fridge. I didn't know anyone had a corded phone anymore. When I pick up the handset, I hear nothing. No dial tone. I check the phone in the living room too, but that one has no dial tone either.

Bloody hell.

I search the house for some clue that Torcall has internet access, but I can't find anything. He must be one of those people who dislikes modern technology. I'm trapped here with no way to call for help. I assume the Mac-Taggarts and their mates thought stranding me and Fiona here would mend our relationship, but instead, she abandoned me here. Oh, aye, that's the way to become unstoppable—to sit here complaining about my life. Fiona will be impressed by that behavior.

I stalk outside and glare at the DC-3. Errol can fly that plane, but I can't.

Walking it is, then.

At least there aren't any midges this morning.

I head down the driveway and out onto the road, beginning my very long journey back to Loch Fairbairn. I'm in excellent condition, but twenty miles is a hard slog. *Do it for Fiona,* I remind myself again and again. The clock on my phone shows me the time, so I know I've been walking for about fifteen minutes when I hear a familiar sound.

The grumble of a motorcycle.

I keep walking even while that noise grows louder and louder, and I begin to hope that the biker will stop to give me a ride. But that's unlikely. I don't look like a harmless laddie who got lost in the forest, not after tackling Easton and rolling about in the dirt. No, I resemble the sort most people would shy away from if they bumped into me on a deserted road.

But as the motorcycle comes into view, rushing toward me, I swear I recognize that bike. It can't be, but it seems like it. Why would Callum MacTaggart ride all the way out here? He's the only one I know of who rides a Harley, and that is definitely the sort of bike that's coming my way.

I move to the side of the road and wait for the biker to arrive.

He stops a few yards away and shuts off his motorcycle, setting the kick-stand. Then he dismounts the bike and removes his helmet.

"Magnus? What are you doing on Callum's Harley?"

"He lent it to me. Someone needed to come retrieve you. Who better than a bounty hunter."

"I thought you preferred to call yourself a private investigator these days."

Magnus MacTaggart shrugs. "That's my official, legal title. But everyone agrees that bounty hunter is sexier and more threatening to the villains."

"Why didn't you drive a car? Dinnae want to hug you for twenty miles."

"It's me or nothing. Swallow your pride, Domhnall, even if you choke on it." He opens up the storage box attached to the rear of the Harley and pulls out a pink helmet. "Here. It's your turn to be humiliated. Hugh Parrish wore Kate's helmet, so you can too."

"Hugh Parrish is a Brit, and he used to call himself Lord Steamy. Dinnae be comparing me to him."

Magnus tosses me the pink helmet. "Gavin sent a message for you. 'Suck it up and be a man,' he said."

"Aye, that's a very inspiring speech." I blow out a breath and pull on the pink helmet. "Kate must have a large head, eh? This fits me."

Magnus chuckles. "We bought a helmet just for you and painted it pink."

The MacTaggarts are irretrievably insane.

We both climb onto the Harley, and I'm forced to hug Magnus as we roar down the gravel road. Dust plumes up in our wake. Luckily, we're wearing full-face helmets. That shields us from the dust. Magnus drives fast, exceeding the speed limit, but that doesn't fash me. Flying in Errol's plane might give me pause, but only because he flies like a deranged bat that escaped from the depths of hell. Aye, I've ridden in his plane before. He took me and Fiona on a short trip to show us the aerial view of Loch Fairbairn.

As we emerge from the forest, I see the village of Loch Fairbairn in the distance. We're almost there.

But Magnus races right past the sign that points toward the village.

"Where are you going?" I shout. "You missed the turn."

He shakes his head.

Does that mean he couldn't hear what I said, or that he meant to bypass Loch Fairbairn? Since I can't talk to him while we're careening down the trunk road, I'll have to wait to ask him about that.

Magnus veers around a corner onto a road I recognize. It leads to Dùndubhan.

Didn't Gavin tell me I had to "earn Dùndubhan"? I have no clue what that meant, but I assumed it involved more than spending a night in

Torcall's house. Maybe we aren't going to the castle. He probably intends to turn down a different road at some point.

Magnus pulls over at a petrol station to gas up. We both remove our helmets. That gives me a chance to interrogate him.

"All right, Magnus, tell me what the plan is."

"That's top secret."

"We're going to Dùndubhan, aye?"

He ignores me and goes about filling up the bike's tank. Even when I ask him a direct question, he continues to ignore me. I call him a rude name, and still he won't respond.

I give up and go into the petrol station's shop to use the bog. When I return to the Harley, Magnus is gone. I search every corner of the shop but find no sign of the bounty hunter. When I walk back outside, I see a car pulling out from behind the building.

Magnus waves at me from inside the vehicle. His wife Piper, who sits behind the wheel, waves to me as well. Then they drive away.

What the bloody hell? They dumped me here and left.

The Harley still sits there waiting, already fueled up. When I approach the bike, I find a large cardboard envelope resting on the front seat. It has my name scrawled on it. I tear open the envelope and flip it upside down to shake out the contents. The Harley's key tumbles out first, then a folded sheet of paper slides out too.

I hook the keyring around my finger as I read the note.

Callum is letting you borrow his precious Harley, the note says. *If you crash it or get a scratch on it, the penalty will be death. Drive to the coordinates below to start phase two. Use your mobile's GPS.*

They won't actually murder me if I scratch Callum's motorcycle. The MacTaggarts love hyperbole.

I don't recognize the address I've been given. I could ride away on Callum's bike and do whatever the bloody hell I want, but I won't do that. Maybe I should. But I know Fiona would want me to go through with this nonsense, and I will do anything for her.

Magnus stowed the pink helmet in the box at the back, so I pull on the black one and start up the engine. As I roll out onto the trunk road, I feel a strange sense of freedom. Not because of the Harley. No, I feel this way because I've given in to the insanity and will do whatever the MacTaggarts and their mates tell me to do. Why not? I'm cocking everything up on my own.

I think a night in Torcall's cottage infected me with his barmy attitude, but I don't care. Whatever sort of bizarre scavenger hunt they're sending me on, I might as well play along.

The coordinates in the note take me to a remote part of the Highlands, half an hour away from Loch Fairbairn and Dùndubhan, far from any of the places I know. It doesn't seem like anyone comes here often, if ever. This is the backside of Beann Dealgach, the mountain behind Dùndubhan. The castle lies at the base of the craggy peak. From this side, it appears far more forbidding, with many ridges and steep drop-offs.

My coordinates have brought me to the base of the mountain, in a clearing, but I have no idea what I'm meant to do now.

A figure races out of the trees, aiming straight for me. "Domhnall! You're finally here. Took ye long enough, eh?"

"Errol, you bloody annoying dafty. Why have you brought me here?"

The Fire Starter, as he's known, halts several yards away and glances back to shout at the trees. "Get your erses out here, ladies! Domhnall's in a fankle, for sure."

Ladies? Errol might drag his wife here, since she's as much of a bampot as he is, but he wouldn't bring…

Fiona jogs out of the forest with Ashley right behind her.

I stomp up to Errol. "Why did you bring Fiona here? She doesn't want to see me."

"Are you sure about that?"

The lasses reach us, and Ashley wraps her arms around Errol. Fiona stops just behind him and only glances at me sideways.

"What's the meaning of this?" I ask Errol. "If you want to strand me out here, I dinnae care. But leave Fiona out of it."

"Oh, no, I can't do that. This only works with both of you searching."

"Searching? For what? Your lost wits, I assume. Don't you have a GPS tracker in your brain?"

Errol laughs. "Very funny. But no, that's not the plan."

"Spit it out before I pound you into the dirt face-first."

"All right, all right, calm down." Errol plucks a folded-up sheet of paper out of his jacket pocket. He hands it to me. "This is your map."

"To where?"

"Not where. What." He spreads his arms wide and grins. "You and Fiona are going on a treasure hunt."

I look at the lass. "You don't want to do this, aye? Hunting about in the forest for whatever barmy clues Errol set out for us? It's rubbish."

She marches up to me. "I want to go on a treasure hunt. I'll do it by myself if you're too uptight to try something new."

"Uh-uh-uh," Errol says while wagging a finger at us. "It's both of you or nothing. You have ten seconds to decide. Ashley, count it down for us."

"Sure thing. Ten, nine, eight, seven—"

Fiona lifts her chin. Her defiant expression makes me want to drag her onto the ground and shag her relentlessly. "I am doing this, Domhnall."

"Then so am I."

Ashley cheers. Errol throws his arms up and whoops.

Fiona throws me a sideways glance—more of a sideways glare, actually—and speaks to Errol. "How do we start? I've never been on a treasure hunt before. Do we get to keep whatever we find?"

"Of course you do. But the treasure might not be what you expect. It's personal, not monetary."

I cross my arms over my chest and shake my head. "Ye mean the so-called treasure will be a pile of rubbish."

"Not entirely. We aren't forcing you to dig up rotting animal corpses. The items you uncover will be of a personal nature." When I try to speak, he holds up a hand to silence me. "Nothing embarrassing. What you and Fiona decide to do with your finds is entirely up to you."

"This sounds like a children's game."

"Children?" Errol says with a laugh. "No, I wouldn't set mines in an area where children might be."

"Land mines?" I almost roar those words, and my voice echoes off the trees. "That's it, you bloody lunatic. I'm taking Fiona home."

Chapter Twelve

Fiona

"Don't go yet," Ashley says. "Errol is pulling your leg. There are no land mines or anything else dangerous."

Domhnall squints at Errol. "Good. Then I don't need to rip him limb from limb."

I make an exasperated face. "Och, Domhnall, do ye always have to threaten violence? You need to learn how to take a joke and improve your sense of humor."

"Your brothers make the same sort of jokes. Besides, you love my humor."

Maybe I do, but that's not the point right now. Domhnall won't listen if I try to explain that, though, so I won't even bother. To be fair, I don't think Domhnall knows anything about Errol's land mines. His reaction isn't completely without merit. My cousin can't accidentally set off those mines because he triggers them via an app on his mobile.

Errol clasps Ashley's hand. "Time for us to go."

"Not yet," Ashley says. "You forgot to give them the satchel."

"Och, you're right." Errol trots over to a bush and retrieves a satchel from behind it, passing it to Domhnall. "Here you are. These are supplies to keep you hydrated and stave off hunger. Now, we are really leaving this time."

"Wait," Domhnall says. "What have you done with Easton Yates?"

My cousin grins. "We let the Three Macs handle him."

He means my brothers. Letting them "handle" Easton sounds like a recipe for disaster, but I need to trust Lachlan, Rory, and Aidan to do the right thing. They aren't rabid animals.

"We really need to go now," Errol says. "You two have everything you need to uncover the treasures we've set out for you. Good luck."

Domhnall grasps Errol's arm as he and Ashley walk past us. "What if there's a storm or a mob of midges? We need a way to get out of this place."

"Aye, you've got the Harley."

"But we can't ride it into the forest."

"No, of course not." He holds out his hand, palm up. "Give me your mobile."

Domhnall compresses his lips and doesn't move for a moment, while Errol stands there waiting with his hand still thrust out. Then Domhnall grumbles and sets his mobile on Errol's palm.

My cousin fiddles with something on the device, then hands it back to Domhnall. "There, you're all set. I just created a bookmark for you in the maps app, and that will help you find your way back to the Harley. It will also assist you in hunting down the treasures, but you'll need to figure that out on your own. It's a learning experience."

He and Ashley hustle past us and the Harley, going into the trees and disappearing from view. A moment later, we hear a car engine revving up. A moment after that, a vehicle races out of the trees and speeds off down the two-track.

"They hid their car?" Domhnall says. "Your family and friends are going to extremes."

"Aye, that's what we do. You know that. You witnessed it firsthand at Alex and Cat's wedding, and you even participated."

"That was different. Meddling in *my* life is unacceptable."

And yet he's here. Participating. Ready to hunt for hidden treasure. And he's doing it for me.

Domhnall unfolds the map Errol had given him. "Best get started. We want to finish before sunset."

"Are you afraid of the dark?"

"No, ye cheeky lass." He winces. "I don't want to be here when the midges come out."

Just knowing that Domhnall is worried about insects makes me want to hug him. He is the strongest, most virile man I've ever met, and I used to believe nothing could faze him. But I was wrong. He essentially admitted to being afraid of midges, and that makes me wonder what else I might get him to share with me if I do it carefully.

I never wanted to break up with Domhnall. He gave me no other choice, but I still hold out hope that he will open up to me.

Domhnall lifts his gaze from the map, and his brows crinkle in the sweetest way. "What do you think they've done with Easton?"

"I hope they locked him in the dungeon at Dùndubhan."

"You and your entire clan have always insisted there has never been a dungeon in the castle. Now you're saying there is one." He slants toward me and smiles with a devious twinkle sparkling in his blue eyes. "I knew the MacTaggarts were lying. I'd wager your brothers have tortured many men in that secret dungeon, just to keep suitors away from their sisters. Who knows how many men they've dispatched."

"Lachlan, Rory, and Aidan have never murdered anyone." I lean closer, our lips a hair's breadth apart. "But they might make an exception for you."

We hold perfectly still, gazing into each other's eyes, while a sensual thread of desire wends its way through me. No, we cannae shag out here in the open. Well, we *could*. But it would be inappropriate and send the wrong message to the stubborn man whose golden brown eyes have transfixed me. But I can't help it. Domhnall's rough, deep voice had lit a fire inside me. Aye, the most annoying part of breaking up with him is that I still want him like mad, and that means he can wheedle his way back into my trousers, and perhaps my heart too.

Has he ever left my heart? The answer is a depressingly firm no.

Domhnall straightens and focuses on the map again. "What do you think Errol meant when he said we should use the maps app on my mobile to find the treasure?"

"He meant we should follow the map. And that app can do more than show us the best route to wherever we need to go. It also can tap into the GPS built into your mobile."

Domhnall stares at me as if he has never seen me before. "You understand all that GPS rubbish?"

"Not all of it. But yes, I understand the basics of how it works."

"There are satellites in space, and they beam information down to earth. That's all I know."

I point up toward the sky. "The satellites are in geosynchronous orbit around the earth, which means they're always aimed at the same spot on the planet. It's a network of satellites that blanket the globe."

He offers me the map. "You are clearly the brains of this operation. How do you suggest we find the treasures?"

Domhnall wants me to take the lead. I get a lump in my throat just knowing that. Domhnall Sterling is an alpha male, for sure, yet he's handing the reins over to me. He has never done that before.

I study the map Errol had drawn on this large sheet of paper and try to figure out what it's telling us.

Domhnall moves behind me and leans over my shoulder to scrutinize the map. "Isn't this what Errol, Ashley, and Munro did together? They hunted for a mysterious hoard in the Grand Canyon. Your cousin is obsessed with treasure."

"Errol is a genius at this sort of thing. This map might be inspired by the ones he and Ashley found."

"Are you sure we're looking at it the right way round? Errol didn't specify which end was up."

"Yes, he did. Look." I point at the top of the map. "The trail starts up here, which means we need to flip the map." I do that and point at the little arrow that shows us the way. "We follow the signs, literally. Each arrow tells us where to go next."

"And those little symbols must point to the general area where each treasure can be found."

"Seems reasonable to assume that." I hesitate, because I've suddenly realized I should have asked him a question. "Have you ever taken part in a treasure hunt? Or have you ridden a Harley before?"

"The answer is no, I have never hunted for treasure. But I have ridden a motorcycle before, just not a Harley."

I had no idea he had ever ridden a motorcycle. Do we not know each other as well as I thought? That realization spurs another question. "The other times when you rode a motorcycle, was that before you met me?"

"Aye. Does that matter?"

"Not sure. I guess I'm still confused about the scope of all the things you never told me or refuse to tell me."

He scowls and snatches the map away from me. "Let's go. The sooner we start this bloody stupid game, the sooner it will be over."

"I thought you wanted me to be the keeper of the map. You said I'm the brains of the operation."

Domhnall sighs and thrusts the map at me. "Aye, you are the brains. I'm the brute strength. If you need a human crowbar to crack open our first treasure, I'm the man for the job."

"That's not what I meant."

He stalks off into the forest, leaving me to scurry after him. I catch up easily, which suggests that he slowed down to make sure we wouldn't lose track of each other. I've known since the day we met that he has insecurities caused by his wife cheating on him for years. But I suspect there's more to it than a bad marriage. I hope my family and friends haven't simply sent us on a pointless hunt just to force us to be in the same place together. They might've hoped doing that would help us.

Not so far.

Domhnall stays alongside me but slightly ahead, as if he wants to make sure he's always close enough to protect me. From what? The wildlife? I reckon that impulse is an artifact of his past too. I need to use this treasure hunt silliness as a chance to push him to explain—without him knowing I'm pushing. Oh, aye, that's a simple task.

We stop at a spot that looks like the first treasure on the map. Both of us glance around in search of the item, but we can't see anything unusual. Domhnall suggests we should hunt for our booty in a circular pattern, expanding the search area with every completed circle. That's probably a remnant of his military training, though I still have no ruddy idea what his job was back then. I don't even know which branch he served in, much less what happened to him during his service.

"Fiona!" Domhnall calls out. "I think I found something. Bring the map."

I race over to him. "What is it?"

He points at the earth just in front of his feet. "Does that look like a fresh wee mound of earth? As if it's been recently disturbed?"

"Could be. Should we try to dig there?"

"Sounds like a plan."

He crouches and begins to brush away the loose soil. His efforts expose a curved object made out of metal and plastic. It seems to be attached to something beneath the surface.

"Is that a handle?" I ask. "Like the ones on toolboxes?"

"Could be." He thrusts his fingers into the dirt, clawing out large clods of earth until he at last excavates the body of the metal toolbox. He rises and holds the box up by its handle, grinning. "I found your treasure, *gràidh*."

I leap up and kiss his cheek. "You are my hero."

"Best hold back your praise until we see what's in the box."

"No, I will not hold back. You found our first treasure."

"*We* found it. I couldn't have done this without my best lass by my side."

I get a strong pang in my chest, all because he called me his "best lass" and declared he couldn't have found that old toolbox without me. I bounce on my toes, ridiculously excited—about our treasure, yes, but mostly because of what Domhnall said. "Open it up. Let's find out what we have."

He pries the rusty lid open, and his brows draw together. He tips his head to one side, then the other, while his gaze narrows. "I don't understand what your family is trying to accomplish."

Since Domhnall is facing me, I can't see what's inside the box. The lid didn't fall backwards all the way. It's blocking my view.

"What is it?" I ask, as I attempt to hoist myself up on my tiptoes to peer around the box's lid. "Is it empty?"

"No, there is something inside." One side of his mouth warps, and he shakes his head. Then he plucks the item out. "Here you are, lass, for what it's worth."

He hands me the item.

I can't help laughing. "This might not be useful, but it is adorable."

"What are you going to do with it?"

"Hug it." I clasp the stuffed animal to my chest. The wee Highland cow is the sweetest thing I've ever seen. I kiss its head. "I love it, even if you don't think it's useful."

"What is a stuffed animal meant to tell us?"

"That you're a cuddly bull with a rusty exterior?"

He gives me a sly smile. "Maybe it's a cuddly female cow."

"Either way, I'm keeping it. We can debate the meaning of this treasure while we move on to the next one."

Domhnall holds up the rusty toolbox. "Should we take this with us?"

"Aye. I'll stuff it into the satchel."

While he does that, I pet my new plush toy and consider its characteristics. "You know, I think this is a bull. The horns are shorter and thicker than a cow's would be." I bump my shoulder into his arm. "So, this is you—a big, hairy Scottish bull."

I kiss the bull's forehead and snuggle it against my chest.

Domhnall shakes his head.

Chapter Thirteen

Domhnall

"Are ye planning to sleep with that silly wee thing?" I ask. Fiona hasn't stopped cooing over the stuffed animal and speaking to it in baby talk. First, she says it's a cow version of me, then she treats it like a bairn. I am not a child. As we continue up the path laid out on Errol's map, I need to get clarification from Fiona. "You're comparing me to a cow. Is that an insult or compliment?"

"I called you a bull, not a cow."

"And ye also said that toy is big and hairy like me. But I am not overly hairy, not like the way Munro used to look. That barmy Wild Man showed me pictures of his unkempt beard and hair. Mine are well-groomed."

She's been walking beside me, but now the lass jogs a few paces ahead and turns round to walk backwards while facing me. "I know you're well-groomed. But I never claimed you share all the same traits as this toy."

The lass holds up her furry bull and grins at me. Then she moves the toy's front legs to make it seem as if the bull is waving at me.

I'm relieved that she feels relaxed enough to tease me, but I still think her comparison is ridiculous. I look nothing like that stuffed creature. At least I have possession of the map. Fiona hadn't wanted to give up her treasure. I'm amazed that she would relinquish control of the map simply to snuggle with a fuzzy cow that looks nothing like me.

Fiona spins around to face the path ahead, but she starts humming the tune of "The Bonnie Banks o' Loch Lomond." And she skips down the trail.

I stifle a groan. Women can be very confusing.

The path we're following isn't a prepared trail of the sort found in official parks. It looks more like a game trail, being narrower than any walking path I've ever seen.

Fiona finishes that song and begins another one—"Flower of Scotland."

"Dinnae ye know any modern songs?" I shout to her. "Feel like I'm marching in a bloody parade with the Royal Regiment."

Fiona switches to marching and raises one arm in a salute—while still holding on to the Highland cow that looks nothing like me.

I have never seen her behave this way. She's mature and calm, which explains how she managed to rein me in and stop me from ruining Alex and Catriona's wedding, not to mention how she helped me see that I'd been a flaming ersehole to Jessica and Grey. I have no idea why either of them speaks to me after all my boorish behavior. They can't have…forgiven me. I know they both said they did, but I assumed they were being polite.

"Fiona, wait a moment."

She halts and half turns toward me, giving me a sweet smile. But that expression swiftly fades. "What's wrong, Domhnall?"

I shake my head because I dinnae trust myself to speak. She is the bonniest, kindest, cleverest, strongest woman I've ever known. But... "I don't deserve you, *mo chridhe*. Why in the world did you stay with me for two years?"

She lets her shoulders slump. "I thought we were having fun with our treasure hunt. How did you go from smiling to looking like you just found out your best friend died? It's only been a few minutes since you were happy."

"I'm sorry, *gràidh*. I don't mean to ruin your fun. Please go on—"

"For heaven's sake, Domhnall." She marches up to me, tipping her head back to meet my gaze. "Do you expect me to prance about singing 'la-dee-dah' while you're miserable? You tell me you don't deserve me, and that means we need to have a conversation."

"Not now. I shouldn't have said anything."

"You won't talk to me."

"Later. Let's finish this barmy treasure hunt first."

"All right." She thrusts her Highland cow toy at me. "Take this. It will make you feel better."

I grudgingly accept the plush toy, though I'm fair certain I'm making a semi-disgusted face.

Fiona smiles with her cheeks dimpled. "Would you rather have a Barbie doll?"

"Those are my only choices?"

"Relax. I doubt Errol buried a Barbie out here." She taps a finger on her chin. "Although, Ashley might do that."

I grasp the wee Highland bull by his midsection. "If I must have a toy, I'll take this one. At least it's male."

"Give him a hug, Domhnall. That's what he's for."

She turns and starts walking down the trail again while humming. The song is not Scottish, though I can't remember its title. Some variety of pop song, the kind women like and men cringe at whenever they hear it.

Fiona pauses to glance back at me. She feigns a scowl. "You're not hugging the stuffed bull."

Since I know the stubborn lass won't give up, I cradle the toy in my arms like a babe and murmur rubbish to it.

"I know that's not genuine love," she says. "But I'll take it."

As we continue through the forest, something odd begins to happen to me. I find myself smiling and whistling along with the song Fiona is humming. It's an old one made famous by Dean Martin. The words compare love to getting kicked in the skull, and that seems highly appropriate for me. I've needed multiple kicks in the head, but the effects haven't stuck.

"I found it!" Fiona shouts. "This is the second location on the map."

The lass waits for me, rather than trying to dig up the treasure on her own. I had gotten a wee bit behind, so I jog to catch up. She points down at a spot on the ground directly in front of her feet.

I hand the cow back to her, then crouch to study the disturbed earth. "Aye, this does look similar to the way the first treasure was hidden. It has the same sort of mound on top. But I don't see a toolbox handle, or any sort of attachment for pulling a box out of the earth."

"Did you expect Errol to make it easy? Besides, he's not the sort who does the same thing every time."

"That's true." I slide the satchel's strap off my shoulder and set it on the ground. "I'll dig it out with my bare hands and a wee shovel."

Fiona's brows wrinkle. "A wee shovel?"

"Aye. Watch and see." I reach into my back pocket and bring out my utility knife. Then I pull the Swiss army knife I always keep with me and stab it into the earth beside the wee mound. "This is my shovel."

She seems rather skeptical of my claim.

I use the dull side of the blade to carefully search under the dirt while I figure out what sort of shape lies beneath the surface. I get a rough idea of the overall size, then I pull the knife out and flip it to the dull side. I use that to break up the earth and loosen it enough that I can start to dig with my hands. I go slowly and move cautiously to ensure I won't damage whatever the object is. At last, I've cleared enough of the dirt that I can pull the object out.

And I set it on the ground near Fiona's feet. "Here it is, our next treasure."

She studies the small burlap sack, tipping her head this way and that. "There must be something inside it, aye?"

"Most likely. But with Errol, who knows." I wipe the dirt off my knife and fold it up, tucking it back into my hip pocket. "Time to unveil our treasure."

I untie the string that holds the package together, then carefully peel the burlap back until the object inside is revealed. I need to peel open one of the paper napkins wrapped around the item too. "Your cousin is definitely insane."

"Actually, I think this is a brilliant gift. I'm getting hungry. Aren't you?"

"Well, aye, but—" I sigh. "You're right, this is a useful treasure, unlike your furry friend."

"Oh, but I do love *Dòmhnall an Tarbh*."

"Are you calling me a bull? Or are you talking about your silly toy?"

"Both." She hugs the toy to her chest as she gazes down at our booty. "Let's eat our Scotch pies and drink some water. I'm glad Ashley and Errol provided nourishment for us."

"I'd rather drink whisky."

Her cheeks dimple again, and the sun coming in through a hole in the forest canopy makes her brown eyes twinkle. "Maybe the next treasure will be a bottle of Glenfiddich."

"We'll see."

Hiking this far has left me famished and my mouth dry. I drag out two bottles of water and open them while Fiona unwraps the four Scotch pies and sets them on the paper napkins. She gives me three. I set one of mine on her paper napkin. She tries to hand it back.

I hold up my hand. "We both eat two, or I eat nothing."

"Suddenly you're interested in equality? This from the man who insists on carrying in all our messages by himself, no matter how many there are."

"That's called chivalry. You buy so much at the supermarket that it takes a former wrestler to haul it all in."

Fiona kisses my cheek. "I love that side of you. But I also love your *Dòmhnall an Tarbh* side too."

"I am not a stuffed animal."

"No, but you are a strong, hardheaded bull of a man." Her gaze flicks down to my lap. "And you both have impressive loins."

"Are ye talking about my *slat*?"

She nods slowly, then shoves half a Scotch pie into her mouth and devours it just as slowly, like she wants to savor every last bit of it. Crumbs and juice cling to her lips. Instead of using the paper napkin, she drags her tongue over her lips, top and bottom, to wipe the remnants away.

My cock is awake now, for certain.

Fiona bites off another large chunk of her pie, consuming it in the same manner.

"Ah, *gràidh*, stop that now. You're eating like ye want something other than a meal."

"I have plans for second course." She rubs her lips together as her gaze drops to my groin again. "Something much bigger and meatier."

"You're trying to make me hard."

She nods and smirks.

I stuff an entire Scotch pie into my mouth. Crumbs and juice get stuck to my mouth and chin, but even more crumbles onto my lap. I finish off the second pie as well, in record time.

Fiona drinks half of her bottle of water, sighing with satisfaction. Then she shakes the crumbs off her paper napkin and wets it with her water bottle so she can wipe that over her throat. As she drags the wet paper napkin down the center of her chest, her hand grazes the slope of her breast. The stiff peaks of her nipples push against the fabric of her shirt.

Mhac na galla. I want to lay her down on the grass and make love to her.

No, that's not the way to win her back. But why is the lass teasing me this way? She can't want me to shag her, right here in the forest, on the ground, where any casual hiker might see.

Fiona drinks the rest of her water so quickly that I can see the movements in her throat. Even that turns me on. Almost nothing could make me not want her, which means I'm in for a right trial during the remainder of this treasure hunt, since she seems determined to drive me off my head with that body.

I won't give her the satisfaction. Even though I want that satisfaction.

We gather up our used paper napkins and water bottles, tucking them into the satchel. Neither of us wants to litter the forest with our rubbish. Our love of nature is one of the things we share, but we have much more in common than that. We're a perfect match, in my estimation.

Fiona walks alongside me as we continue to follow Errol's map, though she doesn't hold my hand. I wait a reasonable length of time before I slip my hand into hers. She threads her fingers with mine, and I do the same. I determined what a "reasonable" length of time was based solely on how long I could stand to wait before I felt myself getting irritable about it. Now, we're both relaxed as we amble toward our next stop on the itinerary created by Errol Murdoch, the laddie with explosives for a brain.

Up ahead, I hear the rushing of water.

We slow our pace as we draw closer. The trees thin out a wee bit, though they hadn't been dense deeper into the forest either. The trees in this part of Scotland aren't like the ones I'd gotten used to in America, when I lived in Washington State. The forests of the Pacific Northwest are thicker and taller, but also more densely packed in many places. I'd gone hiking with Jessica sometimes while we were together, but my ex-wife had abhorred the outdoors. I think Jess only went along on those hikes to make me happy. She enjoyed nature, but only in short excursions.

Fiona loves nature. She loves hiking. We've gone on multi-day treks into the wilds of the Highlands. Aye, that's another reason why we're perfect for each other.

And why I cannot ever give up on us.

Chapter Fourteen

Fiona

We walk with care as we move closer and closer to the river, since we can't tell what the terrain will be like there. Domhnall keeps hold of my hand, gripping it a wee bit tighter as if he's worried I might fall into the water. The sounds I hear suggest the river has a waterfall. We slow down now, almost tiptoeing as we approach the source of the rumbling water.

Domhnall stops us both. We can tell the ground falls away sharply just ahead of us, which means we have reached our destination. Errol's map shows the river, but I hadn't realized until right now that the odd little squiggles on the map must indicate where the waterfall is.

"Let me go first," Domhnall says. "I'll scope out the area to check for obstacles and spots where the cliff might be weakened."

"I'll wait here. You've done far more hiking than I have."

And that means I trust him. Why didn't I say that? He must realize I've placed all my faith in him during this little expedition. But I should have told him that I know I can rely on him all the time.

Well, except when he refuses to talk about his past.

I hug myself as I watch Domhnall creeping up to the precipice.

He glances left and right, up and down. Then he stomps his foot several times. Finally, he gives me the thumbs-up sign. "Come over here. It seems safe, and I need your help figuring out where the next treasure is hidden."

I tromp over to him—and experience a brief moment of anxiety as I gaze down at the river far below us and the rocky ledge that creates a ten-foot-high waterfall. The rumbling water spills into a large pool, though I can see that the river narrows again a short ways past that. I've never been afraid of heights, but hovering on the edge of a cliff, one that seems at least thirty feet high, gave me a twinge of fear.

"Fiona, are you all right?"

"Aye, fine." I tear my focus away from the waterfall. "I had no idea Beann Dealgach had this kind of terrain."

"You didn't know?" Domhnall raises his brows. "But this is your brother's mountain."

"It's not Rory's mountain. Beann Dealgach happens to lie within the estate that he owns, but he doesn't think of it as his."

Domhnall studies me for a moment. "Why does it seem like you've never seen this place before?"

"Because I haven't. None of us has ever hiked up Beann Dealgach, except for the eastern face where Dùndubhan is."

"I see." He glances down at the water, then scans the earth and trees around us before looking at me. "I haven't noticed any mound of dirt. Does the map give us any additional clues about where to find the treasure?"

"Let me study it for a moment."

Domhnall leans against a tree and gazes out at the river and the trees.

I contemplate Errol's map, but all I can tell is that our next find must be somewhere in this vicinity. Like Domhnall said, there aren't any obvious wee mounds of disturbed earth, like the ones we'd found earlier. But something about the squiggles on the map seems…not right.

"Domhnall, take a look at this."

He shuffles up to me and stares down at the map. "What am I looking for?"

"This." I point at the squiggles. "These water symbols… Don't they seem as if they're pointing straight up into the sky?"

Domhnall squints at the sheet of paper, bending his head to get even closer to the symbols. "They do seem to be oriented sideways to the river. But then there's another symbol beneath the, ah, squiggles."

He clearly didn't want to speak that word. Men can be silly about such things.

I lean forward too, and our heads bump against each other as we scrutinize that very small symbol. "Could that be an arrow?"

"Maybe." Domhnall flips the map around, so it's now upside down. "I think we've been looking at this wrong. Our hike might have begun on the downriver side of the slope, but the map doesn't tell us that. What if that symbol is meant to be pointing up toward the waterfall? We've been walking up the mountain, but the river flows down."

I plant a big kiss on his cheek. "You are a genius, Domhnall."

"Dinnae give me a Nobel Prize yet, *gràidh*. I have no idea how our next treasure could be in the river."

Aye, that is a conundrum. Then again… "Errol loves to tell the family how he, Ashley, and Munro discovered the Grand Canyon treasure. At one point, he dived into the Colorado River to find a clue that was under the water."

"I thought the fact that those three found the treasure was a secret, since they didn't have permits to search in the Grand Canyon."

"That's true. But you're missing the point." I point down at the rumbling cascade. "What if our next treasure is hidden down there? In the river? We can't retrieve it."

"Yes, we can."

Domhnall kicks his boots off, then removes all his clothing. He approaches the edge of the cliff and performs a few stretches, as if he means to leap off the precipice and into the water.

I grab his arm. "What are you doing? You can't jump into the water. What if it's only three feet deep? You'll crack your skull open."

He smirks and raps his fist on his head. "Hard as steel, *gràidh*."

"Domhnall, don't—"

Before I can finish my sentence, he leaps off the precipice feet first.

I watch him sailing down, down, down, until he hits the water and sinks below the surface. He bobs up again a few seconds later. The pigheaded man grins and gives me the thumbs-up sign, then dives under the water again, this time headfirst. All I can do is watch and wait.

The waterfall rumbles below me. Leaves rustle in the trees above. And I stand here wringing my hands while I count the seconds that he's been underwater.

Oh God, Domhnall, you barmy bull. What are you trying to prove now?

He springs up out of the water and whoops. Then he raises one arm straight above his head, waving it to show off the black box he holds in one hand. "I found it!"

"Brilliant. How do plan on getting back up here?"

"It's easy, love." He fiddles with the box, revealing a long black strap, and slings that over his body diagonally. "Watch and learn."

"This cliff is at least thirty feet high. That doesn't seem easy to me."

He ignores me and swims toward the waterfall, though I can't imagine how that will get him up to the top of the precipice again. He reaches the waterfall swiftly and climbs on top of it, then jumps onto a narrow ledge beside the river. I don't see anything that he could grab onto in order to climb up here. But I trot over to the area where Domhnall stands on that ledge and wait to see what he means to do now.

Domhnall lays his hands on the sheer cliff and slides them left, right, up, and down as if he's feeling for something. Then he stops.

I want to shout to him, but that might distract him so much that he falls down. So instead, I bite my lip and keep my focus glued to his every movement.

He pulls himself up, apparently having found something to help him. Though I can't see exactly what he's doing, he keeps finding new handholds and footholds as he gradually makes his way up the sheer cliff. When he reaches the top, he slaps both hands on the edge and levers himself up and onto the ground beside me. Domhnall is breathing hard but seems to be hardly sweating at all. He landed on his belly but now flips over onto his back. The black box is still strapped to his torso.

Domhnall aims the sexiest smile at me. I haven't seen him smile like that in months, maybe longer. Seeing that expression now makes me feel warm and wet and breathless with anticipation. For what? All the things I know he can do to me with that body.

I kneel beside him. "*Dòmhnall an Tarbh*, you are my hero."

He raises himself up on one elbow to face me. "You are my inspiration, *mo leannan*. I could lift this whole mountain if I knew that would impress you."

"You have impressed me. I had no idea you could free climb—or free dive."

"I'm an athlete. You've seen me toss cabers and play shinty."

"Aye. But that's nothing like what you just did here on Beann Dealgach. That was the most amazing feat of strength and agility."

Domhnall sits up and peels the strap of that black box off his body, setting it on the ground. "Want to have a poke?"

"You know how I feel about outdoor sex."

He cups my cheek in his hand, leaning in until our lips brush against each other. "But I performed a valiant feat, and you called me your hero. Doesn't a hero deserve a good, hard shag?"

"Och, you're a stubborn man."

"Because I want to fuck you? No, lass, that's hormones, not stubbornness." He slings an arm around my waist to tug me into his hard, hot, wet body. "Jumping into the river to retrieve that box got my adrenaline up. I need to feel your *brillean* wrapped around me while I push my *slat* inside you. Ahm already getting a *crann* for you. But if you'd rather I *fannadh* while you watch..."

"No, Domhnall, I need you inside me."

He rises and picks me up, then methodically strips away all my clothing. Once he's done that, he pulls me close until our bodies are in full contact.

"Tell me, *m'eudail*, would ye like me to take you the way *Dòmhnall an Tarbh* would?"

"Aye, please, whatever you want." I have no idea what he means to do, and I don't care.

"Get on your knees, Fiona, facing away from me."

I fall to my knees.

"Now, set your hands on the ground too."

Without any reservations, I obey his command. The tone of his voice, deep and firm and rough, gets me even more aroused.

He kneels behind me and pushes my legs apart a wee bit more. Then he presses his mouth to my erse and drags his tongue from one cheek to the other. He palms my bottom with both hands, licking his way up my spine, and just when he reaches the base of my neck, he pushes his stiff cock between my erse cheeks. I gasp and dig my fingers into the soft, damp earth. He rocks his hips back and forth to tease my folds while he reaches beneath me to take my tits in his hands and pinch the nipples. A cry bursts out of me.

Domhnall fists one hand in my hair, forcing me to tilt my head back, though not enough to cause pain. When he thrusts into me, I let out the most pathetic whimpering noise, but I dinnae care. He pumps into me hard and fast, his movements so vigorous that my tits flap wildly and I'm pushed forward with every violent thrust. His *bagais* slap against my erse, the sound echoing through the forest along with our cries.

He drops onto all fours and keeps fucking me.

I feel the orgasm rising fast, speeding through me like a runaway train. When he nips my throat and growls, I come. My inner muscles pulsate, and a strangled cry explodes out of me. Domhnall keeps thrusting until he finally can't hold back anymore. He slams into me so hard that I slide across the grass, and he roars like a rampaging beast. I've hit my peak, but I know he isn't quite done yet.

Domhnall pulls out and comes all over earth, groaning with deep satisfaction.

I lie down on the grass and gaze up at him with what must seem like a lazily contented expression.

He stretches out beside me, rolling onto his side to drape an arm across my belly. "I should have brought condoms. Never could've imagined a treasure hunt in the forest would lead to an incredible shag."

Neither could I, but I have no words to express how much I loved what we just did. Now that he's relaxed, it's time to drop the gauntlet.

"Domhnall, why won't you talk about your past?"

Chapter Fifteen

Domhnall

I groan and sprawl out on my back. An opening in the trees above us lets the sun shine down on our naked bodies, but I can't appreciate the beauty of Fiona's figure, not after the question she just posed. Question? No, it was a demand with a question mark at the end meant to push me to tell her everything. I should tell her, I know that. But I can't make myself do it.

What if the things I tell her make the lass run away? For good this time?

Fiona sits up and assumes a cross-legged position, facing me. She sets her hands on her knees and keeps her chin up. Aye, I recognize that posture. She always does this, or something very like it, whenever she thinks I'm being a bloody annoying ersehole.

"Talk, Domhnall. Or I'll push you off the cliff and run away with all your clothes."

"You would abandon me to the midges?"

"Aye. So start talking."

"What do you want to know?"

She eyes me with a hint of suspicion. "Are you implying that you'll answer any questions I ask?"

"I'll try. That's the best I can offer."

Fiona puckers her lips and drums her fingers on her knees for several seconds. Then she blows out a breath and nods. "I agree to your terms."

"Thank you." I debate with myself whether I should sit up or stay lying down. I decide on the latter, linking my hands under my head as I keep my focus on the sky. "Ask your questions. Be specific, though. None of that 'tell me everything' bollocks."

"All right." She drums her fingers again, but this time chews on her lip instead of puckering it. "Why did you insist that Jessica should stop being friends with Grey Dixon?"

"I told you all of that two years ago."

"The abridged version. Now I want the details."

Of course she does. Fiona deserves the whole truth, but ahmno the sort of man who blethers about himself. I gather that's the point of this exercise—to push me to open up. So, I sigh and do it. "I worried that Jessica would leave me for Grey, and I was right about that. Might've taken years for it to happen, but she did push me aside for a bloody business intelligence analyst. I dinnae know what that means, except that it's computer rubbish, but it sounds dead boring. I couldn't understand why Jess would prefer him."

"You feel inferior because Grey is clever and good with computers."

"That's rot. I do not feel inferior to that Sassenach."

Fiona's lips curl into a closed-mouth smile. Oh, aye, it's a smug expression, for dead certain. I've seen that sort of smile on her face before, and it always means she thinks she knows something about me that I refuse to acknowledge. For once, she's right. I just stop myself from grimacing. She's probably right every time she gives me that look.

I cover my eyes with my hands and groan.

A soft, warm weight settles onto my body. The scent of her surrounds me, though I don't mean that she's aroused and I can smell her cream. No, it's the way she smells all the time.

I peel my hands away from my face. "What are ye doing, lass?"

Fiona is currently lying on top of me with her hands clasped on my chest and her chin resting on them. She also wears a sweetly smug smile. Only Fiona MacTaggart could combine those two seemingly opposite expressions. Even Jess hadn't looked at me this way.

"I repeat, what are ye doing, lass?"

"You need encouragement. I'm giving it to you."

"Every last one of you MacTaggarts is insane." I rest my hands on her back. "But I'll overlook that flaw and be honest about my feelings anyway."

She laughs in a soft, sweet way. "You make that sound like I mean to strap you to a rack and stretch your bones until they break."

"It's the mental version of that." I take a deep breath to calm myself before I turn into a raging ersehole again. And now it's time for me to admit the truth to myself and Fiona. "Aye, you're right. I felt inferior to a bloody business intelligence analyst. Most women love my muscles and don't bother to look past the exterior and get to know me. I never used to mind that—or at least, I convinced myself I didn't mind it. Jessica wanted to dig under my skin and learn more about me, but I never let her."

"Because of Sophie. She cheated on you for years, and you had no idea that was going on."

"Until I caught Sophie and her lover going at it. Two years ago, I told you about that and said I might have been able to forgive her if she'd been shagging a different lover every time. But she had a relationship with one man for all the years of our marriage. She loved him."

Fiona places a soft kiss on my throat. "That hurt more than a casual betrayal, didn't it?"

"Aye. But honestly, it would've destroyed me even if she'd been having a poke with lots of men."

I close my eyes for a moment, letting the warmth of her penetrate my skin and begin to chase away the emotional chill. Christ, I've never admitted even to myself that Sophie's betrayal destroyed me. Six years I wasted with that lass. Six years of loving her and trying to be a good husband. Six years of pain. And no children, though I wanted them. Sophie didn't.

Fiona doesn't push me to say anything else. She simply gazes into my eyes and waits. She is an incredible woman, and I hope one day I can deserve her.

But right now, I need to keep going. "By the time I met Jessica, I was too scarred by my marriage to be any good for her. I should never have gotten involved with Jess, for her sake and for mine. We had good times, but I couldn't let her in the way she needed me to, and she couldn't fully commit to being with me. For her, the impediment was Grey and the fact that she couldn't admit even to herself that she loved him."

My thoughts reel backward in time to the day at the nudist resort when Fiona had confronted me in an attempt to talk me out of harassing Jessica. I still remember the exact words she spoke. The memory rushes through me, and I feel as if I'm back in that moment.

"You're a braw man who could get any woman he wants," Fiona had said. "Why are you banging your head into a brick wall trying to make Jessica love you?"

I'd known she was right even then, but I shoved the truth aside in favor of my obsession with reclaiming a woman who didn't want me. Fiona's question hit too close to home, and so I lashed out. "Keep your bonnie wee nose out of my business."

"If you want to keep banging your head on those bricks until your skull caves in, it's your choice."

Then Fiona had walked away, casually, as if she hadn't just confronted a snarling beast. Aye, I'd been a bastard back then. After Fiona left, I'd caught

Jessica coming out of the caretaker's cottage and forced a confrontation with her.

"Give it a rest, Domhnall. This is bordering on obsessive behavior."

"I love you, Jessica. I can't give up on us."

"There is no us. And you still haven't answered my question. If you love me so much, why did you wait four months before you tried to get me back?"

Oh, aye, she had asked me that question earlier. Naturally, I couldn't give her an answer because I didn't understand it myself, not yet. "You needed time to think, that's what I assumed. I waited for what seemed like a reasonable length of time."

The lass had laughed at me, and it wasn't a friendly sound. Sweet Jessica O'Connor had scoffed at me. "A reasonable length of time? It was months, Domhnall. I may not be in love with you, but I can still tell when you're full of shit. Did you ever think that maybe you took so long because you don't love me as much as you want to think you do?"

Jess had been spot on with that question. I didn't love her the way I should have if I meant to marry her. We'd been engaged, until she broke it off. I wouldn't listen, being a stubborn *bod ceann*. But Jessica might as well have driven a knife straight into my heart with her confession.

"I never loved you, Domhnall."

Even now, while I'm remembering that day, I still get a hard pang in my chest because of those five words she uttered. Jessica never really loved me. That means she would have left me anyway, even without my ultimatum that she must choose either me or Grey. She chose him, of course. And I couldn't handle that. Two years later, I feel that pain all over again when I remember what happened back then.

I explain all of that to Fiona, then I reveal something I haven't been able to think about until this moment. "Jess asked me why I didn't come for her sooner after we broke up. I waited four months. And I've finally accepted the reason for that. I never loved her. I wanted to feel that way, but I couldn't. Sophie ruined me."

Fiona's expression remains neutral, as if she's waiting for me to continue.

"That's why I've ruined our relationship," I tell her. "I keep expecting you to walk away, and finally, I fucked up so badly that you had no other choice."

"I didn't want to do it. I love you, Domhnall."

"And I love you. But I have too many scars. You deserve a better man than me."

She sits up, resting her palms on my chest. "You're wrong, Domhnall. You are not a bad man who's too damaged to love or be loved. But I know what you've told me is only part of the problem. Someday, I hope you'll share the rest. But not today. This was enough for now."

I stare at her for a moment before I can comprehend what she said. "You're letting me off the hook?"

"For today."

Why she would want to do that confounds me. But I've learned the hard way that women are inscrutable.

Fiona rises to her feet and waits while I pick myself up off the ground. We both brush ourselves off as best we can, then get dressed. Once we've done that, she clasps my face in both hands. "You're wrong, Domhnall. Sophie didn't destroy you so badly that you could never be good for any woman. If that were the case, Jessica wouldn't have become your friend after the two of you broke up. But she is your friend now, and so is Grey. Everyone has forgiven you for your bad behavior at Alex and Cat's wedding, which means it's time for you to forgive yourself."

"You just said it isn't true that I'm no good for any woman. But then you went on to explain how I'm only acceptable as a friend. That contradicts your claim about me."

She sets her hands on her hips and shakes her head at me. "You insist on interpreting everything I say through the lens of 'Domhnall is an ersehole who can't be loved.' Jess loves you as a friend." Fiona boosts herself up on her toes to gaze into my eyes. "And I love you, full stop."

Then she turns away and walks toward the black box I'd left on the ground.

I stand by my assertion that Fiona is off her head.

The lass picks up the satchel and the black box, which she brings over to me. "There must be something inside this. How are we meant to open it?"

"Ask your cousin. Errol probably wants us to divine the answer by tossing runes or going into a psychic trance."

She wags a finger at me. "Dinnae revert to Domhnall the Ersehole. I like *Dòmhnall an Tarbh* much better. He knows how to shag a lass, and he's quite heroic when he dives off a cliff to unearth hidden treasure."

"Flattery won't help us unlock this box." I take the contraption away from her and study every side of it. "Look at this. It has a combination lock. Now, if your cousin would have left us a clue that would help us figure out the combination…"

"The lock has numbers, and there are six of them. What does that tell us?"

"We're buggered. That's what it tells us."

Chapter Sixteen

Fiona

"Och, Domhnall, you are the most pessimistic man." I brush dirt off the box and try to think of what numbers Errol would assume we would know. I can't think of anything offhand, and Domhnall seems to be doing no better. "Why don't we ring Errol and ask him for a hint?"

Domhnall huffs. "I'm sure he would love to give us a hint, but we won't understand it because he's insane. A few months ago, I asked him for directions to a shop in Fort William, and he gave them to me in the form of a riddle. I never did crack his bloody code. When I told him so, he grinned and slapped my arm. He's a bampot of the first order."

"Errol is very clever. But aye, he's an unusual man. Why don't we at least try ringing him?"

"If you insist." Domhnall brings out his mobile and dials the number, tapping his foot while he waits for my cousin to answer. After a moment, he gives up. "No signal. I thought Dùndubhan had cellular service throughout the property."

"No, it has service on the eastern side of Beann Dealgach. We are on the western side."

"Perfect. Your crackbrained cousin has left us with no way to open this ruddy box."

I bite my upper lip while I consider the problem. "There are two options. Either Errol forgot to provide a clue, or this box is a practical joke."

Domhnall groans. "If we don't finish the treasure hunt soon, we'll be spending the night on Beann Dealgach."

"It won't come to that. The combination must be something that Errol is sure we would both remember. Since it has six digits, I wonder if the combination is a calender date."

"Let's head for the next spot on our itinerary while we think about that."

"Good idea."

We follow the path on the map, which corresponds with what seems like a trail created by animals, most likely deer. The terrain becomes a bit steeper, though not steep enough to tax our muscles or make us breathe harder. The map is leading us along a path that skirts the river. We can hear the rushing of the water, though it doesn't sound as if it's close enough that we might stumble into it and drown.

After ten minutes or so, Domhnall suddenly halts. Since he's been walking right beside me, I stop too and turn toward him.

"What is it?" I ask. "You look stunned."

"I think I've had an epiphany."

"About what?"

He crouches and sets the satchel on the ground, then brings out the black box. "I think I know what the combination is."

I kneel facing him. "What gave you the answer?"

"You did." He sets the box on his thigh and turns the tumblers on the lock. A click indicates he has opened it. His eyes widen. "I was right. I did it." Domhnall flips the lid up—and seems puzzled. "What are these lunatics trying to tell us now?"

"What's inside?"

He plucks an item out of the box and holds it up for me to see.

I can't help laughing. "Errol gave us a wee figurine of a Scottish piper."

Domhnall holds the figurine between his thumb and forefinger, turning it this way and that as if he can't believe what he sees. Then he shakes his head. "They can't know. But they must."

"Who can't know what?"

He stuffs the wee piper into the satchel along with the box. "Let's move on to the next treasure."

Domhnall takes off down the trail at a good clip, every step crisp and precise. Oh, aye, that's a reaction I've seen before. He walks that way when something has disturbed him but he doesn't want to talk about it.

No, he won't get away with that anymore.

Domhnall has gotten ahead of me since his legs are longer. I need to sprint briefly to come up alongside him again. He ignores me, naturally. With his jaw firmly set and his lips flattened, he has most definitely shifted in stoic mode.

"What was the combination, Domhnall?"

He grunts.

"Tell me. If ye dinnae do that, I'll be forced to torture the answer out of you."

When his lips tick upward the slightest bit, I can tell he isn't angry—not at me, anyway. But when he slows his pace and switches to a more relaxed gait, I know he has recovered from whatever disturbed him about that box. Which means I have an opening.

So, I halt and grasp his arm to stop him too. "Explain yourself, Domhnall. What about that combination fashed you so much?"

He bows his head, wincing as he grips the back of his neck. "Those were our numbers."

"Dinnae understand. Our numbers? I wasn't aware we had our own digits."

"It's a calendar date." He winces even harder. "And it's, ah, the day we met."

"Oh." I feel almost as stunned by that fact as he had been when he opened that box. "Why would Errol and Ashley make the combination be the day we met? How could they know we would remember that date?"

He rolls his eyes sideways to look at me. "I remembered. Did you?"

"Aye, of course. I remember every milestone in our relationship."

"So do I. May we continue our barmy quest now?"

"Of course."

I'm fair certain he remembers every milestone too, not just the day we met, and that knowledge makes me feel almost giddy. I manage to hide excitement from Domhnall, I think. He might not appreciate it if I jumped on him and tackled him to the ground so I could rip his clothes off. Men can be sensitive about that sort of thing.

Our second to last treasure lies up ahead of us, and the map leads us out of the trees and into a bonnie wee clearing. A jagged rock rises out of the ground at one side of the open area. The map indicates we should go there. Domhnall insists on holding my hand as we make our way over to the boulder, which makes me feel slightly giddy again. He hasn't been this affectionate in months, ever since I demanded to know more about his past.

At the base of the boulder lies a small, rectangular cardboard box. Domhnall snatches up the box and lifts the lid to reveal the object nestled inside it, surrounded by crumpled tissue paper. He turns the box toward me just enough that I can read the words on the bottle's label.

"*Collaidh Sgeul-Rùin* Black Label Highland single-malt whisky. A tantalizing secret blend with a sensual undertone designed to rouse the passions of whisky lovers."

Domhnall grunts. "Sounds like rubbish to me. But I reckon the tourists love it."

I lean in to scrutinize the smaller words printed at the bottom of the label. "Distilled with only the most authentic, pure Highland ingredients sourced locally on the outskirts of Loch Fairbairn. I had no idea there were any distilleries in the vicinity of the village."

"Neither did I." He closes the lid of the box. "What does a bottle of whisky have to do with our relationship?"

I shrug. "The name means 'sensual secret.' Maybe that's meant to get us randy."

"Dinnae need whisky for that. All I need to do to get you randy is jump into the river."

He tucks the whisky box into the satchel, and we continue on our way. One more treasure to go. That's good, since the sun will begin to set in a wee while, and we don't want to get caught out here with the midges.

Domhnall doesn't want that, at any rate.

Our last stop takes us around the side of Beann Dealgach, skirting the slope without scaling it. Rory's mountain, as Domhnall calls it, isn't as tall as Ben Nevis. And besides, we've stayed at the lower elevations. Errol's map guides us to a lovely little overlook where we can see the sprawling forest around the mountain as well as the village in the distance. I can just make out the peak of the tallest tower of Dùndubhan, but nothing else of the castle. The forest thins out beyond the perimeter and the land it encompasses.

Clouds have begun to move in, but it doesn't seem like rain coming.

When I turn round and tip my head back, I catch sight of the rocky summit and the sparse greenery that surrounds it. I return my attention to the vista in front of the mountain to find Domhnall standing there with his hands on his hips and a look of intense concentration on his face.

I come up beside him. "What do you see?"

"Nothing. Where has your cousin hidden the last treasure? It must be invisible."

"Och, no. Errol can't make objects invisible, only ink."

Domhnall squints at me. "I didn't think we were up high enough for you to suffer from altitude sickness, but I can't think of any other reason you would talk like a nutter."

"It's a good thing I know you well enough to realize you're teasing me. Errol makes his own invisible ink. It's from a medieval recipe."

"Why in the world would he do that?" Domhnall holds up a hand when I'm about to respond. "Never mind. It's irrelevant at the moment. Just help me find our treasure so we can go home and eat a proper meal."

"And enjoy the whisky Errol gave us."

"Dinnae tempt me. I might open up that bottle right now."

I rotate in a circle, slowly, examining the area for clues. Then I sigh and let my shoulders flag. "We should fan out again and hunt for the ruddy thing, whatever it is."

Domhnall and I start walking in opposite directions in a rotating figure-eight pattern that he suggested might be the most useful. I've never heard of such a thing, but if he wants to do it this way, I'll go along. We bump into each other now and then, and every time, he gives my hand a squeeze and flashes me a smile.

After several minutes, I stop to examine the area more thoroughly.

Domhnall whoops. "I found it! Over here, Fiona."

I whirl around and spot him standing between two small trees. He swivels his head around to grin at me. I rush over there.

He holds up his treasure—another sodding lockbox. That means another combination we need to puzzle out. But Domhnall is still grinning, until he notices my expression. "Why do ye look so defeated? We found the last treasure."

"But it has a combination lock. More numbers. Errol wouldn't put the same combination on both lockboxes."

"Let's try it and see." He turns the wee dials until he has selected the date that corresponds to the day we met. The lock does not disengage. His posture sags. "Bloody hell. What other date would Errol use?"

"Something he thinks is important to us."

"I'll try your birthday." He spins the dials again, but he still can't open the box. So, he tries his birthday, with no better results. "Do you have any suggestions?"

"Um…" I bite my lip and lean in close to study the wee dials. Numbers. We need six of them. Something related to our relationship. "Try the day we moved in together."

He does that—and sighs miserably. "Try again."

"Are you sure you remember the date correctly?"

"Of course I remember it." He gives me a devilish smile. "We shagged on the living room floor before we brought the new bed in. That made it a memorable date."

"I love that bed. It's just the right size for you, and it provides us with plenty of space to have a poke in any way we like."

Domhnall holds the box in both hands, tapping his fingers on the bottom of it.

I freeze. Did I just see.. Cannae be sure. "Stop tapping your finger, Domhnall. I think I see something on the bottom. It's black on one side and white on the other."

He flips the box over and peels away the strip of black duct tape that had held a small, thin plastic bag in place. Inside the bag lies a folded sheet of paper.

"Eureka!" I shout, though I doubt I've ever used that word before.

Domhnall holds the box out to me. "You peel the tape off and read the note. There must be one."

I remove the tape and unfold the paper. "Aye, it is a note from Errol. He says that he made this task more difficult because he knows we can handle it. The coordinates to our next location are in the note as well. Errol says the only clue he will provide about the final treasure is that you need to remember Munro's advice."

"What?" Domhnall frowns. "I'm beginning to despise your cousin."

"Did Munro ever give you advice?"

He scrunches up his mouth. "Aye, but it's not something I should tell you yet."

I decide to ignore that statement, for now. "Do you remember exactly when he offered you that advice?"

"Aye. It was the evening of Munro and Natalie's engagement ceilidh." His face goes blank briefly, then lights up as he furiously rolls the dials—and a click tells us the lock is open. He grins. "We did it. We solved the last riddle."

"What's inside the box?"

Domhnall lifts the lid halfway, then swiftly shuts it. "I, ah, need to keep this one to myself."

Chapter Seventeen

Domhnall

I tuck the smaller lockbox into the satchel and use focusing on the map as an excuse to avoid looking at Fiona. I need a moment to compose myself after seeing what Errol had hidden inside the box. He told us the final treasure would be personal, not monetary, though I don't think kitschy trinkets are worth much. Nothing we found had any intrinsic value until we found this item. The idea of it doesn't disturb me. Not knowing how Fiona might feel about it does. We've had a good time here on Rory's mountain, and the treasure hunt lightened the mood and brought us closer together. That's how it seemed to me.

How could Errol have known what I meant to do?

I suddenly remember what Thane Buchanan had told me back in the car when he and the others abducted me. *We know what you're after, but you'll need to prove yourself first.* Whether that statement has anything to do with the item in the lockbox, I have no idea. As for what Munro told me… I can't tell Fiona that her cousin advised me to be unstoppable. It's not helpful.

The lass in question punches my arm. "Wake up, Domhnall."

"I am awake."

"Physically, aye. But you're mentally in a coma."

"Blokes in comas don't speak."

She glances at the satchel. "Are you going to show me the last treasure? This is meant to be a shared experience."

That bloody Errol. He did this on purpose, for dead sure. Whether to humiliate me or to force me to tell Fiona what I did recently, I don't know. This doesn't seem like the right time.

"I think Errol intended for me to keep this until it's needed."

Fiona puckers her lips. "You're trying to repair our relationship, but you insist on keeping more secrets instead of less."

"No, I'm not. It isn't the right time to tell you, that's all."

"When will it be the right time?"

I pinch the bridge of my nose and shut my eyes, feeling the first pangs of a headache. "Please, Fiona, let's talk about this another time. We need to make our way back to the Harley before dusk."

"Aye, we do."

I open the maps app on my mobile and find the pinned location Errol had set for us. We backtrack our path, following the GPS, and Fiona stays in step with me all the while. We reach the base of the mountain much faster than we had climbed it and jog over to the Harley. Fortunately, no one stole it. But I reckon Beann Dealgach is too remote for anyone to think of hunting for goods to steal on this mountain.

Fiona wraps her arms around me as we drive off down the road. She even rests her helmeted head on my shoulder.

I thought she was angry with me. Women are impossible to understand. But I relish the weight of her head resting on my shoulder and the warmth of her wrapped around me. We reach our next location just as the sun begins to sink toward the mountains. The note had indeed told us where to go, though it's not where I had expected we would end up. Now, we find ourselves riding the Harley up a bumpy gravel two-track through the forest.

I never knew it could take so long to drive round the base of Beann Dealgach and find the outer gate of Dùndubhan.

The metal gate is hanging open, waiting for us.

We reach Dùndubhan in a matter of minutes, mostly because I wanted to get off this ruddy motorcycle and so I drove much faster. Fiona doesn't seem to care, though she hugs me tighter. I'd call that a fringe benefit of wanting to get to the castle quicker.

I park in the courtyard near the vestibule entrance, sliding in alongside vehicles I recognize, though I can't attach a particular person to any of them. That might be Munro's car or Alex's. I've never been a car fanatic, and I pay little attention to what sort of vehicles other people drive. Though I offer my hands to help Fiona dismount the Harley, she ignores that and slides off it on her own. When she removes her helmet, her hair stays flattened, but the lass doesn't seem to care. On anyone else, that would look ridiculous. But Fiona is bonnie and sexy no matter what she wears or how badly her hair gets mussed.

The vestibule door swings open, and Errol steps outside just enough to hold the door open for us. "Hurry up! The festivities are about to begin."

Festivities? Nobody warned me about that. I'm too bloody jeeked to dance or chat to anyone except Fiona.

Despite not wanting my help to dismount the bike, Fiona takes my hand as we approach her cousin.

I stop on the threshold of the vestibule door, twisting my head around to glare at Errol. "What sort of festivities are going on here?"

He grins and chuckles. "You'll see. Logan and Alex arranged everything."

Perfect. A former spy and his former con artist mate arranged "festivities" for us. That sounds like barrels of fun, if "fun" means a keg full of piranhas.

Fiona and I enter the vestibule, then Errol slams the door shut and rushes ahead of us while waving for us to follow him. He keeps grinning too, like a ruddy eejit. I know Errol is a clever laddie, but his behavior always baffles me. He leads us upstairs, but we breeze past the first floor and the great hall, continuing up to the second floor which houses the long gallery. A lengthy strip down the middle has been covered over with some sort of white flooring that lies atop the wood floor.

Errol slaps my arm. "Here we are. The game will commence shortly."

"What game? I'm getting bloody sick of the secrecy."

"Can't you tell what we're about?" He waves his arm to indicate the white surface. "It's indoor curling."

"You are insane. Curling is a winter sport, and it requires ice."

"Get with the times, Domhnall. Modern technology is amazing, and it allows us to have curling matches any day of the year thanks to synthetic ice."

Ice that isn't ice? I've never heard of such a thing, but then, I've never been interested in curling or hockey.

"What are we waiting for?" I ask. "Looks like your barmy family is already here, along with that man who sat beside me in Munro's car when he and Gavin kidnapped me."

"They kidnapped you?" Fiona says. Then she scowls at Errol. "No wonder Domhnall is grumpy."

I am not grumpy, but I won't defend my demeanor in front of everyone.

"Never mind that," Errol says, waving a hand dismissively. "You wanted to know what we're waiting for. The answer is you and Fiona—and the laddies who are bringing the rest of our equipment. We have the synthetic ice rink. Now, we need the curling stones and target mats, plus pusher sticks for the old gents who can't bend over anymore." Errol points at someone behind us. "I'm talking about you, Iain, and Torcall too."

Iain MacTaggart comes up beside us. "I am not that old, ye *cacan*. But I can't expect a wee bairn to appreciate the maturity only a man over fifty can achieve. I'll kick your erse, Fire Starter."

Errol grins again.

Aye, he loves his nickname—the Fire Starter—and even calls himself that sometimes.

The barmy laddie leans toward me and speaks in a whisper. "How did the treasure hunt go? I assume you found all the items Ashley and I left for you. But did your search inspire any, ah, romantic moments?"

Fiona's eyes flare wide. Then she turns her head away as if she's embarrassed.

I aim my hardest glower at Errol. "None of your bloody business."

Errol throws his hands up. "All right, calm down. Did you at least find the treasures?"

"Aye, we did."

"Brilliant! Did you show the last one to Fiona?"

"No."

"Why not?"

I wince and scratch my neck. "Well, ah, it didn't seem like the right time. And you're bloody cheeky sod to include that in our treasure hunt."

"But it's for her. You're meant to give it to Fiona to show her—"

"At the right time. Now haud yer wheesht, Errol."

Fiona swivels her head toward me, her eyes wide.

She doesn't know what the last treasure was, and I dinnae want to tell her, not yet. That means I can't give the thing to her now. We're in a room full of her family and friends. When I decide it's time, I will reveal the final treasure to her.

But the lass keeps gawping at me.

Footfalls pound up the vestibule stairs. It sounds like an elephant rampaging toward us, but as the newcomer mounts the last step and heads our way, I realize that is no elephant. It's Magnus MacTaggart. No, I never actually thought it was an elephant. But I've never heard anyone create such a racket in the stairwell.

Errol, Fiona, and I spin around to look at the bounty hunter. He seems a bit winded, but not as out of breath as I would have expected. He just ran up three flights of stairs while carrying what appears to be a heavy bag, based on the way the handles are stretched and the main compartment bulges.

"What have ye got there, Magnus?" I ask. "Looks like you're carrying a bag of severed heads."

Magnus sets the bag on the floor. "No severed heads tonight. The first of every month is my manslaughter day, and this is the fifteenth."

As with all the MacTaggarts, I can't tell if he's being facetious. I assume he doesn't literally kill people. He takes them in to the police.

Munro jogs over to us and snatches up the heavy bag that Magnus had set down a moment ago. "About bloody time. What took you so long to get the stones?"

"You forgot to leave the boot of your car unlatched. I had to pick the lock."

"Ah, sorry." Munro crouches to unzip the bag and reveal its contents—several thick, disk-shaped curling stones. "Now we're ready."

I strap my arms over my chest and give these laddies my best hard stare. "You lot had better not be wanting me to take part in a curling match. I've never played the sport before."

"Relax, Domhnall," Errol says. "It's easy. We'll explain the rules, then we can all ignore them like we do when we're playing shinty and cricket and the Highland games."

"Best not be thinking I'll play cricket. I've never participated in that sport either."

Magnus picks up one of the curling stones. "Ready to learn a new game?"

"Aye. Why not." They probably won't let me leave the castle, anyway. The MacTaggarts enjoy holding people hostage in the name of meddling.

"Iain and I will demonstrate for you. It's more of a mental challenge than a physical one. You need to calculate the perfect trajectory for the stone."

Since the MacTaggarts also enjoy having me on, I can't decide if what Magnus just said is true. I've played shinty with his clan, and they paid little attention to the rules of the sport. They make up their own instead.

Magnus and Iain lead me over to the synthetic ice and set a stone down at my feet.

Iain points at the shiny rock disk. "Do you see that L-shaped red object attached to the top of the stone? That's called the handle."

"Aye. I'm fair certain even a five-year-old could figure that out."

"Excellent. You've grasped the concept easily." Iain crouches and grips the handle. "You hold onto this and release the stone at a swift pace."

Magnus shakes his head. "Iain, you know bloody well that a curling stone should maintain an average speed of three to four miles per hour. This isn't a high-speed race."

"It isn't? Errol taught me the game, and he insisted it must be lightning fast."

"And you believed him? Errol loves to tell porkies."

Errol steps up beside me. I'm trapped between him and the bounty hunter. "I never lie, Magnus. You know that."

He snorts. "You're a consummate actor. I watched you con Dilara Terzi into showing you the computer rubbish at the headquarters of Sovereign World Industries. Then you conned her into confessing to murder."

"She was guilty."

"Aye, but she wouldn't have confessed if you hadn't talked her into it."

"Dilara was—"

"Enough!" I shout. "Have any of you ever actually played this game before?"

Magnus, Munro, Errol, and Iain all exchange bemused expressions and shrug.

I scrub a hand over my eyes. "Ye haven't, aye? Not one of you has ever attempted to curl or do curling or whatever the proper term is."

Errol hunches his shoulders. "Not as such."

"Then why are you pushing me to do this?"

Iain claps a hand on my shoulder. "It'll be good for your mental and emotional health. Jack said so."

"And is Jack here right now?"

"No. He's at home with Autumn and the bairn."

Munro slaps my back more firmly than seems necessary. "Might as well give it a go, eh?"

"First, I want to talk to Errol. Alone."

The Wild Man slaps my back again—three times. "Go on, then. We can wait for you. Fiona, why dinnae ye find your sisters? They're in the tower bedroom doing…whatever women do."

Fiona must be standing behind me because I can't see her in my peripheral vision. Now, she strides past me without even glancing in my direction. At the closed door to the tower bedroom, she grasps the knob and pauses to glance back at me. Her lips form a tight smile.

I open my mouth as if I mean to speak, but I can't think what I intended to say. She wouldn't hear me, anyway. The MacTaggarts and their spouses and friends are having conversations that the cavernous room amplifies.

Fiona opens the door and disappears as it shuts behind her.

She must still be irritated that I wouldn't show her the last treasure or share with her what Munro told me. I want to run after the lass and beg her to forgive me, but that wouldn't make her happy. She fell for me because I was *Dòmhnall an Tarbh*, the sort of man who boxes and wrestles and plays shinty with virtually no rules. Of course, I'm also the man who cheated at the Highland games just to embarrass Grey Dixon.

I crook a finger at Errol, guiding him away from the crowd and to the spot furthest away from the others. "What was that treasure hunt bollocks really about?"

He speaks as softly as I had done. "Helping you and Fiona. What else would it be about?"

"I have no idea. That's why I'm interrogating you. Seems like you are the one orchestrating all of this nonsense."

"You need help. That's what it's all about."

I study him for a moment, suddenly wondering if I've misunderstood Errol's motives. "Do you want me to convince Fiona to take me back?"

"Of course. We all want that."

"You're claiming all your family and friends want me to succeed."

"Aye."

Though my mouth opens, I can't produce any words. I'm most likely gawping at him too.

Errol leans back against the wall and considers me with a canny look in his eye. "I admire you, Domhnall. You and your mate Mick started a company from nothing and turned it into an international chain. Sometimes I think you like for everyone to assume you're nothing but a brainless lout, but MacTaggarts aren't that easily fooled."

"You aren't a MacTaggart."

"Half of me is. My ma was born Finella MacTaggart and only changed her name once she married Jock Murdoch, my da."

"Thank you for the genealogy lesson, but I want to know why you arranged that treasure hunt and why you put that…thing in the last lockbox."

Errol chuckles. "Thing? That sounds like something Munro would have said back when he was a grumpy sod. Well, he still is one. But he outgrew his fear of intimacy and rejection." He glances around as if he's worried someone might overhear. "We should talk about the 'thing' later. Right now, you need to start curling."

"What will playing a sport I've never participated in before do for me?"

"That's what we aim to find out."

I'm developing a strong urge to find Fiona, throw her over my shoulder, and stalk out of here. These people seem insane, on the surface, but I've spent enough time with most of them to realize their lunacy is purposeful.

"Ye have twenty minutes to convince me that curling is worthwhile, Errol. Then I'm away."

One side of the laddie's mouth ticks upward in a sly expression. "As long you're not away with the fairies, it will all work out."

I give up on trying to get information out of Errol and return to the makeshift curling rink or whatever they call it. Synthetic ice doesn't sound appealing, but I did agree to do whatever these people want me to do.

Fiona and her sisters emerge from the tower bedroom.

Aye, I will do anything for that woman.

Chapter Eighteen

Fiona

Curling is a strange sport. I had heard of it before, but I never watched a match or met anyone who participated in the sport. Everyone I know prefers shinty and Highland games. Curling seems like a cross between hockey, golf, and discus, though it's not really like any of those things. The player slides across the floor until he slowly releases the handle and stops. Meanwhile, two other men whisk wee brooms across the floor as they shepherd the stone toward the target zone.

Iain has just played the first round, or whatever it's called in curling parlance, and his stone reached the target.

Are we meant to cheer? I sweep my gaze over the crowd, but it seems like no one has a ruddy clue how to react. After a moment of unintended silence, someone finally dares to clap and whoop. That would be Rae, Ian's American wife. Their teenage daughter, Malina, joins in her mother's revelry.

"Way to go, Dad!"

Malina races over to Iain and hugs him. Rae takes a wee bit longer to reach him since she holds their youngest child in her arms.

"The match isn't over yet," Munro shouts in his grumpiest voice. "May we continue, please?"

"We had to celebrate," Rae says. "This was Iain's first attempt at curling, and he rocked it."

Malina nods vigorously. "Yeah, Dad is awesome at curling. Does he get a trophy?"

"Not unless his team wins." Munro sounds even grumpier now, but that's nothing new. We all know and love the Wild Man. His crusty exterior hides a heart of gold. "Would ye get yer erses off the ice? Your fellow team members would like to have a go too."

Iain stoops to let Malina climb onto his shoulders, then they lead the way back to the other end of the playing area with Rae and the bairn in tow. All the spectators are on either side of the long strip of synthetic ice, with a wide exclusion zone, as Magnus called it, surrounding the rink. Once they've reached the other end of the playing area, Malina rejoins the crowd with her mother and the bairn.

Iain is playing for the Loch Fairbairn team, while Domhnall is on the Dùndubhan side. My brother Rory had invited Domhnall to join his team, and I nearly fainted from shock when I heard that. I know my brothers don't hate Domhnall, but they do love to harass him, so I assumed they would send him to the other team. But they asked him to play on their side.

No one here knows how the scoring is meant to work, so they will count each stone that reaches the target as one point. Why didn't they get on the internet and search for information before they decided to mount a curling match? Men are eejits.

Domhnall steps up to the ice and kneels to grasp the handle of the curling stone. He nods as Munro gives him advice. Then he sets his stone gliding down the rink. He drops to his knees and slides along with the stone until he reaches a certain point. I have no clue how players decide when to release the ruddy thing. But once Domhnall lets go, Evan and Aidan shepherd the stone toward the target without ever touching it. I think they're sweeping away bits of ice or something to make way for the stone.

"It's in the house!" Iain shouts. "We think that means Domhnall scored."

"Of course it does," I shout, though I don't understand the scoring. I'm supporting my big, sweet bull. "Go, Domhnall! You're in the house, and apparently, that's a good thing."

Domhnall flashes me a bemused look.

The match goes on, and still no one bothers to Google the rules of the sport. Well, it doesn't matter. This is part of Domhnall's rehabilitation. That's what Jamie and Cat claim. Jamie broke up with Gavin at one point, before they were married, because he refused to share all of himself with her. Catriona despised Alex after he shattered her heart years ago, but later, she rehabilitated him too. My sisters believe Domhnall won't be as pigheaded as Gavin or Alex. I hope they're right.

The Loch Fairbairn team scores again. The teams have been taking turns, which means everyone gets a chance to slide a stone across the fake ice. Serena, Logan's wife, brings out a whiteboard on wheels to help everyone keep score. She and Keely, Evan's wife, keep track of the men's progress with erasable markers. Every score results in cheering, no matter which side earned the point.

Errol finally takes a turn, stepping up to the starting point. He rubs his hands together, and his tongue pokes out between his lips. I think that means he's concentrating and calculating the best trajectory. The long gallery goes silent as everyone waits for the Fire Starter to make his move. Errol drops into a crouch. He brushes his hand over the synthetic ice, then just sits there staring at it.

"Hurry up, ye bampot," Munro shouts. "You're holding up the match."

Errol rises and steps backward several feet. Then he rubs his hands again and races forward, hurling himself at the curling stone, grasping its handle as he drops onto the floor flat on his belly. The stone is moving so fast that it drags him along with it. Evan and Aidan try to shepherd the stone, but they can't keep up with the speed of Errol's path down the rink. He begins to whoop and shout. Finally, he lets go of the stone a few feet from the house, which is the target, and the stone rushes inside that zone.

And it keeps going. And going.

With a thunk, the curling stone hits the far wall of the long gallery.

"Errol, ye bloody *cacan*," Rory snarls as he stalks over to his cousin. "If you damaged my castle—"

"Chill out, Rory." Errol crawls on hands and knees to inspect the wall. "It's fine. Zero damage to your precious castle."

Rory aims his patented steely glare at Errol, but our cousin pays no attention to that. My brother sighs and heads back into the crowd to find his wife. Their twin bairns have been shrieking with delight every time someone sets a curling stone gliding down the rink.

Or crashing down it. Only Errol has done that, though.

Iain glances about until he sees the man he'd been searching for, then he lets out a sharp, piercing whistle. "Domhnall, you're up next." As Domhnall trots over to the starting point, Iain says, rather more loudly than necessary, "Dinnae feel pressured to ride your stone down the rink. Errol has haggis for brains, after all. You are an intelligent laddie."

"You expect me to be offended," Errol pronounces. "But that won't work. Having haggis for brains is a compliment, to my mind."

Only Errol would say something like that. He loves to stir things up.

Domhnall gets ready, assuming the appropriate position again—or at least the same position as before. Who knows what the correct stance is. He surges forward while gripping the stone's handle, dropping to his knees and releasing the stone once he feels it's on the right trajectory.

I clasp my hands and track the motion of the stone with gaze nailed to its trajectory. I feel ridiculously anxious, as if Domhnall's life depends on his ability to play a strange sport.

The stone reaches the house.

Everyone cheers. I leap up and down while clapping.

The long gallery falls silent as Iain and Munro engage in a secretive conversation. Then Munro nods.

Iain faces the crowd and raises his hands. "We have declared the winner of the first-ever Dùndubhan Curling Competition. Welcome the champion—Domhnall Sterling and his team!"

Even louder cheers erupt, and several people whistle. Some of the lasses shriek. The men slap Domhnall's back.

I race over there.

The other men see me coming and fan out to make room as I fling my entire body at Domhnall. He stumbles backward half a step but never loses his grip on me. I pepper his face with kisses, then crush my mouth to his.

And the cheers turn into catcalls.

Domhnall sets me down and takes a wee step backward. His face is cinched up into a pained expression.

I lay a hand on his chest. "What's wrong, *leannan?*"

He clears his throat but still seems uncomfortable. Out of the corner of his mouth, he hisses, "Everyone is watching."

"Since when do you care about that?"

"This is your family."

Evan and Aidan sprint over to us, and Evan holds up a statuette that features a figure pushing a curling stone. He offers it to Domhnall. "The winner receives this trophy. Congratulations."

Domhnall accepts the item, but he still seems uncomfortable. He bows his head to study the trophy, turning it side to side.

I clear my throat, then announce, "Domhnall and I are going home. It's been a long day."

"The treasure hunt left ye jeeked, eh?" Iain says. "You can't go home, though, not yet. You're staying the night here at Dùndubhan. It's already been arranged, which means you are not permitted to decline our generous demand. Ah, our generous *offer.*"

Iain winks and smiles.

Munro and Natalie lead us away, but not to the bedrooms upstairs or downstairs. Instead, they take us across the long gallery. We need to hop over the synthetic ice, then Munro holds the door open for us as Natalie guides us up the steps and into the tower bedroom. I've been in this room before, though only briefly. I've never spent the night in here—or anywhere else in the castle. Rory often invited me to stay, but I had a home of my own for all the years when I ran a dress shop in the village. When that closed down, Catriona and I shared a house for a while, until she reunited with Alex.

After that, I met Domhnall. We lived together for two years.

Until I booted him out. I feel a touch queasy when I think about that.

Natalie shoos me over to the foot of the bed and won't stop until I do what she wants. So, I settle onto the mattress. It's so tall that my feet don't touch the floor.

Domhnall marches up the steps, followed by Munro.

The Wild Man, as everyone calls Munro, grips Domhnall's shoulder and gives him a strong shake. "You two need some alone time."

Domhnall twists his mouth into an irritated slant. "With all the spacious bedrooms in this castle, why did you bring us to the smallest, most cramped one?"

"It's a teaching moment. That's what Iain says."

Munro crooks his finger at Natalie, and she trots over to him. They exchange odd looks, then hurry out of the room, pulling the door shut behind them. A lock chunks.

Domhnall's nostrils flare, just like a bull. *Dòmhnall an Tarbh* has roused from his slumber, and I can't deny that side of him gets me randy—and makes me stifle a laugh. But he is not amused or aroused. Domhnall grabs the knob and tries to pull the door open, but it won't budge.

"Could've told you that was locked. I heard the sound of it."

He ignores me as if I'm a ghost haunting the room and he refuses to admit such things exist. Domhnall tries the knob on the other door, the one that leads to the top floor, but he has no better luck.

"Aye, I could've told you that one would be locked too."

Domhnall stomps over to the bed and sits down beside me at the foot. His shoes reach the floor, unlike mine. "I'm acting like a *tolla-thon* again, just the way I did when we first met."

"No, you are not an asshole now, nor have ever been one." I suck in a big breath and shout toward the door, "But my family and friends have become bloody annoying lately. Maybe we should move to France to get away from them."

"Two Scots in France?" Munro shouts with feigned revulsion. "The frogs would never let you in."

"But I love frogs. They're adorable, and they ribbit."

"We're leaving now. You two are irredeemably insane."

"Don't be such a grump, Munro," Natalie says. "We are leaving, Fiona, for real this time. Have fun."

I hear their footsteps receding, and I know this time they won't hang about to eavesdrop. Once they're gone, I gesture toward an object in the corner. "Why is there luggage in here?"

"Dinnae know, dinnae care."

I nudge him in the side with my elbow. "No grumpiness, Domhnall. Why did you mutate into an ogre after you won the curling match?"

"Because it was a ruse. I'd wager all your relatives know the rules of curling, and they're pretending to be ignorant."

Well, I can't say my family would never do such a thing. They have pulled similar stunts, but always for a good cause.

With a heavy sigh, Domhnall hoists himself off the bed and approaches the mysterious luggage. He kicks it with the toe of one shoe.

"I doubt it will reach out and bite you, Domhnall."

He grunts. Then he crouches to pull the first piece of luggage out and unzip the bag. "Your clothes are in here including, ah, unmentionables."

"When did you become shy about my nightgowns?"

"Not shy about anything. These garments aren't nightgowns. They're… something else." He zips up the bag and gives it a hard shove. The piece of luggage slides across the wood floor, halting near my feet. Then he pulls out a larger bag and opens it up. "These are your clothes."

"Isn't there anything of yours in those bags?"

He rummages around in that dark corner and brings out two more pieces of luggage. They're both larger than the previous ones. Domhnall opens one up. "Here are my clothes."

"Whoever packed for us must wonder why you don't own any underwear."

"They can sod off. I will not explain my clothing choices to your family."

He drags out the last bag and opens it up. His face blanches. I swear it does. Never have I ever seen Domhnall Sterling appear even slightly shocked, but whatever is in that bag has left him speechless. I can't see what he found, since his body blocks my view. The second I leap off the bed, he zips up that bag and kicks it into the corner, behind a chair.

Despite the way he scowls at me over his shoulder, I hurry to Domhnall and try to pull that mystery bag out.

He thrusts an arm out to block me. "You do not need to see this."

"Is it a dead body? I've always wondered where Logan stores his enemies' remains after he dispatches them."

"You are a cheeky lass. Did ye know that?"

"Me?" I point at myself and feign innocence. "*Dòmhnall an Tarbh* frightens me ever so much, and I feel a wee bit faint. I wouldn't dare mock you."

"Now you've done it, *mo leannan*. You've summoned the beast." He scoops me up in his arms. "Your punishment is to be ravished by the bull."

Who knew a silly plush toy would lead to having a poke. But I have to be honest with him. "Afraid I'm too exhausted to shag, Domhnall."

He sighs. "Aye, so am I."

Domhnall carries me to the bed and, despite his tiredness, yanks the covers off with one hand. Then he gently sets me down on the mattress. Every bedroom in Dùndubhan has the softest sheets and pillows. Emery must have chosen them, because I cannae see my brother Rory shopping for such things. Domhnall strips off all his clothes, then delicately undresses me too. We cuddle under the covers together and soon fall asleep.

Someone had left the curtains open, before Domhnall and I were brought to the tower bedroom. That means I can watch the sunrise creeping up toward the window, casting its warm glow on the room. The light spills across the bed, inching toward us as the sun gradually rises. Since I'm lying on my side, facing the window, I can admire the view very well.

Domhnall slings an arm over me, tugging me into his firm body. "*Madainn mhath, mo gaol.* Did you sleep well?"

"Very well." I wriggle my erse, just to make him gasp. I can feel his growing erection. "Did you sleep well, *gràidh*?"

"Mm, there's nothing like sleeping with your body nestled against me."

"I feel the same way about your body." I wriggle my erse again, and this time, he groans and cups my mound with one large hand. "Do ye think we have time for a quick poke? Or will our captors bring us breakfast in bed at any moment?"

"More likely, they'll burst in and drag us down to the great hall while we're still naked."

"Aye, that is a possibility." I roll over to face him. "You haven't been this randy in months. We were going through a severe drought in the bedroom."

Domhnall squints at me. "If you're implying I have some sort of problem in that area, that's rot."

"No, I wasn't implying anything. We hadn't made love in months, not until this week."

"I know. We'd been arguing and—"

Someone bangs on the door.

We both sit up, waiting for the visitor to make an announcement, but none comes. That person bangs on the door twice more.

Domhnall leaps up and rushes over there.

Chapter Nineteen

Domhnall

I pull the door open and stare at the man who stands just beyond the threshold. Aye, I've seen him before. But I still have no idea who he really is. All I've learned about Thane Buchanan is that he prefers not to speak. Well, he did speak to me once—producing two full sentences. *Fiona is a wonderful woman, and I dinnae take kindly to anyone hurting her. We know what you're after, but you'll need to prove yourself first.*

That was all he said. And it made no sense.

Now, Thane eyes me up and down while his brows lift slightly and his lips curl into the faintest of smirks. He crosses his arms over his chest and meets my gaze. "Get dressed."

I glance over my shoulder. Thane couldn't see Fiona's naked body, since the bed covers conceal her. That's bloody good news for Thane Buchanan, because I dinnae like to rip someone's eyes out first thing in the morning. "We'll go downstairs when we feel like it."

"No, ye won't." Thane brushes past me and takes up a position in the corner adjacent to the door. "I'll wait while you two get dressed."

I clench my jaw so tightly that it hurts, hissing words out between my teeth. "You will not watch Fiona putting on her clothes, not unless you're wanting to be disemboweled."

Thane maintains a disinterested expression. He doesn't even glance at the bed, which is the only reason I haven't tossed him out the window.

"Best shut your eyes, laddie," I say. "Or do I need to blindfold you?"

"I have no interest in embarrassing Fiona."

Thane closes his eyes.

Fiona scrambles off the bed to find her clothes and get them on again. I do the same, and all the while, I keep wondering who in the world Thane Buchanan is. He's even stranger than the MacTaggarts. Once we're fully clothed, I decide to ask a question. But I aim it at Fiona, not Thane.

"How do you know this bloke?"

She winces. "Does it matter?"

Her expression convinces me it does matter. "Who is he to you?"

Fiona opens her mouth, but instead of speaking, she glances back and forth between me and Thane. Then she squeezes her eyes shut. "We dated briefly once upon a time."

"How briefly?" I veer my gaze to Thane, but he still has his eyes closed. "Fiona, did you—"

No, I won't ask the question in front of this man. I'll have to wait until we're alone again.

Fiona's pinched expression has mutated into a stubborn one. "Are you going to explain your past?"

She knows the answer. Whether she's using my past as an excuse to avoid talking about her relationship with Thane, I can't say. But her reticence gives me an opening to avoid discussing my past.

Yet I suddenly realize I don't want to walk through that opening.

I claim Fiona's hand. "We should talk about this when we're alone."

"Let's go downstairs," Thane announces. "*Tha mòr-fheum air cofaidh*, eh? Good thing we brewed up a barrelful."

Fiona's posture sags, but she allows me to lead her out of the tower bedroom as we follow Thane. Aye, we there is a great need for coffee this morning. A barrelful of caffeine sounds brilliant, though I might need to spice up my morning brew.

"Got any *uisge-beatha* on hand?" I ask. "A wee bit in my coffee wouldn't go amiss."

Thane glances at me over his shoulder, brows raised. "Ye want whisky first thing in the morning?"

I sigh. "No, I reckon not."

"Dinnae mind if ye do want a dram. We have put you and Fiona through the wringer lately."

"It hasn't been as much of a trial as I expected. We enjoyed the treasure hunt."

"Glad to hear it."

The first time I met Thane, he barely spoke to me. He maintained an inscrutable demeanor too. But this morning, he became talkative. I feel a wee bit stunned by his sudden flood of words. For anyone else, a handful of sentences wouldn't qualify as a flood. But Thane is clearly not an average man.

As we cross the long gallery, I notice that the synthetic ice is gone. A wave of relief rushes through me when I realize that means no more curling. What a stupid sport. I'll take shinty over curling any day. To be fair, though, I've only experienced the MacTaggart version of the game, so maybe I would enjoy a normal match.

Thane leads us down the vestibule stairs and even begins to whistle a cheerful tune that I don't recognize. He hops down the steps two at a time while dancing.

What the bloody hell? The man who wouldn't speak has turned into Fred Astaire. I glance at Fiona, but she simply shrugs. That makes me wonder how deeply involved she was with Thane. No, I will not get jealous. I lost that tendency when I lost Jessica O'Connor to Grey Dixon and then lost the Highland games to the business intelligence analyst too. Humiliation taught me a powerful lesson. But might I have taken that lesson too far? Is that why Fiona threw me out of the house?

Maybe I've gone too far in the other direction. On the western face of Beann Dealgach, I became my old self again, leaping off a cliff and diving into the deepest hole in the river to retrieve a lockbox. Then I took Fiona like a wild bull who hadn't seen a cow in years, which inspired her to call me *Dòmhnall an Tarbh*. A plush toy of a Highland cow had set off a chain reaction.

And I had never felt more like myself than I did on that mountain with the woman I love.

I don't get the chance to delve into that revelation, because Thane is taking us out the vestibule door. "Where are you going? The dining room is in the guest wing."

"We won't be dining inside the house."

"Breakfast outdoors? I hope the midges aren't out this morning."

Fiona snorts, which seems to have happened because she was struggling not to laugh.

Thane slows down to walk alongside us as we wend our way around the cars parked in the courtyard. "Do you have a fear of midges? Or is it all insects?"

"I am not afraid of the wee beasties. But I dinnae relish the idea of getting bitten up by them." I pull Fiona close to my side. "And I never want you to get bitten up, *mo chridhe*."

She smiles up at me sweetly. "Thank you, Domhnall. I can honestly say no man has ever worried about protecting me from midges."

The lass might be joking, partly. But I know she also means it. Midges might not be the most horrifying beasties out there, yet she appreciates that I care about protecting her from them.

Our escort directs us toward the garden doorway and halts there to wait for us to enter the walled garden first. Once we've crossed the threshold, Thane jogs ahead of us to make sure we don't miss the dead obvious thing in front of us. A table has been set up under the arbor, where climbing roses cover the trellises and almost form a roof. Someone has placed all the appropriate items for a meal—plates, bowls, and other dishes, plus two glasses for each of us. One is for water. The other contains wine, and I reckon the bottle came from Rory MacTaggart's stash. Dùndubhan boasts a healthy selection in the wine cellar.

"Isn't it a bit early for alcohol?" I ask, gesturing toward the table. "And why are there only two place settings?"

Thane plants a hand on my back and another on Fiona's, then gives us both a shove to propel us toward the arbor. "Sit down, and I will answer your questions."

I pull out a chair for Fiona and push it in once she's sat down. Then I take my own seat.

Thane rolls his shoulders back and lifts his chin. "This is a private breakfast designed for lovers. You will be drinking a dry Riesling that's the perfect wine for a morning meal. A mate of mine who lives in France grew the grapes and nurtured them so they would become an exquisite breakfast treat. This wine did not come from the Dùndubhan cellar."

"Will you be serving us our meal?"

"Aye. The MacTaggarts thought a neutral party should see to your breakfast, though I didn't cook the food. Malina is taking care of that."

Fiona's eyes widen. "Malina as in my cousin Iain's daughter?"

"That's right. She's a clever sixteen-year-old and fast becoming a gourmet." Thane's lips twitch as if he wants to smile but can't quite manage it. "She won't give you food poisoning, that's for certain."

"I never thought she would. Malina is a good lass."

Thane picks up a small towel that had been lying on the table and drapes it over his forearm as if he's a waiter. "I need to check on the meal, so if you need anything, simply shout 'garçon' and I will hasten to fulfill your wishes."

Garçon? Hasten? He's having us on.

Our waiter—no, I will not call him "garçon"—insists on placing napkins on our laps. "Allow me to open the wine for you."

He reaches into his pocket and brings out a strange-looking metal device.

"What on earth is that?" I ask. "If you're planning to kill us, that won't do the trick."

"It's not for murdering. This is a combination sommelier knife and corkscrew." While Thane flips open the two folded sections of the device,

I watch with an odd fascination. He uses the knife to carefully remove the foil wrapping, then switches to the corkscrew to open the bottle. "Now, permit me to decant the wine for you."

He's going overboard with this display, but Fiona seems to enjoy watching Thane do his garçon routine. Everyone here is Scottish, not French. But I grudgingly find myself admiring his fluid, elegant technique for opening the bottle and pouring the wine into our glasses.

"What do you do for a living, Thane? Dinnae seem like the sort who would be a waiter. I've had the impression you're former military."

"Based on what evidence?"

"Gut instinct. Military men can spot each other a mile away."

"Let's not talk about me. This is a special event for you and Fiona." He pockets his double-duty knife. "But I will tell you one thing. I own a distillery just outside Loch Fairbairn. The rest you'll have to wait to find out."

"What kind of spirits do you make? Or is that too much to ask?"

He winks. "I make whisky, of course."

Though I'm itching to interrogate him further, I don't get the chance. Thane bows, then hustles back toward the vestibule door. I could interrogate Fiona instead to learn more about Thane, but that would ruin our garden meal. So instead, I take a sip of my wine.

Fiona does the same. Her eyes widen a touch, briefly, and she hums with pleasure. "This is delicious wine."

"Aye, it is. Did you know that Thane owned a distillery?"

"No. Honestly, I don't know him well. He started out as a friend of Logan and Magnus because they are all former military. When Gavin got involved with my sister Jamie, he joined the unofficial club started by Thane, Logan, and Magnus. Munro is in the group now too."

I was also in the military, but I don't blether about that or join any groups. The MacTaggarts and their mates haven't invited me into their wee cabal. Could that be what they're trying to do now? All these tests and other bollocks might be preparing me to join their club.

Not that I want to join them. I have one real friend—my business partner, Mick Dalton—and that's good enough for me.

Fiona raises her wine glass to her lips and gently swirls the contents. "You were in the military. Why haven't you joined the club?"

"I am not the club-joining sort."

Her cheeks dimple with a teasing smile, and her eyes sparkle with humor. "Is that so? I never would have guessed you don't like joining groups or making friends."

"I have friends."

"Other than Mick Dalton?"

"Well, ah…" I swig a mouthful of wine and avoid looking at her. "I suppose Munro has become a mate."

"Of course he has. You don't make it easy for anyone to get to know you, but some of us have managed to break through that *tolla-thon* shell of yours."

"I reckon that's why Sophie shagged another man for our entire marriage, and why Jessica would never move in with me. I'm impenetrable."

Fiona holds perfectly still, almost as if she's mutated into a stone statue. She doesn't blink. Her gaze remains locked on me, and she still holds her wine glass near her lips.

What did I say? I thought she wanted me to open up and share my past with her. Yet I've done that, and she doesn't seem happy about it.

The lass carefully sets her glass down on the table. She wriggles in her chair and clears her throat. "Domhnall, I… Thank you for sharing that with me."

Her response is hardly encouraging. She must agree that I'm an impenetrable *tolla-thon*. For a moment that feels like forever, we sit here languishing in an uncomfortable silence as if neither of us has a ruddy clue what to say next.

Then Fiona leans forward to grasp my hand. "Whatever made you the way you are, I'm here to listen when you're ready to talk about it."

I relax a little.

She squeezes my hand. "You are wrong about one thing, Domhnall. You are not impenetrable or a *tolla-thon*. You're the best man I've ever known."

"Excluding your brothers and cousins."

"No. You are the best with no qualifications."

Thane walks into the garden carrying a tray full of food, and I get a reprieve from talking about my past while we eat. Fiona thinks I'm better than her brothers. Isn't that what she just said? Maybe I should give her the last item from our treasure hunt, but it still feels too soon.

After all, it's a diamond engagement ring.

Chapter Twenty

Fiona

For the rest of our breakfast, Domhnall continuously sips his wine and nibbles on his food—to avoid conversation, I'm fair certain. I gave him a compliment. He acts like I accused him of being in league with the devil. Since I have three brothers, I realize what's going on here. Domhnall is embarrassed because I told him he's the best man I've ever known and because he revealed a little more of himself.

Thane had brought our food and immediately left. He seemed to recognize the tension between me and Domhnall, and he has the grace to avoid interfering.

Will I ever understand Domhnall? Completely?

As I enjoy my meal, I can't stop wondering why he hasn't pushed me to explain my past with Easton Yates. Malina cooked us a splendid breakfast, yet I can't stop worrying about my relationship with the man sitting across the table from me for long enough to fully appreciate how talented that lass is in the kitchen.

I've eaten half of my food, but I push my plate away and lean forward. "Please tell me more about your military service. I don't even know which branch you served in."

"Why does that matter?"

"Because your past is a part of you, and I want know everything about the man I've lived with for two years."

Domhnall claps his fork down on his plate and leans back in his chair. "If ye dinnae know me by now, you never will."

"What does that mean? Stop being so cagey and talk to me. Please. I love you, Domhnall."

He stares down at his lap with his lips compressed.

Oh, aye, he is the stubbornest man on earth. "Would it help if I fell to my knees and begged you to confide in me?"

Domhnall lifts his head and rolls his eyes. "Dinnae be a dafty."

"That is not a valid response." I stretch my arm out to clasp his hand. "Please, tell me something about your time in the military."

He slumps in his chair, and a breath gusts out of him. "I served during wartime, Fiona. I saw things I wish I could forget, but I never will."

"Were you in the army like Munro?"

"No. I was a pilot in the RAF."

I must be gawping at him, though I had no intention of doing that. I've known and lived with Domhnall for two years, yet I had no idea he'd been in the RAF or that he served during wartime. How can I know so little about him after two years together? I hadn't tried very hard to learn more about him. He hadn't volunteered and, until recently, I hadn't bothered.

Does that mean our relationship is doomed? No, I will never believe that.

Thane rushes into the garden, breathing hard.

We stare at him while he bends his knees and sets one palm on his thighs as if he needs extra support to stay standing. He holds up his other hand in a staying gesture. Once he's caught his breath, he straightens. "Intruder alert. Easton Yates has breached the first gate and is on his way to the main entrance."

"What?" I leap out of my chair. "How did he find me here?"

"He will answer that question once we have him in custody. For now, please come with me."

Domhnall scoffs. "I will not run from a cowardly *cacan*. If he wants a rematch, I will take him down with a KO on the first punch."

"We have a plan. Lachlan, Rory, and Aidan had intended to have a conference with you after breakfast. This development simply moves up the time line."

To my complete shock, Domhnall nods his agreement. "Aye, we will go with you."

He clasps my hand as we follow Thane back into the house, passing through the vestibule to make our way up to the first floor, which is actually the second level. Thane leads us across the great hall and straight to the open door of Rory's office. Our guard loiters in the great hall, ambling over to the high windows, where he leans against the sill.

Domhnall and I enter the office.

Rory sits in the executive chair behind his large mahogany desk while rocking slightly. He also has his elbows on the chair's arms and his fingers steepled. That's my brother in professional mode. "Sit down, please."

He gestures toward the two chairs across from him.

While we take our seats, I notice Lachlan leaning against the book-shelves behind Rory. Aidan sits on the window seat with one knee bent and his shoe planted on the cushioned seat. My youngest brother is not known for being aggressive, though he has proven himself to be a capable fighter, during the two sieges of Dùndubhan. Lachlan, as the oldest in our family, takes on the role of moderator and leader. Rory is the Steely Solicitor, the man no one wants to battle in court. But like Aidan and Lachlan, he also fought in those sieges.

I hope Easton doesn't plan on starting another battle. He would lose.

Rory taps his steepled fingers. "I assume Thane informed you that Easton Yates is on his way to my castle as we speak. He has a vehicle, but I'd wager it's a hire car. Logan rang his contact at the Home Office, who tapped into surveillance cameras to track Yates's movements. He left his home in Milton Keynes three days ago and slowly made his way into Scotland, stopping at various hotels and bed-and-breakfasts. He ran up quite the credit card debt in the process."

"That doesn't sound like him," I say. "But then, I hadn't seen him in a long time. He used to be well off, though not a millionaire. He had a trust fund from his parents, who died in an airline crash when he was at university."

"Aye, he had a trust fund. But he blew through it like a high-speed hurricane. The laddie is skint."

"If he thinks I have money, he's mistaken. Everyone knows I've failed at every business I tried to run and every job I accepted."

Domhnall clasps my hand. "No, *gràidh*, you didn't fail. Events beyond your control ruined your chances. Those businesses you worked at mismanaged their funds and shut down. Your dress shop suffered from an economic downturn. You did the best you could under hard circumstances."

I lay my hand atop his on my arm. "Thank you, Domhnall. You always come up with the right words to make me feel better."

Rory and Lachlan exchange self-satisfied looks, and when I glance at Aidan, he's doing the same. It's bizarre.

"What are you three so smug about?" I ask. "You haven't done anything to earn it."

Lachlan approaches Rory's desk and rests his hip on the corner, facing me. "We had a number of events planned for you two, intended to prove one way or the other if you belong together. But Easton Yates escaped his confinement."

Domhnall aims his flinty stare at my oldest brother. "Best explain what you lot did with Easton if he wasn't here the whole time. Errol told us only that the Three Macs would handle him."

None of my brothers get the chance to respond to that statement. Thane has just sauntered into the office, and he halts beside Rory's desk, inches away from Lachlan. "The Three Macs took custody of Yates once Torcall arrived in Loch Fairbairn. But they sort of…lost sight of him for a wee bit. Just long enough that he managed to steal a car."

I sit up straighter. "Steal? I thought you said he had a hire car."

"He did. But your brothers confiscated it before Torcall brought the captive to them. Couldn't have the *bod ceann* escaping."

"But how did Easton get away from my brothers? They're bigger and stronger than he is."

Rory and Lachlan both wince.

Aidan slides off the window seat and shuffles over to us. "Maybe I should explain. Lachie and Rory Baby are too embarrassed to tell you."

Lachlan and Rory simultaneously glower at Aidan.

Rory snarls, "Dinnae be using that nickname. Only my wife calls me that."

"Aye, Aidan," Lachlan says. "Dinnae call me a name like that either. You know I hate the diminutive."

My youngest brother chuckles and pats Rory's shoulder with one hand, and Lachlan's with the other. "Chill out. Everyone knows your nicknames, whether ye like it or not, so just go with the flow."

Domhnall lets out a piercing whistle. "Can you lasses please get back to the current issue? That would be Easton Yates, in case you forgot."

"Aye, of course," Rory says. "We have allowed Yates to approach the main gates, and we will allow him to drive into the courtyard as well. Then, we'll take him down."

I glance back and forth between Rory and Lachlan, confused by their statements concerning my former fiancé. «He's an annoying *tolla-thon*, but Easton isn't dangerous. You three are acting like he wants to murder me."

"Are you sure about that?" Lachlan asks. "You hadn't seen him in a very long time until he turned up on your doorstep. People can change, especially if something terrible happened to them."

"Do you know something about him? If you do, tell me now. I deserve to know."

Thane looks at Lachlan. "She's right. You should explain what we know and how we know it. Fiona and Domhnall both should understand, and we don't have much time."

Nothing I've heard about Easton in the past few days makes any sense. He stole a car? He searched until he found my home address? The laddie I had met at university was a decent man. Confused and lonely, but not a criminal.

Aidan wanders over to the windows and peers down at the courtyard. "The scunner has arrived."

Rory rises from his chair. "All right. Two things are going to happen in the next ten minutes. You should not be present for either, Fiona."

"Dinnae treat me like a child, Rory."

My brother pretends he didn't hear me, the way only a solicitor can. "Thane, escort Domhnall to the place we agreed on earlier."

"Aye." Thane eyes Domhnall with a touch of suspicion. "I assume you won't be cooperating."

"Not if it means you're taking me away from Fiona."

"What gave you the idea you have a choice?" Thane whips a pair of handcuffs out of his back pocket. His T-shirt is long enough that it covered the upper part of his jeans, hiding the cuffs. Before Domhnall can react, Thane snaps restraints into place around his wrists. "Should I shackle your feet too? Or will you submit to going wherever I take you?"

Domhnall throws me a long-suffering look, then faces Thane. "I will go along with this for now."

"Fair enough."

I watch as Thane leads Domhnall out of the office and through the great hall, out of my sight. Then I round on my brothers. "You had better tell me what in the world you three are plotting?"

Rather than responding, Lachlan pulls out his mobile to dial a number. "We're ready for you."

He ends the call.

I must look as baffled as I feel. "Explain yourselves now, or I will grab the nearest blunt object and batter the lot of you."

Lachlan nods toward the doorway behind me. "You should let him explain."

"Who?" My brother grasps my shoulders and rotates me to face the door. "Alex? Why are you here?"

He ambles up to me, smiling with all the charm of the consummate grifter he is. "Your brothers want me to help you con the truth out of your former love. If that doesn't work, they will wield brute force."

I think I'm actually spluttering. "This is madness."

"Are you saying you'd rather be locked up in the cellar during this operation?"

"No." I pull myself together and straighten my spine. "I can handle it."

"Good girl." Alex offers me his arm. "May I escort the lady?"

"Just get your erse moving, Alex."

He leads the way as the five of us march down the vestibule stairs and out into the courtyard. A strange car does indeed sit in the drive, and I can just make out a figure inside the vehicle. My brothers urge me to halt several yards away while Alex approaches the driver's side.

The British Bastard assumes his best cavalier attitude and pulls the door open. He holds out his hand. "May I assist you in exiting the vehicle, my lord?"

Easton scowls at him and shoves Alex's hand away. Then he scrambles out of the dilapidated car. "Get out of my way, you bloody stupid wanker."

Alex clucks his tongue. "Now, now, there's no need for profanity."

"Who the fuck are you?" Easton demands as he kicks the car door shut. "I'm here for Fiona, so get out of my way."

"Sorry, mate, can't do that." Alex hooks an arm around Easton's shoulders. "We can do this one of two ways. Either you walk under your own power, or one of the Three Macs will kneecap you and haul you into the house draped over his shoulders."

"The three who?"

"Macs. As in *Mac*Taggarts." Alex turns toward me and my brothers, pulling Easton around with him. "Just take a good long look at those gents. They're bigger and stronger than you. Personally, I find them irritating and wish I could dump them into Loch Ness with the creature that supposedly lives there." Alex releases a long sigh, seeming for all the world to wish he could do that to my brothers. "But I shan't do that. My wife is their sister, after all."

Easton throws Alex a seething glare, then tries to shake free of his grip. "Let go of me you bastard."

Alex keeps a firm hold on Easton while he wags a finger in the *cacan*'s face. "Don't steal my nickname. I worked hard to earn it. And besides, I am the *British* Bastard. Do get it right if you're trying to insult me."

Rory clears his throat deliberately. "I believe it's Fiona's turn, Alex."

"Of course. Toss me the cuffs, would you?" Lachlan does that, and Alex catches the restraints. Before Easton realizes what he's about, Alex has the cuffs around his wrists, behind his back. "Go on, pet, the floor is yours."

I approach Easton, halting far enough away that he won't be able to spit on me or whatever he might try. "What do you want, Easton? Why are you harassing me?"

He lifts his chin and turns his head away.

Rory steps up beside me. "All right, then. It's the rack for him."

Chapter Twenty-One

Domhnall

Though I expect Thane to drag me up to the tower bedroom or maybe one of the rooms on the top floor, he doesn't do that. Instead, he keeps hold of my handcuffs while aiming straight for the spiral staircase. We trudge down the steps side by side and halt in the vestibule. I still have no idea what the MacTaggarts and their cohorts have in mind—for me or for Easton Yates—but I need to be out there with Fiona, not locked away somewhere.

"Are we going to the kitchen?" I ask. "Or the guest wing?"

"None of the above." He considers me for a moment, as if I'm a troublesome rodent and he can't figure out how to get rid of me. "Are you jealous because I once dated Fiona?"

"No. But I am getting bloody sick of her former boyfriends turning up to annoy me."

Thane lifts his brows. "Isn't that the same thing as being jealous?"

Aye, maybe it is. But I refuse to admit that to him. Instead, I act like the jealous *bod ceann* he expects me to be. "Did you shag Fiona?"

"Today? No."

"What about in the past?"

"It would be ungentlemanly for me to answer that question." Thane gives my bindings a light tug. "Time to get your erse moving again, Domhnall. We don't want to miss the show."

"What show?"

He ignores my question and proceeds to drag me through the great hall and the dining room. But when we step out of that space into the guest-wing hall, he veers left, where there are no rooms and no door to the outside.

"Seems like you're planning to keep me here," I say. "Just to prevent me from seeing or hearing what's going on outside."

"You make too many false assumptions." Thane keeps hold of my cuffs in one hand while he flattens his other palm on the wall, gliding it down slowly until he stops about halfway to the floor. "Ah, here it is."

"Here what is?"

Thane releases my cuffs and flattens both palms on the wall.

"It's a wall, ye bloody eejit. Are ye meaning to kiss it? Seems that way since you're caressing it like—"

Thane grunts as he pushes against the wall hard enough to make him wince and grit his teeth. And a section of the wall breaks away, receding into a dark space while the sound of stone grinding against stone vibrates in my bones. Once the slab of rock has receded a few feet, Thane stops pushing and turns toward me. "Prisoners first."

"What's in there?"

"*You* will be in a moment, even if I have to toss ye in there myself." Thane steps back into the hallway. "Go on, move your erse or we'll miss the show."

"Must be taking me to a rat carnival under the castle."

He chuckles. "I'm glad you can keep your sense of humor under the circumstances."

I shuffle into the dark space exposed by the rock slab and move just far enough away from it that Thane can squeeze through the gap too. He pulls his mobile out of his pocket and activates an app that turns the device into a torch, spreading white light into the passage. I follow while he marches off down the corridor, seeming as if he knows it well, but I have never heard of a hidden passage inside Dùndubhan.

"How did you know this was here?" I ask. "No one has ever mentioned a secret corridor before."

"We found it recently."

The passage begins to slant downward at a moderate grade, and I can see what looks like another mechanical door up ahead. Thane whistles as we approach the door, and he fiddles with a gear mechanism on the back of the hidden door, which makes it grind open. I stumble out of the way.

Once the door is open, Thane waves for me to go through it.

Sighing, I shuffle into the space beyond—and freeze. "Is this the wine cellar?"

"Aye."

"If you were bringing me here, why the hell did we have to go through the whole bloody castle and down a hidden passageway? You could have brought me in here from the outer door, which is not hidden."

"Exactly. It's dead obvious from the outside, and we don't want Easton Yates to know you're watching the festivities."

"If you mention 'festivities' one more time, I'll give you your head in your hands to play with."

"Would that be literally or figuratively?"

I lean toward him and growl, "Whichever way ye like."

Thane clamps a hand down on my shoulder. "I'm starting to like you, Domhnall. But we need to get our erses in gear."

He keeps hold of my shoulder as he leads me through the racks of wine and toward the door that opens into the courtyard. We pause only long enough that Thane can pull out a pocketknife. Then he drags me to a spot a few feet to the left of the door. With the knife, he pries open a wee peephole.

"No one can see this from outside," Thane tells me. "It was specifically designed to be a secret method of seeing who's out there. Medieval engineers were bloody brilliant."

"Fascinating. And by that I mean I dinnae give a toss and I'm looking for a blunt object I can use to batter you."

Thane steps away from the peephole. "Take a look."

I step up to the wee opening and peer through it. The angle of the hole gives me a perfect view of what's going on out there in the courtyard. I can see Fiona and Alex, as well as Easton who remains handcuffed. Fiona's brothers hover behind her with their arms folded, their chins lifted, and their eyes narrowed. I can't deny those three know how to look intimidating. Even Aidan, the comedian of the trio, pulls off a menacing air.

I twist my head around to look at Thane. "Will we be able to hear what they say?"

"Sounds from in here are muffled, but anything out in the courtyard gets amplified. It's something to do with acoustics. Still, you might want to speak softly to be sure."

"That's what I've been doing."

"Since we reached the cellar, aye. But before that, you were raging like a caged lion."

If he thinks that statement will offend me, he's mistaken. But I'll give Thane the benefit of the doubt since we don't know each other well, not yet. He doesn't know me the way Fiona does, for certain.

"Calm down, Yates. We only want to help you."

Those words echo in the courtyard and filter through the peephole to my ears. I recognize the voice. It's Alex Thorne, putting on his best British Bastard persona, which means he's trying to con Easton Yates. To what purpose, I have no idea.

When I stare out the wee hole in the castle wall again, I realize something strange. "Are these images being transmitted by mirrors?"

"Of course. How did you think it would work? The cellar is half underground, after all. Dinnae worry, though. No one out there can see us in here."

"Are these mirrors a modern invention?"

"The ones in use at Dùndubhan were installed this year. But mirrors in general are an ancient innovation."

I want to know why they installed such things, but then I realize I can guess. Twice, the castle has been literally under siege. Adding a few more precautionary measures is a wise choice.

Out in the courtyard, I can see Alex and Fiona. Her brothers must be hovering just out of view, since I'm dead sure they would never leave their sister out there alone. They trust Alex, but Easton's arrival has put everyone on edge. That means one cocky Brit is not enough of a protection detail.

I need to be out there. I'm itching to batter that *cacan*, but I agreed to do what the Three Macs, Alex, and Thane believe is best. For now. I'll rescind that agreement the second I feel it's no longer appropriate.

"You lot are not trying to help me," Easton says, grinding the words out between his clenched teeth. "You mean to keep me away from Fiona. That's why you're surrounding her and not letting me see her alone."

"No, that's not why," Fiona says. "I decide who I speak to, not my brothers or anyone else. I have nothing to say unless you care to explain your behavior. I hadn't seen or heard from you in at least two decades, until you knocked on my door the other day. So tell me now, Easton. Why are you here?"

That's my lass. Strong, determined, and unwavering.

"I'm here for you," Easton declares. "We belong together."

Fiona barks out a harsh laugh. "That's rot. If we belonged together, then we would have been together all along. I broke up with you, but you're acting like it was the other way round and I begged you to stay with me."

"Come now, Fee darling, let's have a civil conversation—alone. Then I will explain everything."

She makes a rude noise. I think she rolled her eyes too, though it's hard to say for sure from this distance. The wonderful lass locks her arms over her chest in the manner I know means she isn't having any of whatever Easton Yates is trying to feed her.

The *cacan* takes one step toward her. "Don't be so childish, Fee darling. Let's behave like adults, eh?"

Alex approaches Fiona and Easton. "I have no particular stake in this argument, so why don't I moderate the discussion? Let's see if we can deduce what Easton Yates wants from Fiona MacTaggart."

Easton flashes Alex a hot glare. "Stay out of this."

"There's no point in arguing with him, Alex," Fiona says. "Might as well give up. Your way of doing things bounces right off his iron-hard skull."

"Quite right, pet." Alex switches personas in a heartbeat, as smoothly as a drop of rain flows down a pane of glass. "You really have no idea who you're dealing with, do you? Allow me to enlighten you. Several men, who are larger and stronger than you, will do anything to protect this woman. Stop lying, confess the truth, and perhaps we won't toss you down the old garderobe shaft. Or perhaps you prefer to break every bone in your body when you land on a pile of medieval shit."

Lachlan steps up beside Alex, on the other side of Fiona. "Alex is spot on, ye scunner. If you're lucky, the garderobe shaft might have some remnants of the Black Death lurking down there to crawl into your nostrils."

"Oh, please. You morons do not frighten me."

"Ye won't be confessing, then, aye?"

Easton lifts his chin. "Certainly not to you or any of your mates or relatives. I will only speak to Fiona—alone."

"The more times you say that, the less we care about your safety."

"Oh, I'm so bloody terrified of you inbred yobs."

Lachlan looks at his sister. "Have you had enough of him?"

"Definitely."

Her brother seizes Easton's arms and clinches them behind his back before the *cacan* realizes what he's about. Lachlan holds Easton's wrists in one hand while he straps an arm around his throat. The Brit struggles, but Lachlan is stronger and bigger, dragging the *cacan* away. Easton spews vitriol and even splatters Lachlan's face with his saliva, but it makes no difference. He stomps on Lachlan's foot too.

Fiona seems to enjoy watching her brother manhandle her former lover.

Lachlan abruptly shouts and staggers backward just enough that Easton manages to break free and make a run for it.

But he doesn't run for his car. The bastard barrels toward Fiona.

She's focused on Lachlan, and so is Alex. Neither of them sees Easton until he rams into Fiona and knocks her down.

I whirl around and bolt out of the cellar, just missing Thane in the process. I barrel down the hidden passage, then careen through the guest wing and dining room, exploding out of the vestibule door. The gravel crunches under my shoes as I fly across the courtyard, reaching Easton and Fiona just as he grabs her around the waist and hoists her off her feet.

He's facing away from me, and that's his last mistake.

I kick his feet out from under him and latch my arms around his neck to drag him away before he falls on top of Fiona. Despite flailing his arms, he can't get any leverage to escape. "All right, ye damn scunner. No more games. If you don't explain yourself in the next ten seconds, I'll hogtie ye and drive your useless erse to the Loch Fairbairn police station."

Easton lifts his nose and sniffs with derision.

I tighten my grip on his neck just enough to make him gasp. "I'm already on five and still counting."

The scunner's jaw begins to tremble faintly. "Yes, fine, I'll confess. But only to Fiona."

I lift him only enough that he's now balanced on his toes, then lower my voice to a dark whisper. "Try again."

"Please, I don't want to say it for everyone to hear."

"Then just tell me. And maybe I won't snap your neck."

He nods.

I set him down but keep my arms around his throat.

Easton turns his head to the side and whispers out of one corner of his mouth.

Oh, aye, I heard what he said, and I believe him. But the words do nothing to improve his situation. "*Tha thu giùlan lòchran dhi*, eh? You'll never get what you want."

He's still a rotten piece of shite. Nothing will change that.

Fiona moves closer. "What did he say? I couldn't hear it."

"*Tha thu giùlan lòchran dhi.* That's what he told me."

Her eyes go wide, then she swerves her attention to Easton. "You still carry a torch for me? That's insanity. If you loved me, you would have tried to win me back right after I walked out. But you waited more than a decade? Dinnae believe it."

Fiona glances at me, as if she wants confirmation that she's right not to believe what Easton said.

"He's telling the truth, *gràidh*. No man would lie about such a humiliating thing. It's pathetic."

The British *cacan* makes a petulant face. "But she threw you over too. That makes us both pathetic."

Fiona shakes her head slowly. "The difference is that Domhnall tried to win me back as soon as I broke up with him. And he never stopped trying."

Chapter Twenty-Two

Fiona

The moment I spoke those words, I felt the truth of them deep in my soul. Easton's arrival had thrown me for a loop, and it took me a while to understand why. It wasn't simply that he turned up unannounced and claimed he wanted me back. I needed him to go away because his presence made me realize that I didn't want to live without Domhnall. But I sort of resent that need too. I'm conflicted. That's hardly a crime.

I love that big bull of a man.

He shared something of his past with me, but not nearly enough. Yet I've held back too—when I failed to mention that I'd once been engaged, for instance. I could make the excuse that I knew Easton such a long time ago that I'd forgotten about him. But I don't want to play that sort of game. I want us to be open with each other, and that won't happen until we both bare our souls.

Domhnall has done everything my family demanded of him. And he did that for me. He even endured midges and let my cousins kidnap him, though he's much stronger than any of them and could have gotten away. But the most impressive thing he has ever done was what happened a moment ago. When Domhnall exploded out of the house and tackled Easton, I felt something I haven't experienced in a long time. I suddenly knew that he would do anything for me. Aye, Domhnall Sterling is quite a man.

My hero still has his arms latched around Easton's neck, though he loosened his grip somewhat. "Do ye believe him, *gràidh*?"

I study Easton for a moment, then nod. "He's telling the truth, I'm sure of it. But he needs to explain himself."

"Aye, in many ways. You should decide how and when we try to get the whole story out of him."

"Let's go into the sitting room. Just you, me, and Easton."

My former lover twists his head around and tries to spit in Domhnall's face, but the spittle only lands on his shoulder. "I will speak to Fiona. No one else."

Domhnall ignores Easton's demand, and instead, takes hold of the cuffs that still bind his hands. I follow slightly behind the men as Domhnall hauls Easton into the vestibule and down the ground-floor hall. Our prisoner complains the entire time, as we go through the dining room and into the guest wing. He whinges and whines and generally acts like a toddler.

I can't believe I ever lived with that cretin.

Domhnall swerves into the sitting room. Easton stumbles, but he doesn't fall down—and he keeps on whingeing. For heaven's sake, the man should show a little decorum. Domhnall could snap his neck in a heartbeat if he wanted, though I know he would never do such a thing without extreme provocation.

Easton is teetering on that edge.

My sexy bull virtually tosses Easton onto the sofa, where my ex-fiancé lands in a jumbled heap. One leg has fallen half off the sofa while the other is bent close to his belly. He's twisted slightly sideways too, and his hair has gotten tousled.

Domhnall saunters over to one of the high-back chairs near the windows.

With the coffee table between us, I lean over to stare into Easton's eyes. "Start talking."

"Make him go away."

"Honestly, you sound like a toddler." I sit on the edge of the table and shake my head at him. "You could never compete with *Dòmhnall an Tarbh*."

"What did you just say? It sounded like Scottish nonsense."

Surprise flashes on Domhnall's face for a split second, then he resumes his usual demeanor and chuckles darkly. "Oh, aye, it's nonsense, laddie. But folk who spout rubbish can be the most dangerous ones of all. We dinnae care if our prisoners get roughed up a bit, and we have no compunctions about hiding bodies in the forest."

I cup my hand over my mouth, just in case Easton can read lips, and mouth to Domhnall, "Enough. I need him talking."

He seems to understand, since he leans back in his chair and sets one ankle on the other knee. Then he drapes his arms on the chair.

I haven't seen him looking this relaxed and confident in a long time. I'd love to mount him right now, in that chair, but not with Easton watching.

So, I turn toward the *cacan* again. "Last chance. I want to know why you waited all these years before you sought me out. If ye dinnae tell me, I'll set *Dòmhnall an Tarbh* loose on you."

Easton's forehead wrinkles. "I know Domhnall is that wanker's name, but what in the world is *an Tarbh*? I thought his surname was Sterling."

I remain silent, simply looking at him steadily. Talking hasn't made him confess. Might as well try a different approach.

His forehead wrinkles even more, and his brows draw together too.

But I keep staring at him.

Easton puckers his lips and wriggles as if he's got ants in his trousers.

And still, I watch him.

He huffs, and his entire demeanor slackens. "All right, fine, I'll tell you."

"Go on, then."

Easton squirms as if he's trying to get himself into a more upright position, but he cannae manage it. "After you threw me over, I experienced a string of events that were, ah, unfavorable." He squirms again and winds up sinking deeper into the corner of the sofa, which makes him wince. Then he sighs heavily. "All right, you win. The fact is that my life fell apart after that. You know my mum had passed away a year before we met. But after you were gone, my father died too. I had received all the money in my trust fund once I turned eighteen. You know that already, and you know I loved to spend money on frivolous things."

"What does that have to do with why you're here now?"

"I slid off the rails rather spectacularly after my father passed away. I received even more money in my inheritance, and I didn't use it wisely." He lets his head fall back against the sofa and shuts his eyes. "I got into drugs and began drinking too much. I frequented night clubs and gambling establishments, not to mention the prozzies."

Easton had sex with prostitutes? That admission stuns me because he used to be such a mild-mannered boy. But I won't ask any questions until he's done talking.

"I got tangled up with some very bad blokes," he says. "I owed them shedloads of money, but I couldn't pay it back. Only after years of rehab and a rather lengthy stint in prison did I finally clean myself up and become somewhat respectable. That happened five years ago. I had a job as a paralegal."

Domhnall has not moved a single muscle or made any sort of facial expression during Easton's confession. He gazes out the window rather than staring at my ex.

"Last year, the law firm went broke. I was out of a job and skint." He finally opens his eyes. "That's when I started to think about you, about all the good times we had and how much I missed you. Took me until a month ago to rally the courage to find you."

"Why bother hunting me down? After all these years?"

He shrugs. "You were the one bright spot in my life. I know you left me because I'd started to behave oddly, but I've worked bloody hard to change."

"I never noticed your behavior changing. We split up because, after graduation, I wanted to go home to Scotland and you preferred England." I slide round to the other side of the coffee table, directly in front of Easton. "We argued about that off and on for months, until I finally realized we had never been right for each other. We wanted different sorts of lives."

"But I still love you, Fee."

"I don't love you, Easton. I don't think I ever did feel that way. What we had was convenient, not everlasting."

"No, you're wrong. Give me a chance to show you—"

"Stop this, Easton. Whatever you thought might happen, it will never be." I stand up and walk around the coffee table, placing a distance between us. "It's time for you to go home and forget about me."

"But I can't."

"That's not my problem."

Easton struggles to get into an upright sitting position again, then scuttles forward until his erse is almost off the sofa.

"Go home," I tell him. "Get in your car and leave."

"No, I can't."

Easton hurls himself up and into a standing position, teetering without the aid of his arms to hold him upright. He staggers into the coffee table and cries out when he smacks into the hard wood table.

Then he launches himself at me.

What happens next seems to move in slow motion, like a scene in a film, as Easton sails over the table toward me. I'm frozen, too stunned to move.

Domhnall flies out of his chair and races toward me.

But Easton gets to me first. He slams his head into my chest, and the energy of that collision bowls me over backward while it sends him tumbling across the floor. Just as he flings himself onto me, Domhnall reaches us.

He grabs Easton while the *cacan* is in the air, sailing toward me. Domhnall seizes him around the waist and plucks him away in midair so he can tackle Easton to the floor. The bull has caught the chicken, which doesn't seem like a fair fight, but I dinnae care. Domhnall has my ex pinned to the floor with one knee on Easton's back. All the *cacan* can do is wriggle and whimper and howl.

"You're done," Domhnall snarls. "Forget what Fiona said. It's too late to get in your car and leave because you are not getting off that easy." Domhnall glances at me. "Ring the police. They need to take him in and charge him. Assault is a crime."

I dig my mobile out of my pocket and dial the Loch Fairbairn police station. Then I ring Lachlan to tell him we might need help restraining Easton. Domhnall rolls his eyes at me when I say that bit. I have no doubts he could subdue my ex on his own, but Easton had tried to escape earlier. I wonder if he's been taking some sort of illicit drugs. That might explain his behavior. He admitted to being an addict, after all.

My three brothers barrel into the room and halt near the coffee table.

"What's happened?" Rory asks. "Looks like the *bod ceann* gave you quite the row."

Lachlan eyes me with a narrowed gaze. "Did the bastard hurt you?"

"No, I'm fine." When Aidan rushes over to help me up, I give him a grateful smile. "Easton is a desperate, confused man who needs shedloads of therapy."

"We should've brought Jack instead of Lachie and Rory Baby, eh?"

"Maybe you should have."

Domhnall, who is still holding Easton down, glances over his shoulder at me. "No, *gràidh*, leave that to me. I'd love to get him in the ring and show him what boxing is all about."

Aidan clucks his tongue. "No, no, Domhnall, ye can't do that. It wouldn't be a fair fight. One scrawny British erse versus the Scottish bull? It would be a blood bath."

I squint at Aidan. "Scottish bull?"

"Aye. *Dòmhnall an Tarbh.* That means Domhnall the Bull."

"Only Domhnall and I know that. How did you hear the nickname?"

My youngest brother winces and hunches his shoulders. Then he spreads his palms. "Well, ah, ye see…we sort of eavesdropped."

"You did what?"

Aidan jabs a finger toward my oldest brother. "It was Lachie's idea."

Lachlan's eyes flare wide briefly. "Maybe it was, ye tattletale. But Thane Buchanan aided and abetted the eavesdropping."

"Haud yer wheesht!" I shout. "All of you, stop blethering like little old men. How much did you three hear?"

Rory winces and shifts his weight from one foot to the other. "We heard everything since you walked into the sitting room."

"*Mhac na galla.*" I rub my hands over my cheeks, though I have no idea why I do it. This has turned into a monumental mess. "Forget about the eavesdropping. We need to keep Easton here until the constables arrive."

"We will," Lachlan says. "You have our word. If our unwilling guest gets away from Domhnall, we will catch him and lock him in the dungeon."

Rory grits his teeth. "There is no dungeon at Dùndubhan. How many times do I have to tell you morons that?"

I give up and flop onto the sofa. My brothers will never stop harassing each other. But at least I know, without any doubts whatsoever, that they and Domhnall will make certain Easton can't escape.

Chapter Twenty-Three

Domhnall

Fiona and I stand in the courtyard, watching as two constables push Easton into the backseat of their vehicle and drive away with him. I keep my arm around Fiona's waist even after the police car has vanished from our sight. She doesn't seem visibly upset by what happened, but I know she must be feeling anxious and confused right now.

Easton Yates is insane. Or maybe he was simply high on drugs. I don't know, and I don't care. If I ever see the *cacan* again, I will beat him bloody.

The Three Macs have been loitering behind us. I assume that's their way of being respectful or showing solidarity with their sister.

Once I can tell Fiona has grown tired of staring at the gravel driveway, I give her a squeeze and kiss the top of her head. "What should we do now? It's hard to top what happened here today."

Thane comes up beside me and gazes at the empty driveway as if he's hoping to see something out there. "Rory received a call from his contact at the Home Office."

"And that means what?"

"News, obviously. That Beckham bloke wouldn't ring Rory unless he had something important to say."

His vagueness makes me want to clench my fists, but I resist the urge. "I thought it was annoying when you wouldn't speak. But now I realize I prefer it when you're silent. It's better than hearing you spout vague rubbish."

"I never spout rubbish. Every word I say has meaning." He folds his arms over his chest and scrutinizes the gravel path that leads away from the castle. "Beckham did some additional digging into Easton Yates and his background. It seems that he was in a high-secure residential treatment center for three years. He had attempted to kidnap his ex-wife, though she verified that he never hurt her and that he was 'not in a good frame of mind' at the time."

"You mean he's a bampot of the first order."

"Aye. But eight months ago, he was deemed to be ready to return to society."

Fiona stiffens, aiming her sharp gaze at Thane. "Return to society? He assaulted me."

"Aye. The system isn't perfect. I suspect he will be sent back to a high-secure facility very soon."

"Will I need to testify in court?"

"I wouldn't worry about that. Easton Yates wants to win you over, in his own barmy way, so he will probably haver like an eejit in court, proving his insanity without anyone needing to testify against him."

Although Fiona seems more angry than frightened, I still feel the need to keep her close. The warmth of her makes me feel more relaxed. "So, the drama is over."

Thane nods. "I would say so."

Well, at least that *cacan* is gone now and won't fash Fiona anymore. I kiss her forehead. "Let's go home, *leannan*."

"Sorry," Thane says. "Ye can't leave yet. The Easton bollocks might be over, but you still have something to prove."

"That he does," a familiar voice declares from behind us. We all turn to look at Lachlan. "It's time for the Three Macs Test."

I groan. "And what is that?"

"Wouldn't be a proper test if we told you all about it."

"Could we hold off on that for a day or two? Fiona has been through hell today."

Lachlan and Thane exchange meaningful glances, but I can't interpret their expressions.

"You two should rest for a few days," Lachlan finally says. "That will give us time set up the test."

I clasp Fiona's hand. "Let's go home."

Thane clucks his tongue. "Afraid ye cannae do that yet. Neutral ground is required, and that means you stay here."

"How is Dùndubhan a neutral place? Rory owns it, and enough MacTaggarts come and go here to populate the whole of the Highlands."

"It's neutral because this isn't the house where you and Fiona live."

Well, I reckon that does make sense, in a way. Not sure if staying here, after what Easton did, will help us mend our relationship. But I'll give it a go. Besides, I'm certain we won't be allowed to leave yet. Fiona's family and friends will see to that, in their oddly supportive way. Aye, it's a bit like being imprisoned for your own good.

"May we go for a walk?" I ask. "Outside the castle compound."

Lachlan nods. "Feel free to do that. Just be back by one o'clock. We're planning a feast in the courtyard."

"Sitting cross-legged on the gravel doesn't sound appealing."

He seems about to say something sarcastic, but he abruptly shuts his mouth as he studies me. Then he smiles. "You're having me on, aren't you?"

"Mostly. But it's true that I don't want to sit on gravel."

Lachlan slaps my arm. "Maybe we won't need to murder you after all. But dinnae worry. We'll have tables and chairs, even utensils, just like proper gents and lasses."

"Glad to hear you lot aren't barbarians." I link my fingers with Fiona's and smile down at her. "Should we start our walk?"

"Aye. But let's not do another hike up Beann Dealgach, not today."

"We can stay in the vicinity of the castle. The river might be a nice place to go."

"Aye, that does sound nice."

Thane abruptly whirls about and races into the house.

I shake my head. "What is he doing now?"

Lachlan sighs. "Who knows. Thane Buchanan is an enigma. We like him, but none of us understands the laddie. I think he needs a good woman to straighten him out."

That's what they say about every unattached man in the Highlands. "Will Thane be the American Wives Club's next project?"

"You never know. But it's the lasses who decide on the next meddling project, not the men. We're helpless to resist anything our women want. The American Wives Club is a force to be reckoned with."

"I'm well aware of that. The Club instigated all the nonsense with Grey and Jessica at Cat and Alex's wedding."

Lachlan lifts his brows. "Most of that was meant to help you, not Grey and Jessica."

What did he just say? I stand here immobilized as the import of Lachlan's words gradually filters into my brain. But even once I've ingested the information, I still cannae understand. "How was that all for my benefit? Grey needed help to win Jessica's heart. That had nothing to do with me. I was a secondary character in their story."

"Is that what you've believed for the past two years?"

"No, it's what I've known since then."

Lachlan waves to his brothers, who have been loitering near the garden doorway having a blether. Rory and Aidan trot over here, and they have a brief, hushed conversation. Then Lachlan points at me. "Domhnall thinks the mischief at Alex and Cat's wedding was primarily meant to help Grey and Jessica."

Aidan and Rory both chuckle and shake their heads, as if they think I must be barmy to believe such a thing.

"That is what happened," I say. "Tell them, Fiona."

She shrugs and gives me a patient smile. "I can't agree with your statements, Domhnall. I was there, and I know that my brothers orchestrated events at the wedding mainly for you. After all, you were the one who crashed the wedding and caused mayhem. You needed help more than Grey and Jessica did."

My jaw has fallen open. I can do nothing but gawp at the woman I love.

"It's true," Aidan concurs. "Alex and Jack gave Grey all the advice he needed. But you… Ah, Domhnall, you are so pigheaded that ye make Rory look like a sweet teddy bear."

Rory squints at his younger brother. "What are you implying about me?"

Aidan slaps his hand down on Rory's shoulder and leans in to speak in a pseudo-whisper. "You aren't the cuddliest bear, are you? Dinnae worry. Your bampot wife loves that you're a prickly, intimidating grizzly and not a sweet, fluffy teddy."

"I intimidate you. That's what you just said. Too bad Calli married such a frightened rabbit."

"You don't intimidate me, Rory Baby. I meant everyone else."

"Dinnae be calling me by that nickname ever again." Rory narrows his eyes to slits and speaks through clenched teeth, despite everyone knowing he isn't actually annoyed with his brother. "If ye say it again, I'll invent an embarrassing nickname for you."

"Calli already gave me one." Aidan straightens and spreads his arms, grinning with devilish delight. "Aidan the Magnificent."

Lachlan huffs. "Your wife didn't come up with that. You christened yourself Aidan the Magnificent."

While those three continue ribbing each other, I lead Fiona toward the wooden gates, which remain open. We've just crossed the threshold when Thane sprints up to us.

He needs a moment to catch his breath. Then he thrusts a bottle at us. "You forgot this."

I glance at the words on the bottle. "*Collaidh Sgeul-Rùin* Black Label? This is the whisky we found on our treasure hunt."

"Aye. Errol and Ashley placed it there for you to find, but I donated the bottle. It's from my distillery."

"How many bottles did you bring with you to Dùndubhan?"

"None. You brought this bottle."

I pause to consider everything he just said. Then I flatten my lips. "You sneaked into the tower bedroom to steal this bottle from our bags?"

"That's right."

I must look enraged, since I bloody well am, because Fiona rests a hand on my forearm. "Save your angry bull behavior for later, when my brothers do their test. Thane is just being helpful, though he's going about it in a bizarre way."

A long sigh gusts out of me. "I know you're right. Thane, I apologize for stamping my hooves at you."

"Hooves?" He laughs. "Fiona calls you a bull, doesn't she? *Dòmhnall an Tarbh.* I heard about that."

I snatch the whisky bottle out of his hand. "Thank you for the single malt. We're away now."

As Fiona and I turn to leave, Thane says, in a tone dripping with sarcasm, "Just a word of warning, *Dòmhnall an Tarbh.*" He waits until we pause to glance back at him. "I have it on good authority that what the MacTaggarts did for you at Alex and Cat's wedding will be nothing compared to what's coming now. With Fiona involved, they will go further than ever before."

"Is that meant to scare me? If that's your aim, you have seriously underestimated my inner fortitude."

"No, I would never try to frighten you. It's a heads-up, that's all."

Though I shouldn't care, I find myself asking another question. "Why would Lachlan and his brothers go further because Fiona is involved? They must have done similar things to Gavin and Alex."

"Similar, aye. But not to the same degree."

"I still don't understand, and I dislike being taken on a verbal carousel ride. Talk to me straight or dinnae talk at all."

Thane lifts a single brow, and his lips tick up slightly at the corners. "I'm beginning to like you, Domhnall. But I won't betray the plans orchestrated by the MacTaggarts and their cohorts."

He turns and walks away.

And I shake my head for the hundredth time today. "What is that man up to? His mysterious act annoys me."

"He's no more mysterious than you are."

I swerve my eyes toward Fiona. "What does that mean?"

"You know exactly what I'm talking about." She seizes my hand, tugging to encourage me to start walking. "I'll tell you about Thane and Easton if you tell me about your time in the military."

I tighten my grip on her hand as we pass beneath the spot where the old gatehouse had been in medieval times. Iain had told me all about the Dùndubhan of the past, and Thane showed me the hidden passages no one knew existed until recently. Have I been as mysterious as this castle? Withholding all my secrets from the woman I love? Fiona has told me several times over the past few months that I need to express my feelings more directly. But that's not something most men want to do.

As we approach the corner of the castle compound, I wrap my arm around her waist. "I will tell you anything you want to know. Here, today, away from prying eyes and ears. If you want to understand me, I'm ready to let you do that."

She stops, which makes me stop too, and she gazes up at me with her bonnie brown eyes large and glistening. Not with tears. No, it's a sign of surprise and happiness. I might be a numpty sometimes, but even I can deduce Fiona's emotions. Usually. I am still a man, after all.

Fiona raises onto the tips of her toes and kisses me. "Thank you, Domhnall. I know you mean that, and you won't back out."

"I will never pull away from you again."

Her lips tighten into the sweetest smile. "I will never pull away from you again, either."

"Not even if I turn into a *tolla-thon* again?"

"You won't do that. You just told me so." She slides her arm around my waist. "And I know that Domhnall Sterling never reneges on a promise."

Fiona MacTaggart is the only woman on earth who has ever made me feel like I could do anything as long as she's by my side.

We wander down the trail that leads into the woods and follow it when the path curves to the right. The trail used to be nothing more than a walking path worn down by the MacTaggarts. But these days, it is a proper walking trail that's groomed and even has signs indicating various points of interest. When Rory and Emery had turned Dùndubhan into a museum and a bed-and-breakfast, they had garnered funding from their family and friends to improve the entire estate—except for the eastern face of Beann Dealgach. But thinking about that makes me wonder aloud.

"Does your brother plan on making the other side of the mountain into a tourist destination too?"

"I have no idea. Rory and Emery like to keep their plans close to the chest until they have everything plotted out in their minds."

"I see."

We've just reached the first signpost. It declares that the river, which has never been given a name, can be accessed via the offshoot trail.

"Should we visit the river?" I ask.

"That would be lovely."

We keep our arms around each other as we amble down the path, and I grow more curious along the way. "Why doesn't the river have a name?"

"Dinnae know. It just doesn't."

"Rory never thought to give it a name?"

She laughs. "You don't know Rory if you think he never thought about that. I'm sure he and Emery talk about that often. But Dùndubhan is more than Rory's castle. It's a historic landmark too, and I assume that's why he hasn't named it." She tips her head to the side, a sure sign she's mulling over the issue. «But it is odd that in all the years Dùndubhan has been around, no one ever bothered to christen the river with a genuine name."

"Maybe your ancestors did that, but they never wrote down the information."

"That could be, I suppose. We should ask Iain sometime." Fiona halts because we have just reached the riverbank. "But right now, I'm dying to hear all your secrets."

"We best sit down for this. It will take more than a wee while."

Chapter Twenty-Four

Fiona

Domhnall settles onto the ground, so near the river's edge that the tips of his shoes come within millimeters of it. He pats the ground beside him. I heed his call and sit down. He leans back, lodging his palms on the earth behind his erse while I move into a cross-legged position. I wriggle around so that I can watch his face while he tells me everything, at last.

"Before I begin," he says, "I'd like to ask you one thing first."

"Go on."

"Why are you still with me? After all my bad behavior, including the way I conducted myself at Alex and Catriona's wedding and every day between then and now."

I stretch out a hand to caress his cheek. "I stay because I love you, ye numpty."

He turns my palm over and kisses it. "I love you too, ye wonderful lass."

"You will always be my *Dòmhnall an Tarbh*, the sexiest, cleverest, strongest, most incredible man I've ever known."

Domhnall scrunches up his face and squirms, then clears his throat. "Could you stop praising me so effusively? At least until I've told you everything."

I've made him uncomfortable, though I have my suspicions that he isn't embarrassed simply because I praised him. His past has something to do with it too. So, I stay quiet and just listen.

Domhnall bows his head. "I told you before that I was a pilot in the RAF. I was deployed to Afghanistan during the war there. That's something I've never told anyone except for Mick."

Though I desperately want to ask a question, I clamp my teeth down on my lips to stop myself.

He almost smirks, though the expression crumbles away quickly. "Go on, love, ask."

"Did you and Mick become friends because of your war experiences?"

"Aye. We met in Afghanistan, when he was with the US Air Force and I was attached to the RAF. We participated in joint operations a couple of times. But then we were deployed to different areas, and we kept in touch via email and video calls."

I had never known how they met. Though I've only spoken to Mick a few times, I've always liked him, and now I understand why they have such a strong bond.

"The bit you really want to know about happened later," Domhnall says. "My jet crashed in Kandahar Province. Though my co-pilot and I both ejected, he suffered severe spinal fractures from the force of the bailout. I had a few fractures too, but I was able to fully recover. I carried John on my back for nearly a mile before I couldn't walk any further."

"Because of your injuries."

"Aye." He keeps his head down and doesn't even glance at me sideways. "We were rescued eventually, but by then, John was dead."

Maybe I shouldn't ask, but I need to know. "How long did it take for you to recover from your injuries?"

"Several months. The physical therapy was grueling." He bends his knees and rests his elbows on them. Then he drops his head into his raised hands. "I've never forgiven myself for letting John die."

"That wasn't your fault."

"Aye, I know that. But I still feel responsible." He shoves his hands into hair, seeming to grip his head firmly. "I saw many terrible things in Afghanistan, including a suicide bombing that killed schoolchildren. Maybe that's why I'm too damaged to be any good for you."

What can I say to that? Nothing that would make him feel better. If he needs to tell me more, I'll listen. I wish I had known from the start that he'd been through horrific experiences. Maybe I could have... I don't know. Done something. But I think all he needs me to do right now is to listen.

But he doesn't speak. Minutes tick by.

Finally, I can't remain silent any longer. "Domhnall, I'm so sorry you went through all of that. But you're wrong. You are not too damaged to be with me. For as long as I've known you, I have only seen how good you are, how strong and resilient, and how sweet and kind and loving. You are a man with demons, for sure, but that doesn't diminish your character and strength. You keep fighting no matter what. That's the Domhnall Sterling I know."

He holds perfectly still for a moment, and I'm fair certain he's holding his breath too. Then he blows out a gusty sigh and lifts his head to look straight at me. "You have been my salvation since the day we met."

That statement takes my breath away. I'm his salvation. No man has ever said such a thing to me, never in my entire life, until this moment. I'm so stunned by his statement that I blurt out a bloody stupid thing. "What about Jessica and Sophie? They cared for you too."

"Not the way you always have." He leans over to grab me around the waist and hoist me onto his lap. "Sophie destroyed my faith in love, but Jessica tried to save me. She just couldn't do it. I wouldn't let her. I have finally realized that my previous relationships, however painful they were, in a strange way helped me."

"I know it's not the same thing, but I've come to believe that my relationship with Easton is part of the reason why I wanted to help you when we first met."

Domhnall gazes at me steadily as if he needs to decipher the meaning of my words. "You had a *bod ceann* boyfriend, and that somehow made you want to take on another *bod ceann*?"

I can't stop myself from laughing, though it's purely affectionate. "Easton wasn't a dickhead back then. In fact, he was very…benign."

Domhnall barely stifles a laugh. "Benign? That doesn't sound like the foundation for a lasting relationship."

"No, it wasn't." I loop my arms around his neck. "I was young and inexperienced when it came to love. I liked Easton because he never got angry or sad or even enthusiastic. He stayed sort of…indifferent, I suppose."

"Indifferent?" Domhnall's lip curls. "What the bloody hell was wrong with the *cacan*? I can't understand how any man could be indifferent to you."

"Easton was my first boyfriend. I didn't know what romance was supposed to be like."

Domhnall studies me again, but this time, he seems interested rather than confused. "If Easton was your first boyfriend, that means you didn't date in secondary school, when you were a bonnie young lass besieged by randy laddies."

"Well, I wanted to date. But most boys were afraid of my brothers."

"The Three Macs chased them away."

"Not three. Aidan was only a wee laddie and still in primary school. Lachlan was in his early twenties, and Rory was a bit younger and away at university." I sigh as I remember those days. "Lachlan intimidated boys without even trying to do it, and whenever Rory came home from university, he would help Lachlan glare at the laddies who wanted to get into my trousers. The situation got worse as the years passed. I know they only wanted to protect me, but it's hard to date when your brothers are breathing down the necks of potential suitors."

"Is that why you went away to university?"

"Partly. I also wanted to see more of the world. That's why I chose a university in England." I tickle the nape of his neck. "I wish I'd met you there instead of Easton."

"I wasn't even in secondary school yet when you left for England. We met at the time when we were meant to find each other."

I pull my head back to meet his gaze. "Is Domhnall Sterling suggesting that he might believe in fate?"

Rather than responding, he surges to his feet with me cradled in his arms. "Let's go for a swim in the river."

"I didn't bring a swimsuit."

"Did I say ye needed one?"

"Why wouldn't I need—" I giggle like a schoolgirl. "Oh. I see."

"Are ye comfortable with swimming naked?"

I wriggle my legs. "Only if you let me down first. Dinnae want to be tossed into the river."

Domhnall lets me slide down his body until my feet touch the ground. "I might set you on your feet, but I would never let you down, *mo chridhe*."

"I know that, Domhnall."

We both shed our clothes and leap into the river. The water is cold, but not too chilly for us to enjoy a swim. The current isn't swift. Further down the river, it does become more powerful, a fact we both know from our hike up the other side of the mountain. Domhnall splashes me, and I splash him back. We laugh and tease each other and generally have a good time.

After our swim, we pull on our clothes. We didn't think of bringing towels for drying off since taking a dip in the river had been a spur-of-the-moment idea. That means our clothes are wet. And wet clothes mean my brothers will realize that Domhnall and I skinny dipped in the river, since our clothing won't be soaked, but simply damp. If we'd jumped into the water fully dressed, everything we're wearing would be dripping wet.

Domhnall halts just out of sight of the river and gently pushes me back against a tree. Then he cups my face in his hands and presses his lips to mine. I can't stop myself from relaxing and sinking into the sensual delight of kissing Domhnall Sterling. We haven't really done this for quite awhile, ever since we started arguing and gave up shagging. I moan softly as he slips his tongue between my lips and teases me with light flicks, making me go warm and liquid in all the best ways.

I grasp his biceps and arch my back, which makes my stiff nipples rub against his chest. Another, deeper moan emerges from me, and I thrust my tongue into his mouth. I'm desperate to taste him again after so long without his kiss, and without thinking about it, I wrap my arms around his neck while hooking one leg around his thigh. He groans with a depth of hunger that would take my breath away if I weren't already breathless. I glide my leg up until my foot bumps into his erse.

Bod an Donais, I love his taut erse.

He grasps my raised thigh and lifts it so he can rub his rigid cock against my cleft. My clothing isn't enough of a barrier, and I'm dead sure I could come just from the friction he's creating.

Domhnall shoves his hand between our bodies and unhooks the button on my jeans, then yanks the zipper down. When he pushes that hand inside my knickers, he groans with such hunger that it almost sounds like a growl. My back arches as he caresses my folds with two fingers. Something thumps on the ground, but I'm beyond caring about anything except the way he's touching me.

"Oh, Domhnall, please make me come."

He claims my mouth again while rubbing my folds with more vigor.

My mobile rings.

Domhnall pulls his head back and glances around in confusion. "Is that yours or mine?" Before I can respond, he reaches into his back pocket and brings out his mobile, which is not ringing. "Must be yours, *leannan*. Ignore it."

I spot my mobile lying on the ground and snatch it up. "It's Lachlan. If I don't answer, he will come and look for us."

"Bloody hell." Domhnall backs away. A large bulge has formed in his trousers. "Better take the call."

I zip up my jeans first, then answer. "What is it, Lachlan?"

"Are you all right, Fiona? Ye sound winded."

"Hikes are for exercise. That means exertion."

Lachlan chuckles. "Exertion? Once Domhnall's done shagging you, get your erses back to the castle. It's lunchtime."

"We were not shagging, and whatever we might be doing, it's none of your business, Lachie."

"All right, Fifi. Point taken."

I resist the urge to call my brother an unkind name, though he bloody well deserves it. "Do not call me Fifi. Easton used to call me Fee, and I always hated it. Fifi sounds like a ruddy poodle."

"Just get back to the castle. Please."

"Since you said 'please,' we will start back to Dùndubhan."

I rudely hang up on him, but I know Lachlan won't be offended. We're all used to the way Rory often hangs up on a call without saying goodbye. The most we usually get is a grunt. There's a reason his nickname is the Steely Solicitor, and it's not because he loves metal.

"We have to go now," I tell Domhnall. "Sorry we couldn't finish what we started."

"Dinnae worry about that." He pulls me close and nuzzles my nose. "I want to ask you a question, but I need to get something first. I left it in the tower bedroom."

"I'll go with you."

"No." He jerks away from me, having almost shouted that word. Domhnall clears his throat. "I'm sorry. Didn't mean to bark at you. But please, let me go to the tower bedroom alone. It will all make sense eventually, I promise."

"I trust you, Domhnall. Whatever you have up your sleeve, I can wait to find out."

His entire demeanor softens. "Thank you, *mo chridhe*."

Every time he calls me his heart in Gaelic, it gives me a pang in my chest and a rush of sweet warmth. I love "*mo leannan*" too, and also "*gràidh*." Those are all endearments. He is my heart, my sweetheart, and my darling.

We hold hands on our way back to the castle and approach it from the backside. Then we get a surprise when we enter the courtyard via the garden. Several rows of tables have been set up, creating an outdoor banquet that fills the large space. Everyone's cars must be parked outside the walls, though not on the green behind Dùndubhan. I hadn't heard any vehicles arrives, but then, Domhnall and I had been at the river. The forest around us would have muffled the sounds of car engines.

But now, it seems as if the entire MacTaggart clan has gathered here for a massive feast.

Domhnall halts in the middle of the courtyard.

"You want to do your errand," I say. "Go on, I'll survive without you for ten minutes."

He kisses my forehead. "You are the most wonderful lass in the world."

"If you keep lavishing me with compliments, I might faint from shock."

While he jogs toward the vestibule doorway, I amble over to the spot where my brothers and their wives are chatting. But I breeze past them. They glance at me and nod, clearly unconcerned with what I'm doing. Who do I want to talk to right now?

I march up to the man who is gazing up at the sky with a faint smile on his lips. "*Feasgar math*. Are you enjoying the sunshine?"

Thane lowers his gaze to me. "Good afternoon to you too, Fiona. Where is Domhnall?"

"In the house. He forgot something in the tower bedroom but wouldn't tell me what it was."

Thane's smile broadens. "I think I can guess what he needed so desperately that he would abandon you so he could retrieve it."

"And what is that thing?"

"Oh, I can't divulge that information."

I fold my arms over my chest. "Domhnall has told me everything about himself, so there's no reason why you shouldn't tell me about the secret thing he went to get."

"Nice try, Fiona. But I know how to keep a secret even under the worst sorts of duress."

My curiosity rears up, and I have to ask. "What did you do before you started your own distillery?"

His expression and tone of voice shift abruptly and remind me of the way Logan looks when he's in spy mode. "If I told you, I'd have to kill you."

Chapter Twenty-Five

Domhnall

I close the bag and rise from my kneeling position, holding the precious item in my hand with my fingers firmly curled around it. I've waited a long time to do this, and I have no idea how Fiona might react. We've grown closer lately, but that doesn't mean she has forgiven me for everything. Being unstoppable means ignoring all those doubts and forging ahead no matter what.

Fiona and I belong together. I will never give up on us, and it's time I proved that to her.

Now that I have my prize, I jog down the tower bedrooms steps and race across the long gallery. I've never taken the vestibule stairs three at a time, but I do that now. My pulse had sped up the moment I retrieved the item, and now, it revs up even more.

I sprint out of the vestibule and force myself to slow down as I cross the courtyard in search of the lass I need to see. But I freeze halfway to her.

Thane Buchanan is talking to Fiona, and they seem to be engaged in an intense conversation. Not the angry sort of intense. No, Fiona seems deeply intrigued by whatever Thane is telling her. Her eyes are slightly wider than usual, she leans toward him a touch, and she nods periodically as if he's telling her a great story.

Am I jealous? Not one iota. Fiona loves me, no one else.

While I watch the two of them conversing, my thoughts reel backward in time to the week of Alex and Catriona's wedding. I'd met Fiona there, and we had an instant attraction, something so magnetic that neither of us could fight it. Our first kiss had thrown me off balance because it had been so bloody incredible. And I found myself doing things to impress her, like the day when I had performed a nude headstand on the lawn, in front of everyone, simply to see the look on Fiona's face.

Everyone had cheered when I raised one arm while remaining upside down.

Fiona cheered for me the loudest and even winked at me, though no one else appeared to notice that. Her whistling and winking had given me a strange thrill. Had I been falling for her already on that day? Looking back now, aye, I'm sure I had starting falling then. I've kept on falling ever since, and I know I'll never stop. That bonnie, feisty lass is my soul mate. I had never believed in that rubbish, but Fiona MacTaggart changed my mind about so many things.

At the Highland games held during the wedding week, I had also whipped off my shirt and tossed it to Fiona, just to impress her. I can still picture the look on her face when I did that and when she caught my shirt. I swear actual electricity had sizzled between us.

Despite the fact I had cheated during the Highland games, Fiona forgave me for that. And when I finished the games without any treachery, I shook hands with Grey Dixon, and he forgave me too. We're friends now, and I'm glad for that. But on that day two years ago, Fiona had raced up to me and thrown her arms around my neck while grinning. I'd lost the games, yet she behaved as if I'd won. I still remember what she said to me then.

"You didn't cheat this time. Congratulations, ye *cacan*."

"Are you trying to make me feel better?" I'd asked. "You're bloody awful at it."

She patted my chest with both her hands. "Dinnae be grumpy. You get the consolation prize."

"What would that be?"

"You'll find out soon."

I still remember the prize she'd given me. We had gone into the guest house at the resort and shagged on the island in the kitchen. How did I ever get so lucky? Fiona saved my soul and my friendship with Jessica and Grey. Her family accepted me because she convinced them to do it.

I have never been jealous when it comes to Fiona. She has never given me reason to feel that way because she never looks at another man. Now, as I watch her talking to Thane Buchanan, I still don't experience even a twinge of jealousy. Thane might be attractive and mysterious, two things women find intriguing, but he's also strange. He owns a distillery, yet he often behaves like a spy.

Aye, in some ways he reminds me of Logan MacTaggart without the deadly calm stare and uncanny reflexes. Thane seems more like a man used to keeping secrets but who rarely, if ever, has the need to stalk his prey. I'd met spies in the RAF, and Thane does not act like them.

The man in question notices me standing over here and waves for me to join him and Fiona. His waving makes her glance this way too.

She smiles at me, and it's nothing like the way she smiles at everyone else including Thane.

I saunter up to them. "What have you two been blethering about?"

Fiona curls her arm around mine, leaning into me. "Thane was telling me about his former career."

"Ah, I see." I turn my attention to Thane. "So tell me, what was your previous career? No one has mentioned it to me."

"They wouldn't."

"Why not?"

"Because I never told them. Even my parents have no idea what I was doing for all those years when I lived in England."

A mystery man? Aye, this is starting to interest me, and I don't usually give a toss about the lives of people I barely know. "Are you a secret agent, Thane? You remind me of Logan in some ways. That's why I ask."

"I'm impressed, Domhnall. You're more than just a bull with a pretty face, aren't you?"

"Bull? I wish Fiona had never spoken the phrase *Dòmhnall an Tarbh* here at Dùndubhan, where her family can eavesdrop and find out what she said. They're bloody awful amateur spies who are determined to drive me off my head."

Thane chuckles. "You aren't fooling anyone, Domhnall. We all know you love the MacTaggarts and the Murdochs and all the rest of us. You're a softhearted bloke."

I had once referred to Jessica O'Connor as softhearted, though I accidentally labeled her softheaded first thanks to an unfortunate slip of the tongue. She didn't appreciate that. But these days, I have become exactly what Thane called me. I'm softhearted, and it doesn't fash me at all.

But I feign annoyance for Thane's sake. "Are ye going to tell me what your former job was? Or do I need to beat the truth out of you?"

I crack my knuckles, strictly for show.

Thane seems mildly amused. "Och, I'm terrified of *Dòmhnall an Tarbh*. I have no choice but to confess." He slants toward me and speaks in a bloody stupid whisper. "I worked for the Ministry of Defence as a geospatial analyst."

"And that means what in English? I'll settle for Gaelic if it's easier to explain in that language."

He straightens and sighs. "Honestly, it's difficult to explain in any language unless you're familiar with geography, aerial photography, cartography, satellite imagery, environmental science, and all the latest studies related to all of those topics."

No matter how many words come out of his mouth, I still can't understand what geospatial analysis is all about. But I must have a masochistic streak because I keep questioning him. "You're a computer geek like Grey Dixon and Evan MacTaggart, aye?"

Thane's lips flatten. His eyes narrow. But then he blows out a breath and laughs. "Domhnall, I like you more and more every time we have a conversation. You don't ever beat round any bushes, do you?"

"No."

"I have never been called a geek before, but you are essentially correct. I'm adept at using multiple GIS applications as well as coding and other types of IT."

"Of course you are." I look at Fiona, but she shakes her head. I won't get any help from her. "You aren't a spy, then."

"Not technically. But I often liaised with Defence Intelligence. That means I had security clearance. My work was classified."

"Fascinating." But no, I dinnae find it intriguing. That's mostly because I have no idea what any of the jargon he used means.

Fortunately, I'm saved from needing to hear more about Thane's past life. Someone rings a very loud bell and shouts, "Lunch is served! Find the card with your name on it and sit there."

That would be Errol Murdoch. I'd recognize that bampot's voice anywhere.

"But don't sit on the card," Errol clarifies. "That goes on the table. Your erse belongs on the chair."

"Thanks for letting us know," Magnus shouts. "Otherwise, we might have sat on the table."

"Oh no, you wouldn't want to do that. The forks and knifes could puncture your erse."

Thankfully, Errol shuts his bloody mouth.

I grasp Fiona's hand, guiding her down the rows of tables and chairs, hunting for the cards with our names on them. We've gotten partway down one aisle when Errol sprints up to us.

He grabs my arm. "You're in the wrong place, Domhnall. Follow me."

Well, why not? Might as well follow the Fire Starter.

Errol takes us to the first row of tables, at the end where Fiona's brothers and their wives wait for us with her sisters and their husbands. Alex and Gavin seem mildly amused while they listen to their wives havering with Emery, Calli, and Erica.

"Sit here, Domhnall," Errol commands. "Fiona, you take the chair beside him."

"I think we could have figured that out on our own." I pull out Fiona's chair for her, then take my seat. But Errol keeps standing there watching us. "What's your problem now, ye bampot?"

Errol pats my shoulder. "Relax, Domhnall. The hard part won't begin until after lunch."

He spots his wife heading this way and hurries to usher Ashley to her assigned chair. They're sitting across the table from me and Fiona.

Our midday meal includes plenty of good food—though no haggis, thankfully—and enough wine is passed around to empty out an entire winery. Of course, we have a large crowd here this afternoon. We have probably emptied out an entire supermarket too.

Fiona's brothers engage me in sarcastic conversation, during which we rib each other mercilessly. Rory calls his oldest brother "Lachie," and that inspires Lachlan to repeatedly inject the nickname Rory Baby into the jokes simply to fash his younger brother. But they both gang up on Aidan, the youngest man in their family, to tease him about the nickname he chose for himself. Aye, he named himself Aidan the Magnificent.

I could understand if his wife invented that title, but for the laddie to choose that himself... Well, I reckon I shouldn't ridicule him for it since Fiona calls me *Dòmhnall an Tarbh*. At least I didn't choose that for myself.

Near the end of the courtyard feast, Alex Thorne switches places with his wife so he can sit beside me. Then he rests an arm across the back of my chair and angles toward me. "Fair warning, Domhnall. You will be permitted to have a brief rest period to let your meal settle. But then you'll be dragged out onto the green for the Three Macs Test. Gavin and I endured the same trial, at different times. Now, it's your turn."

"If ye think I'm scared, ye dinnae know me."

"The last MacTaggart lass has been claimed, and the Three Macs won't go easy on you. Fiona is more than simply the oldest sister. She is the one most beloved by her siblings."

"What are you getting at, Alex? I know Fiona's family loves her. That's hardly a stunning revelation."

The man who calls himself the British Bastard leans in closer to speak in a ridiculous whisper. "Fiona is special to her brothers and sisters. That's all you need to know. Might want to ask Thane for advice."

I make a slightly rude noise. "I do not need advice on how to survive an absurd test. I was a pilot in the RAF during wartime and got shot down in Afghanistan. I suffered spinal trauma caused by ejecting from my Typhoon jet. Even with those injuries I carried my copilot on my back and started walking. So dinnae whisper to me about how terrified I should be of the Three Macs bollocks."

Alex's brows hike up.

That's when I suddenly realize the entire courtyard has fallen silent. It's so quiet, in fact, that I can hear the breeze rustling the trees and birds chirping in the distance. I survey the courtyard and discover everyone is staring at me with various levels of surprise on their faces. Fiona seems the most shocked.

"Why is everyone gawping at me?" I demand. "Do I have food stuck in my teeth?"

Alex clears his throat and sits up straighter in his chair. "No, Domhnall, that isn't why everyone is gawping."

"What is their problem, then?"

"You were speaking so loudly that we all heard you. In fact, your voice echoed off the courtyard walls."

"What? No, I—" My gaze flicks to Fiona, who clasps my hand under the table. I rotate my gaze to her. "Was I speaking that loudly?"

She nods.

I groan and shut my eyes. "Bloody hell."

"You have nothing to be ashamed of, Domhnall." Fiona squeezes my hand. "It's long past time that you shared your experiences. Keeping it all bottled up inside you hasn't done you any good."

Maybe she's right about that. And maybe it's time I stopped hiding from my past.

Rory rises from his chair and clinks his wine glass to get everyone's attention. "Let's all show our support for Domhnall Sterling, a bona fide hero, with our applause."

Everyone leaps to their feet. Clapping and cheers erupt from every table, echoing off the castle walls.

Lachlan comes round to this side of the table and bends over to clap a hand on my shoulder. "Don't be embarrassed. You've earned all the applause. And now, you are officially a MacTaggart by choice if not by birth. Welcome to the family, Domhnall."

Chapter Twenty-Six

Fiona

I started to cry when Lachlan announced that Domhnall is part of the family now. Tears continue to trickle down my cheeks, but at least I'm not bawling. I knew my brothers might want to recognize Domhnall's military record if they heard about it, but I had no idea they would instigate a hearty round of applause in his honor.

Domhnall is an amazing man. I'm so happy he finally shared that not only with me, but also with my family.

Lachlan still has his hand resting on Domhnall's shoulder. When he notices that the man I love has become somewhat uncomfortable with the applause, Lachlan leans down even more to speak to him. "Nothing you've told us today will leave the family. We know how to keep secrets. If you should want to publicly discuss your history, we will support you in that too."

Domhnall nods, though he seems unable to gather any words.

Lachlan straightens and moves backward a couple of paces. Then he whistles in the loudest, most ear-piercing manner I've ever heard, and everyone quietens down immediately. My brother surveys the hushed crowd with satisfaction. "Thank you for your silence. Everyone, please remember that Domhnall's revelations are for us only. If and when he decides to share his story with the world, that will be up to him. But now, we have an important decision to make."

Domhnall wipes at his eyes, though I doubt anyone not sitting right beside him could tell he had a few tears in his eyes. I kiss his cheek and rest my head on his shoulder.

"Here's the dilemma," Lachlan announces. "Once we've all recovered from this feast, should we still hold the Three Macs Test? Raise your hands if you think we should."

Every man and woman in the courtyard raises their hand.

Domhnall raises his hand too.

I lift my head off his shoulder. "You honestly want to do it, don't you? Even though you've already been accepted into the family."

He smirks. "I can't let Alex be the last man to complete the test. That honor should belong to a Scot."

Alex, who still sits on the other side of Domhnall, holds out his hand to the bull. "Good luck, mate. I look forward to watching you demolish every test. And you're spot on about who should be the last to endure the Three Macs Test. It absolutely should be a Scot."

"Didn't need you to tell me that."

I can tell by the way his lips ticked upward that he's having fun with Alex, not expressing genuine annoyance. I love that he's had so little trouble earning the approval of my family—and Alex is a family member now. His mother and father are in prison on various charges related to their attempt to abduct Alex and Cat.

Family isn't only about blood. It's about a strong bond between individuals. Meeting Alex changed how I look at the concept of family, and that knowledge has changed everything for me. But I still wonder about one thing concerning Domhnall and his parents.

Once everyone begins to leave the courtyard, splitting off into various groups or couples, I claim Domhnall's hand to lead him into the garden. No one else is coming this way. The others have chosen to go indoors. My brothers and their wives offered to clean up the courtyard on their own, but some of my cousins as well as my sisters insisted on helping them.

That means Domhnall and I have the garden to ourselves. We sit down on the stone bench across from the arbor and instinctively rotate toward each other.

"You're wanting to talk," he says. "I recognize that look on your face."

"Aye. You know me better than anyone. But I haven't told you everything about my past, and I want to clear the air between us."

"Don't bother, *mo chridhe*. Your past with Easton doesn't fash me."

"Even knowing I slept with him?"

His lips curl into a teasing smile. "Unless ye shagged him last night, I have no issues with your sexual history. I trust you unequivocally."

"I appreciate that. But you should know the last time I slept with Easton was two weeks before I broke up with him. And we only ever shagged six times in three years."

Domhnall's eyes go wide. "What was wrong with him? The *cacan* had a bonnie lass for his own and he rarely touched you?"

"Not sure if I should divulge this. But since Easton assaulted me… The truth is that he had issues with impotence."

Domhnall struggles to maintain a neutral expression, but he fails. Laughter splutters out of him. "That doesn't surprise me one bit. He seems like the limp sort. Why on earth did you stay with him if he couldn't satisfy you? Couldn't have been his sparkling personality."

"He had a certain shy charm. But I mainly stayed with him because it was easy and safe." I slide closer to Domhnall and lay my arm across his shoulders. "I was young and naive. Now, I know what a real man should be like."

Domhnall winks. "But you still like younger men."

"Easton and I were the same age." I slide my fingers into the hairs at his nape. "But I do love having a poke with a younger man who has an impressive *slat*. It's a Scottish bull for me or no one at all."

"Just to be clear, there is only one Scottish bull. Aye?"

"Of course."

"Thane Buchanan doesn't count."

I climb onto his lap, linking my hands behind his nape. "Are you jealous? I thought you got over all that rubbish after your humiliation at Cat and Alex's wedding."

"Not jealous. But you did say you dated Thane. Is it inappropriate for me to wonder if you slept with him? We want to be honest with each other, don't we?"

"Yes, we do. I dated Thane for two months, and we had sex three times. Does that make you feel better?"

"How long ago was this?"

"Seven years ago. We've been friends ever since." I wriggle to get deeper into his lap. His cock is nestled between my thighs. "You aren't jealous. Just nosy."

He flattens his palms on my back and pulls me into him. "You caught me. I might be somewhat curious about your romantic past, but I could never be jealous. You want me and only me, and vice versa."

"Now that we've cleared that up, let's go for a ride on Callum's Harley."

"You like it?"

"Aye. I like any activity that gives me an excuse to have my body pressed up against yours."

He glides his hands up and down my back, and his voice grows huskier. "We'll need permission from the bike's owner."

"Your tone suggests you want to shag on that bike."

"Callum thinks it's not possible to fuck while riding down the road on a motorcycle. But he admitted he's never actually tried."

I brush my lips over his. "Let's find out for ourselves."

Domhnall leaps to his feet, setting me down. He clamps his hand around mine and stalks off into the courtyard. We don't find anyone there, just bare tables waiting to be carted away, so we continue into the ground floor of the castle.

And we meet Errol and Ashley there.

Domhnall wastes no time on greetings. "Where's Callum?"

Errol pretends to be suspicious, but his phony expression is goofy. "Why are you asking? Do ye need some carpentry work done? Or have ye tripped one of my incendiary devices in the garden and need a firefighter to douse the flames?"

"No. I need to speak to Callum for personal reasons. Where is he?"

"Well, I dinnae know for certain. But maybe Magnus would have an idea."

Ashley elbows her husband in the side. "Don't tease him. Domhnall, Callum and Kate are in the sitting room."

"Thank you."

Domhnall virtually drags me down the hall and through the dining room and picks up his pace as we start down the guest-wing hallway. He flings the door open and storms inside.

Callum and Kate are lying on the sofa kissing and groping. She has her hand inside his undone jeans. Callum notices us first and springs upright with Kate in his arms. "What the bloody hell are ye doing? Never heard of knocking, eh?"

"If ye don't want to be caught in the act," Domhnall says, "then avoid shagging in the sitting room. Anyone might walk in."

"What do you want, Domhnall?"

"To borrow your bike again."

Callum rises and stretches, then zips up his jeans. "Have you forgotten about the Three Macs Test? You can borrow the Harley after the big event."

"I have to do that right now?"

"Aye. Might as well give in and do it, mate." Callum moves closer and cups his hand around Domhnall's ear to whisper to him. Whatever Callum said, it makes Domhnall's brows shoot up. Callum steps backward and slaps Domhnall's arm. "Time to reveal your last secret. You'll feel better after you do that."

Last secret? I thought Domhnall had told me everything about his past.

The bull regains his composure and aims a hard stare at Callum. "I haven't done that in years, ye know. I might be rubbish at it these days."

"Oh, no, a talent like yours never dies. It only goes into hibernation."

What in the world are they talking about? It makes no sense. What talent does Domhnall have? I'll grill him about that once my cousin leaves.

But Callum doesn't do that. Instead, he tell us, "Time for you two to split up for a while, strictly for the test. Domhnall needs to put on his uniform. And you, Fiona, need to go into the great hall for a ladies-only tea party."

I know my family loves to engage in outlandish events, but I do not like the sound of this one. Though I need to ask Domhnall about his "last secret," Callum shoos me away and orders me to go to the great hall. He even gives my erse a shove to get me started in the right direction. Callum is rarely bossy, but he seems to be enjoying the chance to tell me what to do.

I flash him a feigned scowl. "I'm older than you, Callum. Show some respect for your elders."

He laughs. "Should I get you a Zimmer frame?"

"Do I look like I need help walking?"

Domhnall pretends to study my erse. "No, *gràidh*, you're very fit. I can personally attest to that."

And I can attest to how robust he is too. All those muscles, flexing against me...

Callum slaps my erse again. "Get moving, Fiona."

I tear my focus away from Domhnall's body and give in to my bossy cousin. Then I trot upstairs to the great hall. Several small tables have been set up in the middle of the space, with lacy tablecloths and posh table settings too, all featuring a cream-and-blue theme.

My sisters and I have our own table. The rest of the lasses decide for themselves where to sit. Jamie and Cat want to chat about the upcoming Highland games, and they muse about which men will go taps off, if any of them do. I love shirtless men as much as anyone, but I thought this was about my brothers' barmy test for Domhnall, not a full-on round of Highland games.

"Why did you think that?" Cat asks when I voice my confusion aloud. "The tests for Gavin and Alex involved a slightly abridged version of the games. They competed against the Three Macs but also other MacTaggarts."

"I know that. But Domhnall is different."

Jamie tries to stifle her laughter but winds up spluttering. "Domhnall is special, eh? I thought Gavin was special too, and I'm sure Cat felt the same way during Alex's test." My youngest sister gives me an exaggerated wink. "But aye, Domhnall is very special. The games will be tailored to him, and no one will dare to outdo the big bull."

"You are bloody annoying, Jamie."

"My, you are you grumpy, Fiona. Senior citizens can be that way."

"Senior?" I had been lazily swirling my spoon in my tea, but now I smack the spoon down. That makes my teacup rattle in its saucer. "I am not that old, ye *smuilceag.*"

Jamie grins. "You called me a chit again. Oh, aye, you've got it bad for the bull."

"Stop calling him that. It's my nickname for him." Now I sound like a schoolgirl with a possessive crush on a laddie. "Let's talk about something else."

A miracle occurs, because my sisters finally give up harassing me about Domhnall. I don't like discussing him with Jamie and Cat, and I think I might feel that way because I've become protective of him. He's my big Scottish bull and no one else's. Why hadn't I felt possessive of him until recently? For two years, I never wanted to skelp anyone simply because they made stupid jokes about him. Domhnall didn't care either.

The answer is obvious. Our relationship has changed in the past few days, growing stronger, and our love has deepened too. I'm loathe to admit it, but I can't help thinking that we would still be broken up if my family and their mates hadn't intervened. That night in Torcall's cabin nurtured a seed. Our treasure hunt made it sprout to life. And lunch with my extended family turned that sprout into a brilliant bloom.

I really need to stop thinking up gardening metaphors.

Despite the frilly decor, no one at this tea party dressed up for the occasion. We're all wearing our usual everyday clothes. I leave my sisters for a while so I can chat to the other women in attendance—my cousins, in-laws, and friends. I hardly notice the time going by, until Emery unleashes her famous whistle. Since she's married to Rory, she definitely needs to know how to get someone's attention. My brother can be pigheaded.

Everyone has fallen silent.

"Thank you, ladies, for being quiet," Emery says. "We all know the men would never shut up unless a bevy of constables showed up to arrest them."

"For damn sure!" Piper calls out. "Scottish men are big and sexy, but as stubborn as mules."

Emery gives Piper the thumbs-up sign, then continues. "Now, on to the reason I needed your attention." She throws her arms up. "It's time for the Three Macs Test!"

Chapter Twenty-Seven

Domhnall

Lachlan, Rory, and Aidan have escorted me into the vestibule. They kept me in a room on the third floor while they forced me to change clothes, though thankfully, they didn't watch me doing that. The Three Macs were too busy to pay any attention, and besides, Rory let me change in the large walk-in closet in the bedroom he used to share with his wife. They live somewhere else these days.

This bedroom is enormous and peppered with hints of the medieval era, like a dirk that hangs on the wall and a fireplace composed of river rocks. Rory had told me when we walked into this room that he and Emery had renovated it, in part for the sake of the tourists, but also to bring back some of the historical charm of Dùndubhan.

I approach the full-length mirror and study my clothing. "Where did you find a kilt in the Sterling clan tartan?"

"This is Scotland," Lachlan says. "It isn't difficult to find any sort of tartan."

"But you didn't decide until today that you wanted me to take your test."

He gives me a tolerant smile. "We have been planning for this day ever since Cat and Alex's wedding."

"But I had only just me Fiona then."

"The spark was impossible to overlook. And we know our sister. She wouldn't try to help a *tolla-thon* unless she sensed that you weren't what you seemed to be."

"Aye," Aidan says. "Fiona is a clever woman. She chose you for a reason."

Rory stalks over to me. "No more bumping your gums. It's time for the test."

The three brothers lead me down to the ground floor, which involves a long journey from the top level down to the vestibule. It doesn't bother me. If part of the test is to exhaust me before I even get started with the games, the Three Macs have failed.

When we finally reach the vestibule, Lachlan grasps the knob on the vestibule door. "Last chance to back out, Domhnall."

"I am not backing out. If a thunderstorm strikes in the midst of the test, I still won't back out."

Lachlan eyes me with what seems like appreciation. "Munro was right. You are unstoppable."

"Aye. That means nothing that any of you say or do to me will prevent me from being with Fiona."

Rory chuckles. "Ye haven't experienced the tests yet."

He's trying to unsettle me, but Rory is too clever to believe that will work.

Lachlan swings the door open. "Rory goes first, followed by Domhnall, and with Aidan in the rear."

I follow Rory out into the courtyard with Aidan a few paces behind me. We march through the garden and straight to the cranky door that opens onto the green. And we stop there.

Rory struggles to pull the door open but gives up after several attempts. He throws his hands up in apparent disgust, though I dinnae believe his act. "Aidan, give it a go."

The youngest of the Three Macs makes his own bloody ridiculous fake attempt to open the garden door. Then he pretends to fall to the ground on his erse. "I cannae do it either."

I bar my arms over my chest. "You two are pathetic. If this comedy routine is meant to make me feel like a real man, it hasn't worked. I dinnae need you three to show me that. I know I'm a real man."

Aidan scrambles to his feet. "But I honestly couldn't open it. You'll have to give it a go, Domhnall."

"So, Aidan the Magnificent isn't amazing after all. That's what you're trying to tell me." I roll my eyes at the pair of them, then stalk up to the door and yank it open. "There, ye *baothairean.*"

"That's right," Aidan says. "We are eejits. *Dòmhnall an Tarbh* will need to save us if we drop our cabers like Alex did during his test."

I wasn't there for that event, but Fiona told me about it. That's irrelevant right now. "Can we get this test over with, please?"

Lachlan shoves me out the garden door. "Ye wanted to get it over with, so we're obliging you."

Their behavior must be part of the trials they mean to put me through. If they think I'll give up, they're bigger eejits than I thought.

Lachlan and his brothers come up beside me, but it's the oldest one who's in charge. Rory and Aidan trail behind us as Lachlan leads me out onto the green, where a genuine horde awaits us. I've never seen this many people at Dùndubhan, not even when the MacTaggarts host Highland games here. I've met all the MacTaggarts who are on the premises this afternoon, but the contingent nearest to us consists of men only, and they all wear kilts fashioned from the blue and red tartan of Clan Buchanan.

I'm wearing a kilt too, fashioned from the green, yellow, and red tartan of Clan Sterling. It's looks somewhat similar to the MacTaggart tartan. That's an odd coincidence, but I reckon it's fitting since I mean to marry Fiona MacTaggart.

The Buchanans are not wearing shirts.

As I scan the crowd, I realize none of the MacTaggarts are wearing shirts either. I glance at Lachlan. "Why are those men shirtless?"

"Because the dress code today is taps off."

"If you're wanting me to compete bare-chested, why did you give me a shirt? You three are covered up too."

"Not for long." Lachlan nods to his brothers, and as one, they strip off their shirts. "Now you will be the centerpiece when you give the ladies a striptease."

"What?" I think I might have roared that word like a ruddy lion. "I am not stripping in front of this crowd."

"Suddenly you're shy?" Lachlan shakes his head. "What happened to the man who played sports in the nude at Alex and Cat's wedding. You even did a nude headstand. But you can relax, Domhnall. We meant for you to dance about like a laddie in a male revue, but only remove your shirt."

"Oh, I see. That's all right, then." As I survey the crowd, I spot a figure pushing through the mass of people. "There's Fiona. Did you three tell her to come over here?"

No one responds to my question. When I glance left and right, I realize the Three Macs have jogged off to find their wives, which leaves me standing alone at the periphery of the area that has been cordoned off with chalk lines on the grass. This will be the field of competition.

Fiona has broken away from the crowd and now hurries toward me.

I instinctively reach for my pocket and the item I've been carrying with me all day. But I left the ring box in the third-floor bedroom with my clothes. Out here in front of everyone isn't the time to ask her to marry me anyway. I can wait until after these games.

Fiona leaps into my arms. I catch her, of course. She smells like heaven, not that I have a clue what that domain smells like. But it must have this kind of scent—sweet and heady and imbued with everything good in the universe. She pecks a kiss on my nose, then slides down my body to land on her feet.

"I won't wish you good luck," she says. "You don't need it. So get out there, *Dòmhnall an Tarbh*, and destroy your enemies. Metaphorically, that is."

"Best rejoin the crowd. I have a feeling the tests are about to begin."

Fiona scurries back to the group just as Munro jogs over to me. He flaps an arm at me. "Hurry up, Domhnall. It's time to take your place on the green. The other laddies will join you once you've completed your first challenge."

"I thought this was the Three Macs Test. You aren't one of the brothers."

"They devised this challenge. That makes it a Three Macs Test."

"Just tell me where to stand."

Munro flaps his hand again. "Follow me, Domhnall."

I trot after Munro, who took off without waiting to make sure I was coming too. He stops in what seems like the exact center of the playing field and stabs his finger down toward the ground, clearly indicating that I should stand there. I take my assigned position.

Munro spins round and whistles. The ear-piercing sound reverberates across the green.

"Out of the way, the doctor is coming!" Jack MacTaggart emerges from the crowd and halts beside me. He holds up an item I recognize. "I believe this belongs to you."

"I stuffed it in the closet at my parents' house years ago."

"And now it's come back to you. Gordon insisted you should take it back, and Teasag agreed."

My brain has frozen up like a computer, and it takes me several seconds to comprehend what he said. "You talked to my parents?"

"Aye." Jack thrusts the bagpipes at me. "Play a rousing number for the crowd, and impress Fiona."

Jack winks, then walks away. He was shirtless, of course, just like the rest of his barmy clan.

I cradle the bagpipes in my arms, feeling odd about playing them after years of refusing to do it. But I used to love this instrument. Sophie had disapproved, so I had given up on my favorite hobby. Why shouldn't I enjoy bagpiping again? So, I hoist them in my arms and place the bass drone over one shoulder, then begin blowing into the blowstick to inflate the bag and keep it that way.

I grasp the chanter and begin to play. Despite years away from the bagpipes, I remember the notes of all my favorite songs. It comes back to me while I play. "Scotland the Brave" seems like the best choice, considering the circumstances.

The crowd begins to clap in time with the music. The Three Macs start to sing along with my melody. I might know the tune of "Scotland the Brave" by heart, but I have no idea what the lyrics are. Rory has the best voice, and his singing nearly drowns out his brothers. The American lasses in the crowd gather to link their arms and do some sort of dance that they must think is a Highland jig, but they aren't getting it quite right.

Who cares? Everyone is having a good time.

The Scots lasses join their American friends in a dance, and soon, the activity on the green feels more like a ceilidh than a round of games.

As I blow the last note, and the drone winds down, the crowd cheers.

Fiona races over here to hug me. "That was incredible. Why didn't I know you could play the bagpipes?"

I shrug. "It wasn't something I did anymore."

"But you should have told me."

"That was my past, and you were my future. I'm sorry I didn't tell you about my former hobby, but it seemed irrelevant."

She kisses my cheek. "It's all right, Domhnall. I'm not angry. Now, get out there and whup those losers' butts."

I can't help laughing. "You sound like Gavin Douglas."

"Aye, he told me I should give you that message."

Fiona returns to the crowd, taking up a position between her two sisters. The American Wives Club has rallied around her too. The MacTaggart men have moved to one side of the green, at the edge of the playing field, while the Buchanans have taken control of the other side.

The Highland games are about to begin.

Rory steps onto the green between the two teams and raises a bullhorn. "Ladies and gentlemen, it's time for the main event—the Highland games. We have some special treats for you, which means events we haven't done before or that we haven't done in years. This round of games is in honor of Domhnall Sterling. He has agreed to participate in the Three Macs Test, so let's give him a round of applause for being brave enough to give it a go."

Cheers and clapping reverberate off the castle walls.

Once everyone has quietened down, Rory raises his bullhorn again. "The first event is the sheaf toss."

I have never heard of that. It must be an arcane entry in the Highland games tradition. What sort of sheaf will I need to toss?

Lachlan jogs out onto the field and sets a small burlap sack on the ground, then hurries over to Rory. Next, Aidan trots onto the green. He deposits a two-pronged pitchfork on the ground, then he and Rory hustle away and disappear momentarily only to return a few minutes later carrying a step ladder. It's the longest bloody ladder I've ever seen and must be at least twenty feet high when it's upright.

Aidan and Lachlan set up the ladder and both slap my arm as they return to the end of the field.

Rory approaches me. "Have you never done this before?"

"Sheaf tossing? No, never."

"It's relatively simple. The sheaf weighs approximately sixteen pounds. You spear it with your pitchfork and then try to toss it over the middle of the ladder. I will determine the maximum height you achieved, and if there's disagreement about it, Torcall Murdoch will settle the dispute. Agreed?"

"Aye, agreed."

Rory moves away from me and raises his bullhorn again. "The sheaf toss is about to begin. Our first contestant is Domhnall Sterling."

The clapping is rather subdued this time, but I reckon that's because they don't want to interrupt my concentration.

I turn around and pick up the pitchfork, eying the enormous ladder that towers above me. Can I throw a sixteen-pound sheaf that high? Time to find out. I spear the burlap sack and gaze up at the ladder, trying as best I can to determine the angle and trajectory of my toss as well as how the breeze might affect it.

Who am I kidding? I've got no ruddy idea how to calculate all of that. I'll need to wing it. So I plant my feet wide, bend my knees, and fling the sheaf.

It flies into the air, going up, up, up, and… The sack sails between the ladder's legs but only manages to rise halfway up the ladder. That would mean my toss was about ten feet. *Mhac na galla*. That doesn't seem like a winning toss.

Rory shouts through that ruddy bullhorn, "Thane Buchanan will take the next toss."

Chapter Twenty-Eight

Fiona

Domhnall's first toss wasn't exactly awe-inspiring, but then, he has never done the sheaf toss before. I'd never seen it myself. This event hasn't been a staple of any of the games I attended, but maybe they do it at large gatherings in the cities. Domhnall seems a wee bit disappointed, though only for a moment. Then he straightens and steps aside while Thane makes his first attempt.

When Domhnall glances at me, I blow him a kiss.

He winks.

Oh, aye, he'll be fine even if he loses every event in the Highland games.

Thane takes up the pitchfork and spears the sheaf. He adjusts his stance and spits on his palms, though I've never understood why that might help, though I've seen athletes in various sports do the same thing. But I have never seen anyone do what Thane does now.

He tips his head back, closes his eyes, and smiles.

Is he praying? I have no idea.

Thane returns his attention to the ladder and squints as if he's concentrating all his mental energy on the task ahead of him. Then he takes three quick breaths and swings his pitchfork up. The sheaf goes flying through the air, heading for the ladder, rising higher and higher until the sheaf reaches its peak and begins to sail downward. It flops onto the ground below the ladder's peak, a wee bit higher than Domhnall's toss.

I glance at him, but my sexy bull seems completely focused on the ladder. I can't tell if he's just analyzing Thane's toss in his mind or if he feels dejected because Thane threw the sheaf higher than Domhnall could. Well, it was only his first try.

Rory shouts through his bullhorn yet again. "Each contestant will have three tosses. Domhnall Sterling is up next."

"Go, Domnhall!" I shout while clapping. "Destroy your enemy! No offense, Thane."

"Nothing offends me," Thane replies as he saunters away from the ladder and says something to Domhnall that makes him smile.

The men bump fists.

Domhnall approaches the playing area, and this time he analyzes the ladder with deeper concentration. Once he's done with that, he approaches the assigned throwing spot and spreads his legs a wee bit, then bends his knees slightly too. He spits on his hands, rubbing them together, and picks up the pitchfork and the sheaf in one go.

The green has gone silent. Everyone waits for Domhnall's next attempt.

He swings the pitchfork a few times, then hurls the sheaf into the air. It soars up—higher than Thane's first toss, I'm sure—before falling back to the ground directly under the ladder.

Everyone cheers. Thane whistles.

And I scream, "Go, *Dòmhnall an Tarbh*!"

Only a few people seem confused by what I said. The MacTaggarts have a stunningly swift grapevine that spreads news like a wildfire on a drought-stricken prairie. That might be a mixture of metaphors, but I dinnae care.

Thane completes his next throw and gains a few feet over Domhnall's previous toss. When the bull goes again, his sheaf soars all the way over the ladder to whump down on the other side. And now, Thane will have his final turn. He hurls the sheaf high enough that it goes over the ladder, just like Domhnall's had.

It's hard to tell whose toss reached the highest.

"The final tosses from both competitors were too close to determine the winner," Rory announces. "Our tie-breaking neutral party will examine the replays."

No one told me there would be a video recording. I suppose it makes sense as a means of determining the winner in a situation like this.

Torcall Murdoch emerges from the crowd and accepts the tablet device that Rory hands him. Torcall proceeds to study the wee screen. He zooms in and out, which I can tell based on the movements of his fingers, and his expression becomes one of intense concentration. No one makes a sound while the "tie-breaking expert" does his job.

At last, Torcall lifts his head and returns the tablet to Rory. He says something to my brother, though I doubt anyone can hear it. Rory nods and faces the crowd.

"Torcall Murdoch, whose character is beyond reproach, has determined the winner." Rory swings his arm out to point at one man. "By a margin of three inches, the champion of the sheaf toss is…Domhnall Sterling!"

I leap up and down while clapping and whooping.

The rest of the crowd cheers too, though not the way I am. Domhnall seems rather stunned at first, but he quickly recovers and throws his arms up while roaring with triumph. I race across the green and leap on him, showering kisses all over his face. He holds me up with my feet off the ground.

"Silence, everyone!" Rory commands. "The games are not over yet. For our next event, four men will compete to win the strongman contest."

Oh, Domhnall will win that event. It's a dead certainty. Anyone would know that just by looking at his chest and arms. His kilt hides most of his legs, but every time he tossed that sheaf, his calf muscles tautened. That's more proof that he is the strongest man here today. In all of the Highlands, for sure. Possibly all of Scotland.

I might be slightly biased.

"Before the next event, however," Rory announces, "there will be a break for contestants to rest and rehydrate."

The sheaf toss didn't seem to exhaust Domhnall or Thane, but I suppose Rory is trying to turn this into an epic event simply by dragging it out.

While the crowd disperses into discrete groups, I look around for Domhnall. He must have slipped away while I was focused on Rory and his bullhorn. Honestly, I think my brother has gone overboard with that thing. These events take part on the green, which isn't a huge area. A bullhorn is overkill considering that this isn't a massive stadium filled with fifty thousand spectators. Rory seems to be enjoying lording his power over the rest of us, though only during these games. He isn't a dictator.

I wander from one group to another, searching for Domhnall—until someone taps my shoulder. I turn to find my sister-in-law standing behind me. "Oh, hello, Emery."

"You're looking for Domhnall, right?"

"Aye."

"Come with me. I know where he is. Rory thought you might not have seen where Domhnall went."

"I didn't. Where is he?"

Emery crooks her finger at me until I start moving. She takes me to the garden doorway, and we walk through it.

The first thing I see is Domhnall. He and Thane are sitting on the concrete bench while my brothers have taken up positions perpendicular to the bench. Two other men, my cousin Munro and a chap I don't recognize, hover near the arbor.

Emery rushes up to Rory and plants a firm kiss on his lips. "I found Fiona for you. Now, show everyone your authoritative side, Rory Baby. It makes me so hot for you."

My brother rolls his eyes. "How many times have I asked you not to say things like that in front of other people?"

She grins. "More times than even you can count."

Emery hooks her arm around Rory's bicep.

He slides an arm around her waist. "Now that Fiona is here, we can continue with the discussion. We were talking about the sequence of the strongman events."

I raise my hand.

Rory rolls his eyes, which is one of his favorite expressions. "Yes, Fiona, what is your question?"

"What is a strongman competition?"

"Just what it sounds like. The competitors attempt a series of feats, each one harder than the previous ones, until only one competitor is left."

"Um, what sort of stone is it? I mean what size and shape."

"Large, round stones," Domhnall says. "I've never competed in a strongman event, but I've seen videos of them."

"Often, they are round," Rory agrees. "But in this case, they will not be spheres. Transporting round stones to Dùndubhan would have been an arduous and expensive task. We opted for natural stones instead, and we sourced them from here on the estate."

"The Dùndubhan estate?"

"Aye. We searched the river and its vicinity to find the perfect natural stones for the competition."

That does make sense. But I still have questions. "Won't natural rocks be jagged?"

Rory sighs heavily. "Relax, Fiona. Your soul mate will not be cut to ribbons by jagged rocks. The river stones have been worn away by the water, giving them smooth, rounded edges." He holds up a hand when I open my mouth. "Let me finish. For the rocks we harvested from dry ground, we sandblasted the edges to make them safe. Satisfied now, *gràidh*?"

"Aye. Thank you, Rory."

Emery grins. "Isn't it adorable the way Fiona worries about Domhnall?"

My brother shakes his head and rolls his eyes, which he often does when his wife says something he thinks is barmy. Emery saved Rory from a lonely existence as the Ogre of Loch Fairbairn and showed him what real love is. Have I done that for Domhnall? Since I threw him out of our house, it's dead obvious the answer is N-O. I have not shown him what love is. But from this moment on, I will give him that.

When I glance at Domhnall, he's smiling in a way I haven't seen him do in such a long time. His expression is affectionate and sweet, but also slightly amused.

He winks at me. "Thank you for worrying about my safety, *mo leannan.*"

I will always worry about his well-being when it's appropriate. When you love someone, that's what you do.

Lachlan clears his throat. "Fiona, lass, would you like to know who that other man is?"

"Oh, aye." Though I had noticed our guest, my attention had been focused on Domhnall. "Who is that chap?"

Lachlan points to the red-haired man. "That is Cormac Buchanan. He will be the fourth competitor."

Good heavens. Cormac has enormous muscles and tattoos that cover his arms and chest as well as snaking up his throat. He has the face of a bull-dog. When Lachlan introduced Cormac, the man grinned with his teeth clenched and growled softly, like a rabid dog.

My Domhnall is going up against that behemoth?

Aidan chuckles. "Fiona is worried for your safety, Domhnall. She thinks Cormac the Destroyer will batter you into the ground."

Panic floods through me. "The Destroyer? No, you cannae let Domhnall compete against a man like that."

My youngest brother trots over to me and gives my upper arm a gentle squeeze. "I was having you on."

"Cormac isn't really called the Destroyer."

"Ah, well..." Aidan winces. "He is called that, but it's just for show. Cormac is a softy at heart."

My pulse has accelerated like a racecar at Le Mans. I feel a touch light-headed.

Domhnall leaps up and rushes over to me, pushing Aidan out of the way. He pulls me into his arms. "I have never seen you panic before, *gràidh.* This is just a game. No one is going to pummel anyone else. The strongman competition is an individual event that does not involve vio-lence." He glances back at Rory. "That's right, aye?"

"It is," my brother confirms. Then his gaze shifts to me. "I have never seen you react this way to any of the competitions we've held here at Dùndubhan."

"That's because I've never before been in love with any of the com-petitors."

Domhnall hugs me to his body more firmly and kisses the top of my head. "Dinnae worry about me, love. I was a wrestler and a boxer. Whatever happens, I can handle it."

I rest my head on his chest and close my eyes, letting the anxiety trickle out of me. Just feeling the warmth of him eases the tension. Once it's gone, I lift my head and smile up at him. "I'll be fine, Domhnall. And I know you will win every event in today's games. But even if you lose, you'll still be a champion in my eyes."

Munro grunts. "Dinnae worry about the rest of us, eh, Fiona?"

"The Wild Man can take care of himself."

Domhnall faces the rest of the men but keeps hold of my hand. "We have two Buchanans but only one MacTaggart and one Sterling. Doesn't seem quite fair, does it?"

Rory lifts his brows. "Do you have an alternative suggestion?"

"I would say add two more competitors, another MacTaggart and another Sterling, but I can't think of another Sterling who might be qualified. The strongman contest is about brute strength."

Munro chuckles in the faintly threatening manner that we've all heard many times before. "Who wants to be the other MacTaggart? Besting me will be a dangerous challenge, and a humiliating one for whichever cousin I trounce. Which of you wants that honor, Rory?"

"Iain will do it."

Munro chuckles again. "Iain? He's an old man."

Rory clucks his tongue. "Dinnae be so ageist, Munro. You're no spring chicken anymore. Iain is very strong, and he's only fifty-four. Torcall Murdoch is older than that, and he's no weakling."

"Fine, let Iain humiliate himself," I say. "That still leaves us with the problem of hunting down another Sterling." I turn to Domhnall. "Doesn't most of your family live in the Clashnessie area?"

"Aye, that's right. Most of my kin live there, but my parents moved to Fort Augustus when I was a wee laddie, then I moved to America as an adult." Domhnall scratches his cheek, something he often does when he can't figure out a conundrum. "I've had no real contact with my other relatives, except at one or two clan gatherings when I was still a boy."

Munro's lips stretch into a smug smile. "Oh, dinnae worry about finding another Sterling. You'll soon find out the solution to the problem is closer than ye might think."

I plant my hands on my hips. "If you think you know something, spit it out."

"Ask your brother. He planned it."

I veer my attention to Rory. "What did you plan?"

My brother shifts his weight from one foot to the other and avoids looking at anyone in particular. "Well, Emery and I thought it might be nice to, ah…invite Domhnall's parents to the Highland games. As a surprise."

Emery snuggles up to Rory and gazes up at him with sheer adoration. "It was mostly your idea." She looks at Domhnall. "And it's a great plan. How long has it been since you saw your parents?"

"Six months."

Rory straightens. "Then it's about bloody time we gave you the surprise we arranged."

Domhnall just stares at Rory.

My brother grows a bit smug himself now. "Your parents are waiting out there in the crowd."

Chapter Twenty-Nine

Domhnall

I must be gawping at Rory. The draft coming in between my parted lips confirms that. Why would anyone believe my father would want to participate in a strongman contest? I know Gordon Sterling has never been a weak man, physically or mentally. He doesn't work out in a gym, but he gets plenty of exercise tending to the homestead and to his small herd of dairy cows. I know my father can toss bales of hay about as if they were balloons. And yet I still can't see him holding up large stones in a competition.

Have I been wrong about him for all of my life?

Rory checks his watch. "Time to head back out onto the green."

We all tramp out there and gather in the area marked out with chalk lines. Emery disappears into the crowd, but her husband remains here to resume his apparently self-appointed duty as the ringmaster. Aidan and Lachlan linger just on the other side of the lines. I loiter with Munro, Thane and Cormac Buchanan.

A section of the green, which everyone is calling the field, now holds five wooden barrels with lids as well as a long rubber mat that lies in front of them. Five huge stones sit on the mat, waiting for someone to lift them up onto the barrels. In a normal Atlas stones event, the rocks would each be perfectly round, but Rory already dashed my hopes for that being the case. Instead, I see five smooth but oddly shaped hunks of rock.

Aidan scurries off to search the crowd for our two missing competitors—my father and Iain MacTaggart. The three of them emerge from the crowd a few moments later.

"Did ye ask if they want to compete?" I ask Aidan. "Or is this purely conscription?"

"No one is forced to participate, Domhnall. Once we told them about this event, they volunteered."

My father marches up to me and seizes my upper arms. "I think we have a great deal to talk about, but that can wait. Let's show these laddies what Sterling men can do."

"Aye, let's do that."

Iain MacTaggart comes up beside us. "I see you two have been reunited. There's nothing like a violent sporting event to bring men together."

"Your cousins made it sound as if this would be a violence-free event. I've never known a strongman competition to become a blood sport."

Iain grins. "I was joking, Domhnall. Try not to take everything so seriously."

My father laughs. "I've been trying to convince him of that ever since he was a wee laddie."

Fortunately, the conversation ends. Rory raises his bullhorn again. "The competitors in the strongman competition will now enter the field."

We already are on the field, but I think Rory just likes using that ruddy bullhorn. He probably uses that thing to get the attention of his twin toddlers.

"And now, we will begin with the Atlas stones, otherwise known as McGlashan stones," Rory declares. "Each competitor will attempt to lift all of the stones one by one and place each on a barrel. The stones weigh, in order, seventy kilograms, eighty kilograms, ninety kilograms, one hundred kilograms, and one hundred and ten kilograms."

The longer I stare at the stones, the less virile I feel.

My father claps a hand on my shoulder. "Dinnae worry, *mo mhac*. You are the strongest, toughest man I've ever known. And you're doing this for your lass." He points past my shoulder. "Look at her. When she smiles at you, that'll give you all the energy you need."

I glance back at the crowd and spot Fiona in the first row. She smiles and blows me a kiss. And aye, that simple expression made me feel a thousand times stronger, as if I could lift Beann Dealgach into the sky with one hand.

"Silence, everyone," Rory commands. "We are about to begin. The order in which each man will compete has been chosen at random using Evan's computer rubbish, which he calls an algorithm. He gave me the printout of the list. Contestants will be judged based on how quickly they finish their task."

The ringmaster pauses to search the crowd for someone. When he sees that person, he waves to the bloke, apparently. But no one moves. Then the crowd begins to part, and an older man emerges.

Rory nods to him. "Torcall, you will time each competitor's attempt."

Torcall raises his hand, showing off the stopwatch he holds. Then he sprints onto the field, taking up a position behind the barrels.

Rory clears his throat, and the sound is amplified by his ruddy bullhorn. "First up, Iain MacTaggart. He's an archaeologist who teaches at the University of the Highlands and the Islands, as well as the father of two—"

"Haud her wheesht, Rory! This isn't the Miss Scotland Pageant. We dinnae need to hear his measurements."

"Silence, Errol!" Rory bellows, and this time he forgot to use his bullhorn. He didn't need it. "Iain, make your first attempt now."

The archaeologist approaches the barrels and dances about as if he's adjusting his stance and preparing to lift. Then he picks up the first stone and drops it onto the barrel.

"Go, Iain! Mature men rock."

His wife Rae stands in the front row with their daughter Malina. Both lasses whoop. I'm sure it was Rae who shouted that mature men "rock." Is that a joke? Iain is lifting actual rocks, after all.

Iain has another go, lifting the second stone. He hefts that one with little trouble too, and of course, Rae and Malina cheer. Iain pauses to face the crowd and raise one arm, bending his elbow so he can show off his muscles. All the lasses let out whoops and catcalls.

On his third attempt, his expression becomes strained as he hoists the stone. When he seems about to lose control of his load, he lets out a harsh yell and drops the stone on the barrel. More cheers erupt. Iain cradles the fourth stone with both hands, testing its weight. Then he hoists it a few inches off the ground, but he's clearly struggling to lift it any higher. Refusing to give up, he grits his teeth and sucks in a sharp breath, then shouts as he tosses it onto the barrel. He's clearly winded, and a sheen of sweat glistens on his skin.

That stone weighs over two hundred pounds.

Iain shuffles over to the fifth stone.

The crowd has gone silent, anxious for what might happen with Iain's next attempt. We all could tell he struggled with the fourth stone. Lifting something of that weight off the ground with hands only is much more difficult than throwing a two-hundred-pound bloke over your shoulder.

Iain approaches the fourth stone, which weighs two-hundred and twenty pounds. He cracks his neck and his knuckles, then does a few quick stretches. Once he's ready, he crouches and grasps the stone. Iain lets out the longest, loudest groan I've ever heard and begins to lift the rock. He gets it about six inches off the ground but then his grip seems to slip, and it looks as if he might drop the thing. But at the last moment, he rallies again and, letting out a roar that reverberates off the castle walls, Iain heaves the largest stone onto the barrel.

For a moment, he simply hunches there with his torso draped over the stone while he struggles to catch his breath. Everyone waits in silence. Finally, he straightens and turns toward the crowd.

Everyone cheers.

As Iain walks past me, I pat his shoulder. "That was fantastic. Dinnae know if I can do what you just did."

"I am rather proud of how well I fared, considering that I don't work out as much as you do."

"That makes your effort even more impressive."

"Appreciate the support, Domhnall."

Malina races up to her father and hugs him fiercely, then returns to the crowd.

"Next up," Rory announces, "we have Thane Buchanan."

I watch with deep interest as the mysterious Thane trots over to the barrels and makes his attempt to lift all the stones. He has no trouble with the first four stones, but then he seems to struggle somewhat with the fifth. Just when I think he'll drop the stone and give up, he sucks in a big breath and blows it out, shouting as he heaves the rock onto the barrel.

Thane throws his arms up and yells.

Naturally, the crowd cheers.

"Our next competitor," Rory announces, "is Gordon Sterling."

I shouldn't feel anxious about my father competing, but I do. He's the oldest man in this competition and the only one in his sixties. But my da saunters up to the barrels while smiling and waving at the crowd, seeming quite confident. He even blows a kiss to my mother.

Then he picks up the first stone and sets it on the barrel.

He does it again, and again, and again, and again. The crowd goes wild. A man in his sixties just lifted all those stones without even pausing between attempts. Gordon Sterling waves to the crowd, smiling as if he just won a swimming race instead of a competition for hoisting enormous rocks.

As my father walks past me, he pauses to whisper, "If I can do it, so can you."

"But how in the world did you do that? You're a senior citizen, and I've never seen you lift anything that heavy."

Da pats my chest. "I'm a dairy farmer, *mo mhac*. I've spent my entire life lifting large bales of hay and hoisting cows that got stuck in the mud. Dinnae need a gym to stay in shape."

He doesn't mean that as a dig against me. But he's right. Not everyone needs a gym. Nature can provide plenty of opportunities for strength training.

My father walks away.

Munro MacTaggart is called next. We're all shirtless, but as he approaches the barrels, he takes a moment to face the crowd and shimmy his hips, pretending that he's about to ditch the kilt. The lasses whistle and shout silly things like "take it all off, Wild Man" and "show us what's under the kilt."

Rory uses his bullhorn to declare, "Silence, please! This is not a male revue. Munro, lift the bloody stones and keep your kilt on."

Munro turns toward the barrels, but then he flips the back of his kilt up to give the crowd a flash of his erse. The women cheer, of course. When he finally makes his attempt, he seems to require little effort to lift all but the last stone. That one gives him only a wee bit of trouble. Once he's done, he spins round to face the spectators and spreads his arms.

Then the eejit thumps his chest while yodeling, like Tarzan did in those old movies.

Cormac Buchanan goes next. He looks like a stereotypical brute of a man, and I can't tell how old he might be. Is he as powerful as he seems? Looks can be deceiving, after all. If appearances are correct, though, I'm facing an uphill battle that will make summiting Mount Everest seem like child's play.

When Cormac grasps the first stone, he lifts it so easily that it's almost embarrassing—to the rest of us. He might as well be tossing chunks of Styrofoam. That's how easily he picks up that weight. He raises the second one just as handily, followed swiftly by the third. On the fourth, he slows down a touch, but he still manages to hoist that stone and the fifth one too much faster than any of the other competitors had done.

Bloody hell. Can I do better than that behemoth of a man?

"Our final competitor," Rory declares, "is Domhnall Sterling."

I march up to the first rock.

"Go, *Dòmhnall an Tarbh*! Kick their erses!"

Just hearing Fiona's voice gives me a shot of adrenaline that makes me stand up straighter and feel more confident, so much so that I think I actually could lift the mountain behind us. As I crouch to take hold of the first stone, something unexpected happens. I don't feel anxious. My relationship with Fiona will not crumble to dust if I fail to win this competition. My father will be proud of me no matter what, and so will my mother. The friends I've made among the clans gathered here won't despise me if I fail. That knowledge releases a weight I've held inside me for too long.

Today, I am free.

I lift the first stone with no trouble at all, as if I'd been tossing an empty cardboard box. I leap over to the second stone and hoist it easily too, then jump to the next one and drop it on the barrel without even pausing to prepare. I remain vigilant, though, since I know the next two stones are the heaviest. As I mentally prepare for the weight of the fourth stone, I'm not telling myself in my thoughts that this rock weighs two hundred and twenty pounds. No, I'm thinking about the best strategy for lifting it.

But I only think about that for a few seconds. I need to beat Cormac Buchanan's time.

I slide my hands under the stone, take a deep breath, and blow it out as I hoist the huge rock onto the barrel. Without even a slight pause, I leap over to the next stone and hoist it. Every muscle in my body rebels against the pain, but I ignore those signals, dropping the stone on the barrel.

Then I stumble backward, my chest heaving, my arms and legs shaky. When I've caught my breath, I shuffle around to face the crowd.

Cheers erupt.

"Quiet, please!" Rory commands. "Torcall please come here so we can discuss the results and determine the winner."

His ruddy bullhorn squawks as he attempts to turn it off.

Torcall Murdoch hurries over there. He and Rory engage in a secret conversation that includes a great deal of pointing at the paper on which I assume Torcall noted the times for the competitors. Then the timekeeper nods and returns to the crowd.

Rory turns his bullhorn on again. "By a margin of two point four seconds, the winner of the first-ever Dùndubhan Strongman Competition is…" He waits for seven seconds. Aye, I counted. Then he shouts, «Domhnall Sterling!»

Every sort of raucous noise bursts out of the men and women gathered here. The revelry is so loud that I can't even hear my own breathing over the noise. For a moment, I stand here stunned. I won? Is that what Rory said?

Fiona bursts out of the crowd and barrels toward me to throw her entire body at me from three feet away. I catch the lass and hug her so tightly that it must hurt, but she doesn't complain. Fiona crushes her mouth to mine and kisses me so deeply and thoroughly that I have no choice but to reciprocate. We grope each other too, though she avoids my dokey.

When the lass finally slides down my body to stand on her feet, I feel so bloody good that I can't stop myself. I throw my arms up and roar with triumph. It's barmy. This is nothing but a round of casual Highland games. Yet I feel like I've conquered the world.

The raucous noises from the crowd wind down. But another sort of cheering takes its place.

"*Dòmhnall an Tarbh! Dòmhnall an Tarbh! Dòmhnall an Tarbh!*"

The chant goes on and on, starting with the lasses—and then the men join in too. Their synchronized shouts of support echo across the green.

I've never felt more alive, and it's not because of the cheers. Fiona makes me feel this way. And finally, I understand what Munro meant when he told me to be unstoppable.

Never again will I doubt myself. I am *Dòmhnall an Tarbh*.

Chapter Thirty

Fiona

Silence, please!" Rory bellows through the bullhorn. He waits until the chanting has died away before he speaks again. "Thank you, everyone. Domhnall Sterling has won the first two events in the Dùndubhan Highland Games. But we still have a few more events to go."

Domhnall will win every last contest. I know he will. While I stand here with him, gazing up at his face, I can see the determination in his eyes and his expression. He has become the resolute warrior once again. His humiliation at Alex and Cat's wedding had made him doubt himself and his ability to win any woman's heart. Now, he knows the truth and finally believes it.

"Our next event is the caber toss," Rory declares. "If you gents need a break to recover from the Atlas stones—"

"Nobody needs a break," Domhnall shouts. "Do we, laddies?"

The men who had just finished the Atlas stones competition all voice their agreement with his statement.

"You might not make it onto the field," Rory says. "Evan will run another algo-whatsit and tell us the lineup for the caber toss. We are considering this to be a part of the strongman event."

Evan squeezes through the crowd to reach Rory. And he grabs the bullhorn to make an announcement of his own. "It's called an algorithm, which our fearless leader knows. He likes to pretend he's a Luddite, but we've all seen him playing games on his mobile."

My brother snatches the bullhorn away from Evan. "Do ye have the lineup ready or not?"

Evan thrusts a sheet of paper at him while smirking. Then my cousin rejoins the crowd.

Rory studies the paper before raising his new favorite toy again to blast words at us. "The four contestants are Lachlan MacTaggart, Domhnall Sterling, Thane Buchanan, and Errol Murdoch." Rory glances at Domhnall's father. "Sorry, Gordon. You didn't make the cut this time, but I know you were hoping to toss a caber or two."

Gordon shrugs. "Looking forward to seeing these laddies toss a few cabers. And I know my son will trounce them all."

He jogs over to us and smacks Domhnall's back. "You are the hero of Clan Sterling, *mo mhac*. And you've already received the best gift in the world."

"Aye, that's for certain. I'll win this event for you, Da, and for Fiona."

Gordon wanders away to join the crowd. He finds his wife, and they hold hands while awaiting the start of the caber toss."

My brother gets on his bloody bullhorn with another announcement. "Each toss of the caber will be judged based on several factors. Competitors will run for a short distance so they can achieve enough momentum for the toss. Each toss will be scored based on how well it lands. We're looking for end-over-end throws that have the best vertical angle."

Everyone knows that. Why Rory thinks he needs to explain that to a bunch of Scots, I can't explain. Maybe it's for the benefit of the Americans in attendance.

Several of my cousins carry the cabers onto the green before they hunt for their wives in the crowd. I hurry back to join my sisters and the members of the American Wives Club at the front of the throng. The caber toss is about to begin.

"Attention!" Rory shouts. "The first contestant will be Errol Murdoch."

My cousin approaches the caber and walks his hands up its length to get the tree trunk in a vertical position. Then he crouches and grasps the end of the caber to heft it off the ground. He rises and staggers side to side but maintains his hold on the caber. The wobbling stops when he sprints across the green and hurls the tree trunk.

It tumbles end over end. The angle of his toss looked to me like it was excellent, but I'm no expert.

"Good show, Errol," Rory calls out. "Next up is Thane Buchanan."

Though I'm naturally rooting for Domhnall to win, I still want the other competitors to do well. They're my family and friends, after all. And aye, Thane was once my boyfriend. Thankfully, Domhnall has expressed not one iota of jealousy over that fact, even once he found out that Thane and I had a poke now and then. It was ages ago.

My former lover makes his toss and sends the caber flying end over end like Errol had done, though Thane's toss isn't as elegant as Errol's. The caber wobbled a wee bit, and the angle wasn't as precise. Thane seems quite happy with his attempt, though. Maybe he doesn't usually take part in the caber toss, so he didn't expect to win.

The next competitor is Domhnall.

I know he has competed in the caber toss before, at least once. My family held Highland games at Alex and Cat's wedding. But on that occasion, Domhnall cheated his way into winning. He regretted it afterward and congratulated Grey Dixon on becoming the champion. But now, two years after that debacle, might he feel anxious about tossing a caber again? I know he hasn't participated in any Highland games over the past two years. A few days ago, Domhnall might have gotten anxious about competing. But he has done so well today that I can't imagine he's worried about the caber toss.

Still, I clasp my hands under my chin and bite my lip as Domhnall approaches the caber.

He grasps the nearest end, then starts walking his hands down it to raise the caber into an upright position. No trouble there. Domhnall has all the muscles required to raise a caber—and then some. And then a lot, actually. My gaze lowers from his face down to the muscles on his arms and torso. Those thick, defined muscles. Though his kilt covers his thighs, I can picture them in my mind as they tauten and flex with his every movement.

I need to shag that man so badly.

Domhnall has the caber upright now. He walks his hands down its length until he's crouching at the base. Then he grasps the caber and lifts it. His lips flatten. His features are pinched. With a shout, he runs forward and hurls the caber.

I jump up and down, screaming like a teenager at a rock concert. That looked like a perfect caber toss to me. But we still have one more competitor—my brother Lachlan. Is it wrong for me to want Lachlan to lose and Domhnall to win? No, of course not. Lachie won't mind, as long as I don't call him by that nickname out loud.

Domhnall steps out of the way as Lachlan approaches his caber. He raises it to a perfectly upright position, then walks his hands down the wooden pole so he can grasp the base. With a shout not unlike Domhnall's, Lachlan sends the caber flying end over end across the green.

That one looked excellent. I can't tell for sure which man won this event, but it seemed to me that Domhnall performed the best. I'm completely objective on that matter, naturally.

Rory confers with the two judges, Cormac Buchanan and my cousin Jack. They all nod, as if they're in agreement. Then Rory gets on the bullhorn yet again. "The champion of the caber toss is…Domhnall Sterling!"

I leap up and down again, screaming so hard my throat hurts. This time, I clap furiously too.

Peripherally, I can see my sisters shaking their heads as if they think I'm a bampot. They have no right to look at me that way. Cat and Jamie have behaved exactly this way on previous occasions when their men competed in Highland games. We're all smitten, and I think that's lovely.

Once the other competitors have congratulated Domhnall, I race up to him and wrap my arms around the victorious bull.

He kisses me, then winks.

What does that mean? I don't get the chance to ask him because Rory is shouting through that ruddy bullhorn for the millionth time today.

"Our next event is the hammer throw! The competitors are Jack Mac-Taggart, Domhnall Sterling, Gavin Douglas, and Alex Thorne."

Though Evan supposedly used algorithms to randomly choose who would compete in each event, I'm seeing a pattern here. Domhnall is "randomly" chosen for every event.

"When did I say I'd compete?" Alex shouts. "I'm a lover, not a hammer-thrower. And I'm not even Scottish."

"Are you refusing to be drafted?" Rory asks. "The penalty for that is imprisonment in the old garderobe shaft."

Catriona rushes up to Alex and whispers something to him. Whatever she said makes him smirk, and his eyes light up with a canny glint.

Alex raises his hands. "All right. I shall compete."

I trot over to where my sisters are standing at the front of the crowd, nearest to the area designated for the hammer throw event. My sisters are bickering about whose husband has the best muscles. Och, those two. The answer is obvious.

"Domhnall has the best muscles by far," I declare. "No other man on earth could compete with him."

My sisters both smirk at me. But Cat says, "Of course you think that, Fiona. You are hopelessly in love with him. Has he asked you to marry him yet?"

I ignore her question because it's none of her bloody business. "What did you say to Alex that made him change his mind?"

Cat grins. "I told him all the naughty things I'd do with him tonight if he cooperates now."

"That's all? I would've thought the British Bastard would take more convincing."

"Alex is a sweetheart."

Jamie and I both burst out laughing.

Catriona scowls at us, but she isn't actually annoyed. "He's much sweeter than Domhnall and Gavin combined."

Jamie snorts out a laugh. "If you say so."

As the first contestant in the hammer throw approaches the designated spot, we stop havering and focus on the games again. Jack will make the first throw. Autumn hurries over to Jack strictly to kiss him and wish her husband good luck. Then she jogs over to my sisters.

Jack picks up the long wooden shaft that has a metal ball on the end. I know that ball weighs about twenty pounds. Jack swings the hammer round and round from near the ground to above his head, completing several swings before he releases the hammer. It lands a good ways from the starting point.

The crowd cheers.

Domhnall goes next. His throw flies even further across the green, so far in fact that I dinnae see how anyone could beat that.

Gavin has his turn, and the hammer lands very close to Domhnall's.

When Alex makes his attempt, he doesn't spin the hammer for long enough, and it flops down a mere few yards away. He sets his hands on his hips and stares down at the ground. Then he turns to face the crowd, spreading his arms. "I told you lot I am not the sort who does well in athletic events."

"Good try, Alex," Catriona shouts. "You have other talents that are more valuable."

She means shagging. Her tone made that clear.

Rory and Thane confer to determine the winner. A moment later, my brother wields the bullhorn. "The champion is Gavin Douglas!"

Domhnall didn't win, but he seems relaxed and happy rather than disappointed. He even congratulates Gavin, shaking the American's hand. Alex and Jack also congratulate Gavin. I know this is the first time Jamie's husband has won an event in the Highland games at Dùndubhan since the day when my brothers put him through the Three Macs Test.

"We will take a short break," Rory declares. "Then the competitors for the final two events will be announced."

I trot over to Domhnall, who stands alone on the playing field, gazing out at the hammers that lie discarded on the ground. "How are you feeling? You lost this event but don't seem upset about it."

He slings an arm around my waist to pull me close to his side. "Winning isn't everything, not anymore."

"You learned that lesson two years ago. Aye?"

"That's true. But my experiences today have proved to me that only one contest really matters." He kisses the top of my head. "The battle for your heart."

"But you've already won that battle."

"I reckon I have. But there's one last thing I need to do." His attention shifts to the far side of the green, where the garden door remains open. He seems rather pensive, but that expression vanishes quickly. "Let's talk about that after the games."

Rory is approaching the playing field again—with that bullhorn, of course. I wouldn't be surprised if he carries that everywhere with him after today. My brother has become enamored of that obnoxious device. But his wife will probably disabuse him of that infatuation. Emery is a clever woman and the only person in the world who can talk Rory out of anything. I adore her to bits. She might have let him play with his bullhorn today, but that will be the end of it.

I glance at Domhnall, but he no longer seems pensive. His lips have curled into a soft smile, as if he's contented. Whatever he thought he needed to do, he seems to have set that aside for the moment.

"Listen closely and stop your havering," Rory says. "Evan's algorithms have chosen the following competitors for the second to last event. Torcall Murdoch, Aidan MacTaggart, Cormac Buchanan, and Domhnall Sterling."

Rory pauses, waiting for just long enough that everyone begins to get restless. He hasn't announced the event yet. Finally, he raises the bullhorn. "These four laddies will compete in the hallowed sport of haggis hurling."

A mixture of vocal reactions fill the green, everything from groaning to fake retching, along with some laughter too.

Domhnall edges closer to me and whispers, "Haggis hurling? I've heard of that, but I thought it was a joke."

"I gather the folk of Clan Sterling aren't enamored of tossing a haggis about. Dinnae worry. It's easy. A haggis only weighs a pound or two."

"Not worried about that." He wrinkles his nose in the most charming expression of disgust. "I hate haggis. It tastes like rotten rubbish stuffed into a slimy sack."

His description isn't entirely wrong. That is essentially what haggis is.

"You don't have to eat it," I tell Domhnall. "Just toss it."

Rory's bullhorn slips out of his hand, and he struggles to pick it up off the ground. His hair is mussed by the time he manages to grab it. "Ah, the first competitor is…" He freezes, then squints as Emery whispers something to him. He nods. "Torcall Murdoch."

Errol trots out of the crowd carrying a small barrel that has its bottom cut off. He sets that down in front of Torcall. "Here ye go. Hurl it like a demon and do Clan Murdoch proud."

Torcall gives his great-nephew a long-suffering look.

My cousin Evan emerges from the crowd, carrying two haggises. I assume one is a backup in case the other breaks. Evan sets both haggises on the ground beside the barrel and Torcall.

"Please be quiet while the competitor prepares," Rory says. "Whenever you're ready, climb onto the barrel and make your attempt."

Torcall studies the two haggises for a moment, then steps up onto the half-barrel. Evan hands him a haggis. Torcall turns it this way and that in his hands as if he's sizing it up. Then he pulls his arm back and pitches it the way a baseball player might.

And the haggis flies through the air, whumping down a good distance away.

The crowd claps for him, but they don't cheer as wildly as they had for the previous events. I guess it's hard to get excited about a lump of pudding sailing across the green. We had done haggis hurling at Dùndubhan once before, but that involved Gavin battling Jamie's ex-fiancé, Trevor Langley. Today, no one is aiming to destroy an enemy. Everyone here wants Domhnall to realize the truth.

He deserves to be with me, and we belong together.

Domhnall Sterling is my fairy-tale prince.

Chapter Thirty-One

Domhnall

I watch Aidan climbing onto that wee barrel while holding a haggis in one hand, and I can't stop picturing that sack of putrid pudding sailing through the air and splatting down on the ground. Torcall hadn't shattered the casing. Still, it seems entirely probable that a fastball pitch could burst that sheep's-stomach casing. Aye, I'm dead sure the MacTaggarts made traditional haggis, not the modern version.

Aidan holds up the haggis. "And now, Aidan the Magnificent will show you old men how it's done!"

Cormac Buchanan stalks up to the line that marks the edge of the playing field. "I'm younger than you, ye *cacan*."

Aidan glances down at Cormac, who has a battered face and scars that slash across it. "You're younger than thirty-three? That's impossible. Ye look sixty."

"I'm twenty-eight, ye *gòrach pìos de cac*."

Aidan chuckles. "Maybe I am a stupid piece of shite, but at least I'm beautiful." He shoos Cormac away. "Away now, please. I need to focus on the competition."

Cormac glowers at Aidan but shuffles back to the edge of the playing field.

Aidan hurls the haggis.

The sack of pudding splats onto the ground, and the casing splits open. Pudding spills all over the grass.

"That is a disqualifying offense," Rory declares. "Aidan MacTaggart is out of the competition."

Aidan hops off the barrel and bows deeply. "Thank you, ladies and gentlemen, for allowing me to hurl a haggis."

The crowd claps as Aidan makes his way off the field and to his wife. Calli kisses him passionately. That doesn't disturb anyone, not these days. Fiona told me how Alex Thorne stripped naked on the green when he proposed to Catriona. No, I won't be doing anything that barmy.

"It's your turn now, Cormac," Rory says. "Please take your place on the barrel."

Cormac stalks up to the haggis that Evan just retrieved and set down on the ground. Fiona's cousin hurries away, almost as if he worries the Neanderthal will thrust the haggis in the air and crush the thing just for the sport of it, so he can watch putrid pudding rain down on all our heads. I am not afraid of him, but I dinnae like the brute.

How can Thane be related to that hulk of a man?

Well, at least I beat the Neanderthal in the Atlas stones contest.

Cormac picks up the haggis and climbs onto the barrel. It wobbles just a little. His feet barely fit on top of it. The brute lets out a roar worthy of a rampaging lion and hurls the haggis. It sails across the playing field, passing the lines that mark the distance one by one until I can barely see the flying haggis anymore. When the haggis finally hits the ground, Cormac shakes his fists above his head and roars again.

"No one beats the beast!"

That Neanderthal actually called himself a beast. Well, I reckon he thinks that's a compliment to himself.

Evan and Thane measure the distance, and Thane announces it. "Eighty-one feet!"

Cormac jumps off the barrel, smirking at me as he walks away.

He thinks he's already won the contest. Oh, that self-proclaimed beast needs to lose, just to prove a point. Cormac is going down.

The crowd has begun to murmur, as if they don't know what to make of Cormac. The majority of them are MacTaggarts and Sterlings, after all.

"Quiet, please," Rory says. "The final competitor in the haggis hurling event is Domhnall Sterling."

Time to chuck a lump of pudding.

I march up to the barrel and hop onto it. Evan has just retrieved the sole surviving haggis, and he offers it to me. I take the thing and prepare for my attempt. First, I examine the playing field visually as I try to determine just how far away Cormac had managed to throw the haggis. It had flown well past where the ladder had been for the sheaf toss. It also seemed farther away than the best distance for the hammer throw.

No more analyzing. It's time to trust my instincts.

I pull my arm back and then hurl the haggis.

The thing flies across the green. It keeps going and going and going, seeming as if it will never lose momentum. But the strange package finally begins to slow down as its trajectory turns ever downward.

And the haggis hits the ground.

"Please remain quiet," Rory informs the audience. "Our judges need to measure the distance of the last throw."

This time Evan hurries out to the spot where the haggis fell, and Thane holds onto the other end of the measuring tape. But Evan doesn't immediately announce the result. He jogs back to the barrel I'm standing on first. Then he raises the measuring tape.

"One hundred and ninety feet!"

Rory lifts his bullhorn. "That's a near world record hurl and a lead of more than one hundred feet! Domhnall Sterling has won this event hands down."

The lasses in the crowd scream with joy while the men from all three clans begin to chant, "*Dòmhnall an Tarbh! Dòmhnall an Tarbh! Dòmhnall an Tarbh!*"

I will be called that for the rest of my life, that's a dead certainty. But it doesn't bother me at all.

Once the crowd has settled down, Rory makes another announcement. "And now, it's time for the final event. Tug o' war!"

Bloody hell. The last time I took part in that event, my team lost to Grey Dixon and his mates. It had been a battle between Brits versus Scots. But here, today, I'll compete against other Scots, and this time I will not engage in any dirty tricks. If my team wins, it will be a fair victory.

"We need nine members on each team, including the coach," Rory explains. "The two laddies who hurled haggis the farthest will become the team captains. That means it will be Domhnall's men versus Cormac's laddies. Please approach the playing field if you want to join Cormac."

The Neanderthal throws his fists into the air and shouts, "Team Cormac rules the world!"

Eight Buchanans walk out onto the playing field and stand behind Cormac, who seems far too pleased with himself. Aye, his men seem very muscular and strong, and that's the main component of the tug 'o war event. But strategy is also important. Will Cormac think of that?

Whether he thinks at all is an open question.

"And now, we need volunteers for Domhnall's team," Rory says. "Step forward to join the bull."

Thane hadn't joined the Buchanan herd, but now I see why. He strides up to me and claps a hand on my shoulder.

Seven more men walk out onto the field, all MacTaggarts except for one.

My father approaches me, taking up a position opposite Thane, and claps his hand on my shoulder. "We will destroy the Buchanans. Dinnae fash, *mo mhac*."

"I am not worried. But Thane, aren't you betraying your clan?"

He shrugs. "I'm a libertarian when it comes to tug o' war."

Whatever that means, it doesn't matter right now. Thane is very strange, but I'm glad to have him on my team.

I'm surprised by the group that fills out my team. Munro, Logan, and the Three Macs are well suited for the tug o' war, having large muscles and plenty of strength. But Alex Thorne and Grey Dixon have volunteered too. And those laddies have indeed surprised me.

"Two Brits want to compete with me? I've cheated at the Highland games before, and you both witnessed that."

"But you won't cheat this time," Alex tells me. "You learned your lesson, and everyone understands why you behaved that way. There isn't a man on this green who hasn't made a bloody stupid mistake or two in his life, and I am a prime example of that."

"I reckon that makes a sort of sense." I turn to Grey. "But you… Why on earth would the man whose girlfriend I tried to steal want to join my team? I know you've participated in the tug 'o war once before, but this will be a true rough-and-tumble battle. Cormac seems determined to destroy me."

"I don't give a toss about those Buchanan blokes. All that's required is brute strength. I have plenty of that since I started working out more, and I can offer you an analytical strategy for winning. As for Alex… Well, we all know his grifter skills have saved the day on other occasions. Besides, you and I are mates now. That means I fight on your side, always."

"But you aren't Scottish."

Grey grins and slaps my arm. "Don't discount the computer geek, Domhnall. I took part in the Highland games two years ago, and I managed to survive and win. I'm an honorary Scot now, aren't I?"

"Aye, of course ye are. I reckon, deep down, I still can't quite believe you want to be mates with me."

"Believe it, Domhnall. All that rubbish is in the past." He nods toward the crowd. "And look who's in the front row, ready to cheer for you and your team."

I swivel my head in that direction—and see Jessica smiling and waving at me.

"Go, Team Domhnall," she shouts. "The Scottish bull rocks!"

Alex throws an arm around my neck. "Are you ready to trounce those louts?"

I crack my knuckles. "Aye, they don't stand a chance."

The rope has been laid out. The teams have been formed. All that's left is to do this.

Rory makes one final announcement before the battle begins. "Since I am taking part in the tug o' war, my cousin Jack will take over emcee duties."

Jack emerges from the crowd and accepts the bullhorn when Rory offers it to him. "The teams will take their places once Errol and Iain bring the rope."

Movement from the direction of the garden door draws my attention. I see the two men coming toward us, with Iain holding one half of the rope and Errol holding the other. They break into a sprint, reaching us quickly. Then they set the rope on the grass and stretch it out to its full length.

This is happening. And I feel no anxiety about it. This time, I will lead the winning team with nothing but clean tactics.

Both teams take to the field and lift the rope off the ground. The last man on each side wraps the rope around his back and up to the opposite shoulder, anchoring it for the team. I'm well aware that the MacTaggarts don't pay attention to most of the official rules—for instance, foul language is allowed—but they never condone the purposeful injuring of a team member on either side. Each side maintains a gap of six feet from the center of the rope. Those of us who had already competed in the previous events don't need to change our clothes, but the newcomers had to put on their kilts and remove their shirts. The final preparation ends when Torcall stabs a wooden stake into the ground at the center point of the rope.

Jack picks up the bullhorn. "Listen, everyone. The final event will commence momentarily. The judge for this competition will be Torcall Murdoch. The coaches are Niall MacTaggart and Stewart Buchanan. Team captains are Domhnall Sterling and Cormac Buchanan. Torcall, please verify that the stake is still at the center."

Torcall double checks that, then jogs back to the edge of the playing field. He faces the two teams, remaining positioned directly in front of the center line. Then he gives Jack the thumbs-up sign.

Now, we are ready. The war is on.

As team captains, Cormac and I are at the head of our groups, facing each other. He glowers at me and bares his teeth, growling like a rabid dog. He must be putting on a show for me. I'm not that easy to intimidate. Strictly to annoy him, I squint and flatten my lips while huffing breaths out through my nostrils like a genuine bull.

All of us watch and wait for Torcall to start the contest.

He steps forward a few paces, then raises his arms above his head. "Coaches, are you ready?"

"Aye," say Niall MacTaggart and Stewart Buchanan.

"Take the strain, laddies!"

We all heel in, ready to go.

Torcall drops his arms and shouts, "Pull!"

All the men lean backward with our heels dug in, pulling with every ounce of strength we have. Cormac is bloody strong, but I'm stronger. He gnashes his teeth and curses at me, but I ignore his intimidation tactics and keep pulling. Grey Dixon is right behind me, and he pulls just as hard as I do. I can't glance back at him, though. I need to focus on my opponent and listen for Niall to advise us.

"Ease up a wee bit," Niall says. "Hold like that."

On the opposing team, Stewart advises his men, but I can't hear what he said. I doubt the other side could hear Niall speaking either. Stewart must have told his team to ease up too, because Cormac's expression softens just enough to suggest he isn't pulling as hard as before.

"Pull!" Niall commands. "Pull with all ye got, laddies!"

As one, we pull with all our strength—and the rope shifts toward our side. Cormac's foot slips. We drag the rope in our direction even more so now that we're inches away from that wooden stake. A little more... Almost there...

The Buchanans abruptly yank the rope.

I stumble forward one step. Grey crashes into me from behind, but neither of us falls down. Our side of the rope crosses over the center line, though, which means we have lost this round.

Torcall makes it official. "Round one goes to the Buchanans."

Mhac na galla. But we have two more chances. If we lose the next round, it's over. But if we succeed in the second round, it will be a tie with the third round deciding the winners.

On our second try, we win handily without even breaking a sweat. But we can't assume that will happen again. Round three is our last chance at victory.

Both teams take a break after round two to rehydrate and discuss the strategy for the next round. Niall begins to tell us about his plan, which is a sound one, but I have a gut feeling it won't work. For a few minutes, I have an inner debate about whether to share my idea. Being cautious never used to be my preferred tactic.

It's time to become the fighter who takes chances once again.

"Niall, your plan is sound," I say. "But I'm dead sure the Buchanans will beat us if we stick to the standard tactics."

"Ye have another idea. Aye?"

"I do." Taking a deep breath, I go for it. "We need to forget the rules. I'm not suggesting we should cheat, but we need to stop treating the rules like they're set in stone. Let's think of them as thick mud instead."

"Dinnae understand."

"We need to quickly come up with a few basic hand gestures to communicate our intent instead of saying it aloud. And we also need to push the rules to their very limits without actually violating them." I glance at each of my teammates in turn. "Are any of you on board with my plan?"

All seven of them nod their agreement. Niall studies me briefly, then nods too.

Logan grasps my arm. "Now that's a plan, Domhnall. You know I'm the sort who doesn't care for rules."

"Neither am I," Alex agrees. "If you need a bit of grifter magic, I'm all in for that."

I'm about to say no, grifter skills won't help us. But I suddenly experience the proverbial lightbulb coming on above my head. "Actually, Alex, I think your talents might be that extra advantage we need."

"Brilliant! I haven't had the chance to exercise my conning muscles lately."

"All right, laddies, listen up. Here's the new plan."

We've just finished hashing things out when Torcall announces that the next round will begin in a moment. The teams switch places.

"Pick up the rope," Torcall commands.

Both sides lift that rope and move backward until it's taut. Torcall left the wooden stake on the field, so we simply needed to make sure both captains are six feet from the middle.

Torcall raises his arms. "Pull!"

Cormac's team pulls hard, but we hold back, pulling only enough to keep from getting yanked toward the opposing team. I watch for Niall to signal in the manner we had discussed earlier. Just when Cormac gets grouchy, spewing obscenities at me, Niall gives the signal—and we pull like the devil himself is on our tail. Cormac had slackened his hold, clearly assuming we were too jeeked to pull hard anymore.

That's Cormac's first mistake.

Niall signals again, and we ease up.

Once again, Cormac has kept pulling hard, even more so than at first, and he ignores the commands of his coach. He had told his men to pull like their lives depended on it, and when we let up, the Buchanans all stumbled and nearly hit the ground. They kept their hands off the grass, but only by a hair. Stewart chastises Cormac, who doesn't seem to give a toss.

I glance back at Alex and nod.

He winks.

Aye, that means he knows what to do.

So does Niall. He holds a hand to his forehead and pretends he might vomit. "Och, ahmno feeling well. Don't stop, laddies, keep on pulling. Alex can tell you what to do."

"Someone get a doctor," Torcall shouts, though he has no idea about the wee con we're about to pull.

"That's not necessary," Niall says. "I just need a wee rest."

Niall sits down on the grass, resting his arms on his bent knees.

Alex wastes no time. "All right, gents, let's kick it up a notch. When those wankers over there do something, we will do the opposite. Got it?"

Cormac laughs. "Telegraphing your moves, eh? Not as clever as ye think ye are, Mr. British Bastard."

"Pay no attention to the cretin, gents. He has a brain the size of a walnut."

"You are a *cacan* and an eejit. Cannae understand why a Scots lass would marry you."

Alex puts on his best British Bastard smile. "She was desperate for a good shag, that's why. Scots are so...limp. Honestly, this game is for children. Only Scots would think tug-of-war is manly."

Cormac grins with feral glee, then twists his head around to whisper something to his team.

And they all begin to pull harder than ever.

We continue our moderate pulling, just enough to keep us away from the center line. Now we wait for Cormac to do it. Alex and Niall teed the ball. If I know anything at all, Cormac is about to putt in the wrong direction.

The Buchanans loosen up their hold on the rope.

And we pull as hard as we can, dragging the stunned Buchanans over the center line. They fall into a heap on top of each other, while my team remains standing.

Torcall yells with triumph and throws his arms up. "The MacTaggarts have won round three. And they are the overall tug o' war champions!"

Chapter Thirty-Two

Fiona

The crowd explodes with joyous cheering, clapping, whooping, whistling, and other exclamations I can't even describe. Domhnall is grinning like I've never seen him do before, the expression filled with sheer joy and a kind of confidence I haven't seen in him for such a long time. This is the Domhnall Sterling who crashed Alex and Cat's wedding determined to win over Jessica O'Connor. This is the sexy bull who seduced me in the kitchen at the nudist resort. And this is the man I fell in love with two years ago.

Oh, aye, Domhnall Sterling is back.

A Dhia, I need to kiss that man right now.

But his teammates have swarmed around him to express their excitement over winning and their gratitude to Domhnall for making victory possible. Whatever he had told his teammates during their wee huddle just before the final round, it had done the trick. His friends ruffle his hair, slap his back, and shake his hand. Gordon Sterling pushes through the group to reach his son, and he beams with pride as he takes hold of Domhnall's upper arms.

Then Gordon pulls his son into a bear hug.

Domhnall hugs his father too.

Are they both tearing up? I think they might be. Domhnall has been through so much in his life—joining the military, getting shot down over Kandahar, coming home and starting a business, marrying a cheating slag. And for the past two years, he has struggled to reclaim his self-confidence. Domhnall has every right to get emotional in this moment.

Gordon steps back and grasps Domhnall's wrist, then raises his arm high. "My son, Domhnall Robert Sterling, is the bravest man I have ever known and a true war hero. Let's give him the applause he deserves!"

I didn't think the crowd could get any louder or more exuberant than they were a moment ago, but they do just that. The screams and cheering almost deafen me. But the crowd goes oddly silent for a few seconds. Then I realize why.

Everyone raises their linked hands and begins to chant, "*S e Dòmhnall an tarbh ar gaisgeach*!"

The men who had gathered around Domhnall join the crowd in chanting. I race up to him and clasp his hand with both of mine. His eyes are glistening, and he swallows hard enough that the movement is visible in his throat.

I raise onto my tiptoes to speak directly into his ear. "They're chanting for you—Domhnall the Bull is our hero."

He swipes at his eyes. "I know that's what they're saying. But it's, ah, embarrassing to be the center of attention."

"Since when does Domhnall Sterling shy away from the spotlight? You are a brave and forceful man."

Domhnall gazes at me steadily for a moment while the crowd's chanting gradually diminishes. Then his mouth slides into a sexy smile. "I was only a wee bit emotional, briefly. But thank you, *mo chridhe*, for the moral support."

"You would do the same for me."

He pulls me close and bends down to place his mouth on my ear. "I love you, Fiona Sorcha MacTaggart, and there's something I need to ask you. Not here, though. I know a private place where other people rarely ever go, and it's right here at Dùndubhan."

"Sounds intriguing." I notice a contingent approaching. "But we'll need to wait."

I nod toward my three brothers.

Domhnall glances at them, then kisses my forehead. "Later, then."

Whatever my brothers want now, I wish they would wait so I can hear that question Domhnall wants to ask me. I might be hoping it's a proposal. But I don't want to start speculating.

Lachlan, Rory, and Aidan stand in front of us. Lachlan takes the lead. "You have done very well, Domhnall. We put you through these tests, beginning with your kidnapping, because we knew you could handle all of it. The Highland games were your crowning achievement."

"Thank you," Domhnall says, though he sounds a touch confused. "But the tug o' war was a team effort. And I didn't strictly stick to the rules."

"But you didn't violate them either. You devised a clever strategy for achieving victory, and you did that without cheating. How does it feel to win because of your brains instead of your muscles?"

"Never been accused of having brains before."

Rory pats Domhnall's arm. "You've always been clever. Now, you've finally let everyone see that side of you."

"Aye," Aidan concurs. "Fiona told her sisters how you figured out the combination for those two lockboxes that Errol left for you during your treasure hunt."

"I couldn't have done that without Fiona." Domhnall looks at me and smiles. "We are a bloody fantastic team."

Lachlan grins, then turns to face the crowd. "We have an announcement."

Rory leans toward Lachlan and whispers, "Do ye want the bullhorn?"

"No." Lachlan sighs and starts again. "We have a very important announcement. Domhnall Sterling is now an honorary member of Clan MacTaggart."

Everyone cheers.

As the crowd disperses, with most everyone heading into the castle for a celebratory snack, the last person I ever expected to approach Domhnall walks up to us. Cormac Buchanan holds out his hand.

Domhnall doesn't hesitate. He shakes Cormac's hand. "You are one tough competitor. Congratulations on getting so close to winning the games. Even second place is an achievement worth celebrating."

"Aye, it is."

"No hard feelings, I hope."

Cormac waves a dismissive hand. Then he shocks me when he tells Domhnall, "I pretended to be a big, lumbering, brute of a man. Someone had to take on the role of the villain. I had a bloody great time doing that."

"You don't actually want to destroy me."

"No," Cormac says with a laugh. "Fiona's brothers made up that nickname. I have never been a destroyer."

"Glad to hear it."

Cormac pulls Domhnall into a bear hug and squeezes him so tightly that my sexy bull gasps. Then Cormac winks and walks away.

Lachlan nods toward the garden doorway. "I think it's time for us to go inside and make sure no one inspects Rory's knickknacks and puts them back in the wrong place. He's finicky about that."

"No, I am not, Lachie."

"Oh, you shouldn't have called me that—Rory Baby."

Aidan rolls his eyes at them. "Come on, laddies, let's go inside and eat something. You'll both feel better after a feeding."

My brothers wander away, disappearing into the garden. Only a few stragglers remain on the green, and all but one of them head for the garden too. Thane, however, comes over to us.

"Congratulations, Domhnall. I knew you'd trounce the Buchanans, and I was rooting for your team."

"But you're a Buchanan. Won't your clan be angry that you wanted me to win?"

Thane chuckles. "No, we dinnae give a toss about that. These games were for your benefit."

"I appreciate that. Everyone did this for me, and I'll always be grateful." Domhnall pulls me against his side and smiles down at me with the sweetest expression on his face. "But right now, Fiona and I need to do something—alone. I hope you won't be offended."

"Not at all. See you at the ceilidh."

"I do not dance."

"Rubbish. Everyone dances, under the proper circumstances."

Thane smirks as he trots across the green, vanishing into the garden.

"What did you want to ask me, Domhnall?"

He freezes, and his smile crumbles. "*Bod an Donais.* I forgot to bring the, ah—I need to go get it. Wait right here, *mo chridhe*. It will only take a moment to get the, ah... Well, you'll see."

Domhnall kisses my cheek, then hustles away.

I do exactly what he said. I stay in this spot. The sun warms my face, and I shut my eyes to enjoy the sounds of birdsongs in the distance, feeling more contented than ever. Domhnall and I have reclaimed our relationship, and we will never doubt each other again.

"There you are, darling."

A chill shimmies down my spine. I recognize that voice, and it's not Domhnall. My eyes fly open. "Easton, what are you doing here? I thought you were in jail."

His clothes are rumpled, his hair too, and he sneers at me with a glint in his eyes that does nothing to calm my nerves. "You had me arrested, pet. That's not a nice thing to do. I need to talk to you, and this time, you will not get away from me."

Easton pulls out a switchblade that he had hidden behind his back.

I bolt for the garden door.

He races after me.

"Domhnall!" I shout. "Help!"

Easton tackles me, flipping my legs out from under me and dragging me backward toward him. He sits on my calves and grabs my wrists, pinning my arms behind my back. Before I can shout again, he gags my mouth with a rolled-up cloth that's tied behind my head.

"I'm sorry it has to be this way," he says. "But you gave me no choice."

And he's giving me no choice too. I can't respond to his claim. I can't free myself. When he stands up and hoists me over his shoulder, all I can do is stare down at his feet and his erse. I try to kick him, but he has my legs bound by his arms. Why is he kidnapping me? Easton, the sweet, shy laddie I'd known at university has become…someone else. I know he's been through many ordeals, but this is insanity.

Since I have no choice, I let him cart me away. No one inside the castle compound will hear me if I try to cry out. The gag prevents it.

He sprints across the green and into the forest.

The second his hold on my legs falters for one second, I thrash my legs in an attempt to knock him off balance. He stumbles but catches himself just in time to avoid falling down. And he also readjusted his hold to ensure I can't kick my legs again.

I'm starting to get nauseous from hanging upside down. Every time my gorge rises in my throat, I gulp it down and take a few slow breaths. I'm also getting dizzy, which doesn't help matters. Since Easton had tied my hands behind my back, I've developed pain in my shoulders that keeps getting worse. And I've also developed a headache.

Suck it up and find a way to fight.

I close my eyes and focus on coming up with a plan. The only weapons I have at my disposal are my teeth. But I can't reach far enough to bite him in the erse. What would Domhnall do in this situation? Granted, he would never be in this situation because he's large and strong and trained as a boxer and a wrestler. Easton wouldn't stand a chance against my sexy bull.

A light bulb pops on in my mind. I know that's a silly thing to think of, but I honestly do experience a moment of clarity and insight. I've watched Domhnall wrestle and box enough times that I understand the basics. But the rules don't apply now, and if Domhnall were here, I know he would do whatever it takes to get free. All right, maybe I can't perform any actual boxing moves right now. But I am getting an idea.

Easton tied my calves. He didn't secure my thighs. And he currently has his arm lashed around my lower legs. An opening? Might as well give it a go.

I take a deep breath and exhale it slowly, letting my body relax. Then I thrash my head up to knock him off balance just enough that his hold slackens a wee bit—and I ram my knees into him.

"Fuck!" he shouts as he trips over something, maybe his own feet, and falls down. He lands on top of me, but at least now I'm lying flat. His face is flushed, and sweat dribbles down his temples. "Why did you do that? You can't get away."

He knows I can't answer. The bastard gagged me.

Easton pushes up into a kneeling position.

My pulse pounds in my ears. Now or never.

I lock my legs together, roll onto my side, and slam my knees into his gut.

"You stupid bitch!" His cry is part shout and part agony.

I roll away from him and accidentally crest a hill, tumbling down, down, down and toward the river.

Two feet block my way, preventing me falling into the water.

Easton kneels and flips me onto my back. Then he uses another strip of fabric to tie my thighs together. "Won't do another runner now."

He throws me over his shoulder and tromps through the woods at a slower pace, though not slow enough. How will anyone know where I've gone? Everyone had retreated into the house.

Domhnall will find me. I know he will.

But I refuse to hang limply over Easton's back while he carts me away to who knows where. I make one final attempt to free myself. I summon all my energy to swing my torso up and bash him in the head with my own skull.

Easton shouts but keeps going.

Now, I'm even dizzier and more nauseous.

Finally, he stops. An electronic beep, followed by a click, suggests he's opening the boot of a car. He grumbles what might be words, though I can't decipher them. Then he dumps me into the boot.

My mobile rings, but I can't get it out of my front pocket. I'm trapped.

Oh, bloody hell.

Chapter Thirty-Three

Domhnall

I sprint through the garden and out onto the green with the ring box clutched in my palm. The adrenaline rush of excitement makes me breathe harder and heightens my senses, all because I'm about to ask Fiona MacTaggart to marry me. But something isn't right. I don't see her. She might have wandered a little further away while she waited for me, but the lass wouldn't go so far that I wouldn't be able to see her.

"Fiona!" I shout. "Fiona, where are you?"

My voice echoes off the castle walls. No one responds.

I cup my hands around my mouth and shout, "Fiona!"

No response. The only sound is the rustling of the leaves on the trees.

Fiona wouldn't leave without telling me. I get out my mobile and dial her number, listening as the device dials. After several rings, the voice mail takes over, and I hear Fiona's voice reciting her standard greeting.

Mhac na galla. She always has her phone with her.

Something has happened to her.

I bolt across the green and through the garden, hesitating only long enough to open the vestibule door. Then I pelt up the stairs to the great hall, where everyone has gathered. When I stop, I'm out of breath and can't speak yet.

Thane notices me first and races over here. "Domhnall, what's fashing you? Why are you gasping?"

"Fiona—" I take a few more slow breaths to calm myself. "Something has happened to Fiona. She was waiting for me on the green, but now she's gone."

Thane's expression hardens. He turns around and bellows, "Haud yer wheesht immediately! Fiona has gone missing."

Everyone in the great hall stops talking and rotates toward us. Fiona's brothers rush up to me.

"What's going on?" Lachlan asks. "How can Fiona have gone missing? She was with you."

I shake my head. "Came back inside to fetch something. Only gone a few minutes."

Rory wears his steely glare, though I know he's not angry with me. He faces the crowd. "Evan, Grey, get your erses over here now! Errol and Magnus, get your erses over here too!"

He has called in the computer experts.

The laddies in question nearly knock the other folk over in their zeal to reach us.

"What can we do?" Grey asks. "Don't we need bloodhounds, not geeks?"

"Dùndubhan has security cameras," Rory says. "We need you and Evan to scour the footage to find out what happened to my sister."

"I have my laptop in the car. I'll go get it."

"Never mind that," Evan says. "I installed the security system here, and I have administrative access to tap into the system remotely. We can use the computer in Rory's office. It'll be faster."

The crowd makes way as Grey and Evan hurry to the office at the other end of the great hall and go inside, shutting the door behind them.

Magnus and Errol seem confused, clearly unsure of why they were summoned.

Rory faces them. "You two are geniuses at finding things, including human beings. What should we do?"

Magnus jogs over to the tall windows and peers out. "No new vehicles out there, though whoever took Fiona might have parked nearer to the road if they realized Dùndubhan might have cameras."

"Get in here, Rory!"

We all turn and see Grey poking his head out of the partly open office door. He waves excitedly.

Rory leads the way with me right beside him and the others following us. We flood into the office, and Lachlan shuts the door.

Evan is sitting behind the desk. "It's a bloody good thing I convinced you to put up thermal cameras. That's how I found them. Fiona was carried into the woods by one individual, apparently male, who traveled on foot. He took her to a vehicle that he'd hidden in the trees, a short distance from the road."

Aidan reaches for the doorknob. "What are we waiting for? Let's get out there and batter that bastard."

Evan holds up a hand. "It's too late for that. The car is on the road now, speeding away from Dùndubhan. We need to ring the police."

I shove past the others and rip the door open. "Fuck that plan. Mine is faster."

As I barrel through the crowd in the great hall, I pause only long enough to ask Callum, "Are the keys still in the Harley?"

"Aye."

Then I gallop out of the castle and into the courtyard, finding the Harley in the exact spot where I'd parked it yesterday. I have my helmet on by the time Fiona's brothers reach the courtyard. I've cranked up the engine just as they run up behind the motorcycle.

I glance back at them. "I'm bringing Fiona home, whatever it takes."

"You'll need this." Rory tosses me a handgun. "Magnus is loaning it to you. Bring our sister back, Domhnall."

I stuff the weapon into my waistband, then release the Harley's kick-stand.

Evan comes pelting out of the house, struggling to catch his breath. He holds out his hand to me. "Your mobile. Give it to me."

I toss it to him.

He does something on the screen, then returns the device to me. "I installed an app for you that will let you track Fiona's phone."

"One way or another, I am not coming home without her."

I roar off down the driveway.

Soon, I'm on the road, flying down the asphalt. Evan's app told me I should go straight through Loch Fairbairn. I know the route, so I don't need to look at the on-screen map. The Harley snarls like a hellhound, which gets the attention of everyone I pass as I roar through the village. Kirsty and Luke are standing outside her shop as if they knew I'd be coming this way. Her brothers must have shot the news down the grapevine in record time.

"Good luck!" Luke shouts. "Save the girl, Domhnall!"

The second I've left the village, I give the bike its head. The Harley roars down the road even faster than before, scaring away any wildlife that gets in my path. A cloud of midges tries to swarm me, but even they run off when they hear me coming. Thanks to Evan's app, I need only check my mobile now and then to ensure I'm on the right track. Up ahead, I see a farmer in a slow-moving pickup truck that's carrying a full load of hay. The truck takes up more than half the roadway, which means I'll have to stop and wait for it to go by.

No, I will never stop. Not until I have Fiona in my arms.

I honk the Harley's horn, but the farmer either doesn't hear or doesn't care. He's left me only one option. I twist the handlebar and squeeze even more power from the bike, pushing it to the limit and beyond. The boost gives me all I need. While the farmer beeps his horn, I veer off the roadway and soar over the ditch and onto the grass. Then I spin the bike around and leap back onto the road, hitting hard enough that my teeth clack together.

No slowing down, not anymore. I keep the Harley at maximum speed, rocketing down the road so fast that everything around me becomes a blur.

I dare to glance at my mobile. I'm less than a mile from Fiona, but I need to turn onto a dirt road up ahead. Do I slow down in advance? Not a chance. Even when I can see the turn coming up, I keep the bike running as hot and hard as possible and swerve off the road to jump another ditch and crash down on the dirt road. My erse lifts off the seat for a split second.

Checking the map, I know for certain I'm on the right path.

Hold on, Fiona, I'm coming for you and the cacan who took you away from me.

The trees begin to thin out up ahead, revealing the outlines of a house. That's where she is. But I dinnae want the *cacan* to know I'm coming for him. So, I ease up on the pedal and let the machine gradually slow down, which also has the effect of making the engine noise quieter. Well, as quiet as a Harley ever gets. Five hundred feet from the house, I pull over and set the kickstand. Then I jump off the bike and jog the rest of the way, frequently checking the map on my mobile and walking in the manner Munro had taught me. It makes my footfalls almost undetectable.

A small clearing surrounds the house. I pause at the periphery to examine the area. One car sits in front of the log cabin. Cannae see anyone inside the vehicle, which means Easton Yates must have taken her inside the house. I think back on all the stories Logan and Magnus had told me over the past two years, and I begin to formulate a plan.

I sneak up to the side of the cabin so I can peer through a window that turns out to be a bathroom. No one in there. I inch around the corner to do a visual search of the porch, but I still see no one. As I carefully climb onto the porch and crawl forward on my hands and knees, I keep an eye on the windows. But I see no evidence that anyone is watching me. Once I come up alongside the front door, I stop to listen.

Shuffling. Scraping. Grunting.

If that bastard has touched Fiona—

"Ah!" a male voice cries out. "You bloody cow. You bit me."

Though I want to chuckle, I stifle the impulse. That's my lass. Feisty, determined, and clever.

"No more Mr. Nice Guy, Fee. Time for the gag again."

I raise my head just enough to peer over the threshold of the nearest window and into the cabin. Easton Yates is pacing frantically, like a caged lion without the massive teeth and powerful jaws. He shoves his hands into his hair and starts babbling to himself, his voice too low for me to make out what he's saying. I have a feeling it wouldn't make sense, anyway.

"Why, why, why are you doing this to me?" the *cacan* repeats four times in a row. "Why, why, why, Fee?"

I pull the gun out of my waistband, move in front of the door, and rise to my full height. Then I check the gun's clip. Fully loaded. Snapping the clip back into place, I take two steps backward and kick the door open.

Easton Yates shrieks. He stumbles backward, struggling to stay upright.

I surge into the cabin and aim my gun at him. "Don't move, Easton, or I will shoot you. The MacTaggarts will help me bury the body."

Peripherally, I see Fiona sitting on a wooden chair with her wrists and ankles bound to it. A gag prevents her from speaking. But I can't risk taking my eyes off Easton Yates.

He brandishes a switchblade, flicking it open. "She's meant to be mine. Isn't she? Yes, I agree. What? No, only I can have her. We shouldn't have split up, and you'll make sure she understands. Won't you?"

The bampot seems to be talking to me, though he never looks at me. Nothing he said made any sense. Time to take control of the situation.

"Put the knife down, Easton, or I will shoot. I'm giving you until the count of three. One, two—"

He lunges at me, wildly careening as if he's drunk or high on something. At the last second, the lunatic swerves away from me and toward Fiona with his knife pointed at her.

I leap on him, dragging the bampot away from Fiona. Then I yank his wrist until he drops the knife, whining like a wee bairn. He starts crying too. I snatch up the switchblade and realize it's made of plastic. Must be a child's toy.

While Easton sobs, I undo all the bindings that keep Fiona restrained and pull her into my arms. "Did he hurt ye, lass?"

"No, not really. He dragged me through the forest while I was hanging upside down over his shoulder, but the pain from that was temporary."

I turn sideways, taking Fiona with me, and we both study the *cacan*. I dig my mobile out of my pocket and dial Lachlan's number. "It's Domhnall. I'm with Fiona, and she's unharmed. Easton Yates has gone off his head in every way imaginable."

"We knew you'd save the day," Lachlan says. "Stay where you are. We'll bring reinforcements and constables."

Aye, I know why he made those two separate things. The reinforcements are not police officers. They're MacTaggarts. "What's the plan now?"

"Keep Easton restrained, and we'll be there soon, Domhnall."

I end the call and stuff the phone back into my pocket. "I need to restrain him, *gràidh*. Stay over here just in case. The crazier the lunatic, the more unpredictable they are."

"Aye, I've experienced that firsthand in this cabin." She gives me a tight smile. "Do what you need to do. But be careful."

I grab the materials Easton had used to restrain Fiona and approach the *cacan*, who is now lying on the floor like a human puddle. Since he seems unlikely to get up on his own, I shove my arms under his and hoist him onto his feet. Then I collar his wrists with one hand, using the other to tie his hands.

"You're a bloody stupid wanker, did you know that? The Scottish bull will be castrated soon enough."

"Haud yer wheesht, or I'll gag ye."

Easton abruptly lunges at me.

Pain stabs into my arm, sharp and searing. I gasp and snarl a curse, then slam Easton down on the floor while blood trickles down my left forearm. I have my foot on Easton's back to pin him to the floor.

Fiona cries out and rushes over to me. "You're injured. What did that ersehole do to you?"

I roll my sleeve up and remove the glass shard from my arm. "He found this and must have hid it in his sleeve. But he didn't get he'd hoped for." I stomp my foot on his back, making him cry out, and lean over to look him in the eye. "Not castrated, ye bloody stupid bampot."

Fiona sprints into the open kitchen and returns with a damp cloth as well as a roll of gauze. "Let me clean up your wound, please."

"All right. But I am not moving one inch. You'll have to treat me while I'm standing on Easton's back."

"Fine with me."

Just as Fiona finishes wrapping my wound, I hear multiple vehicles pulling up outside. Voices murmur out there, and doors slam shut. Then I hear the first whine of a police car approaching with its sirens blaring.

Lachlan, Rory, and Aidan burst into the cabin.

"We're all fine," I say. "Easton pricked me a wee bit, but that's all. He needs more help than I do. The mental kind."

Two constables sprint into the cabin, but only one speaks. "Looks like you don't need us after all."

"Only to take this lunatic to the jail," I tell him. "He's a danger to himself and others." I remove my foot from Easton's back. "You can have him."

While the constables take custody of the bampot, I wrap an arm around Fiona and lead her outside with her brothers right behind us. I halt at the Harley. "How do ye feel, *mo chridhe*?"

"Surprisingly good. It's all over, finally."

"Aye."

The lass links her hands behind my back and rests her cheek on my chest. "I want to go home, Domhnall."

"I'm sure your family has already planned a ceilidh for tonight. We can sleep in the tower bedroom."

She lifts her head to look at me. "No, Domhnall, I want to go *home*, as in our house in Loch Fairbairn."

"Oh, I see."

"The question is, what do you want?"

I hook a finger under her chin. "Let's go home."

Chapter Thirty-Four

Fiona

The bonniest sunrise I've ever seen shines through the lacy curtains in our bedroom, and I should be enchanted with the gorgeous shades of pink, purple, and gold that emanate from the sky. But I can't do anything except lie here admiring the man who lies beside me. Domhnall is still asleep, snoring faintly, and he's flat on his back.

I can hardly believe two days have gone by since the ruckus at an abandoned cabin in the forest. The constables told us Easton had not only stolen a car, but he invaded an elderly couple's house. Fortunately, they weren't home at the time. If Domhnall hadn't been there, I don't know what Easton might have done. I don't need to worry about that, though. My sexy bull will always be here whenever I need him, no matter the weather, no matter the danger, no matter what.

These past two days had been a whirlwind. This morning, we finally have the chance to relax and enjoy our rejuvenated relationship.

Only a single sheet covers our bodies. *Perfect.* I peel that sheet away and straddle his hips, gently settling my weight on him. His cock rouses before he does, twitching as if it wants a good hard shag as much as I do. I wait a reasonable length of time—that means about thirty seconds—and then I wake him up my way.

Aye, I clasp his cock and start stroking it.

Domhnall groans and wriggles but doesn't open his eyes.

I push my finger inside my opening to get my cream all over it, then lean forward to wave that finger under his nose.

He still doesn't open his eyes.

Time for drastic measures. I slide off him and take his cock in my mouth, licking and sucking while his shaft begins to harden.

Domhnall grabs me and flips us both over so swiftly that it stuns a gasp out of me. I now lie beneath him with all of that sexy body on top of me. His *slat* has gone fully hard. He rubs it up and down my cleft so slowly that my clit throbs. "*Madainn mhath, mo chridhe.*"

"You were faking it, weren't you? Domhnall Sterling pretended to be asleep."

"Dinnae know about that Sterling bloke, but *Dòmhnall an Tarbh* would do anything for his lass, even pretend to sleep just so he can watch her trying to wake him up."

"Are you going to fuck me now?"

"Not quite yet." He shimmies down the bed until his face hovers over my mound. "Need an appetizer first."

He gently separates my folds while nuzzling the hairs on my mound, which makes me squirm and bite my lip. "I love the scent of you, *mo leannan*. But the taste of you is what always makes me hungry for more. I need to gorge myself on your cream."

"Please, Domhnall, yes."

He delicately feathers his tongue over my swollen folds and traces his fingers up and down my cleft, repeating the motions over and over until I'm writhing and fisting my hands in the sheets. He nuzzles my clit. Pleasure pulses through me. Domhnall licks the flesh all around my nub but stays away from the one place where I desperately need him to devour me.

"*A Dhia*, you're driving me off my head. Please make me come, Domhnall."

He raises his head to smirk at me. Then he grasps my hips to lift them off the bed—and he rubs his cock up and down my swollen cleft. My sensitized skin sends waves of pleasure down my nerves.

A phone rings.

He glances at the nightstand, where both our mobiles lie.

"Don't you dare stop, Domhnall. Finish us both off."

"Aye, I will."

He sets his hands on the mattress, bracketing my body, and thrusts into me so deeply that I feel the crown of his cock nudging my cervix. While the phone rings again, he starts fucking me.

Banging erupts in another part of the house. It's not the sort of banging I want right now.

Domhnall keeps his word. He lunges into me again and again.

"Answer the door," someone shouts. "Answer it now, or we're breaking in."

I freeze. Domhnall freezes. And we both groan at the same time, though it's not an erotic groan. Lachlan had shouted that command.

"Aye, Fiona," Aidan calls out. "Best open the door before Rory Baby knocks it down. Or maybe Lachie would do it."

Domhnall leaps off the bed and scrambles to get his clothes on. I do the same, and we greet my brothers together. What do they want? To be bloody annoying, that's what.

"You're coming to Dùndubhan," Rory declares. «This is not optional. We've arranged a ceilidh for you."

"We said no to a ceilidh the other night." I try to shoo him away, but he doesn't budge. "Honestly, Rory, this is verging on harassment."

Aidan grins. "Not if we're giving you gifts."

What sort of gifts would my brothers give me? Not sure I want to find out.

"Dinnae want a ceilidh or any presents." I push the door partway closed. "Away and boil yer heads now."

The last thing I ever expected happens. Domhnall pulls the door open all the way. "We should let them give us a ceilidh, Fiona. They're only trying to show how much you mean to them."

He's right, naturally. It's annoying but true.

My shoulders slump. "Aye, let's have a ceilidh."

At last, my brothers leave. They came here strictly to order us to take part in a dance and drinks party. I'm beginning to agree with Domhnall that everyone in my family is barmy.

At least I know that Easton is safely tucked away in a high-secure facility, where he can get the help he needs and won't harm anyone else. The constables told us that Easton had escaped while they were dealing with another inmate, and that's the only reason he was able to come after me.

We get the rest of the day to ourselves, and we use that time to talk and make each other laugh. I'm still very curious about Thane. I might have dated him and slept with him too, but that was a long time ago. He's clearly changed since then, and I can't help wondering about his time in England. My questions can wait, though, because it's ceilidh time.

Domhnall and I arrive at Dùndubhan to find the festivities well underway. Music wafts out of the castle, as do the aromas of food. We bump into Thane during the party, and he seems to be having a good time. Domhnall gets a lovely surprise a few minutes later when his old friend and business partner walks into the long gallery. Mick Dalton grabs Domhnall in a big, boisterous hug. Well, they haven't seen each other in person for at least a year. I love listening to them joke with each other and talk about how their partnership began.

Midway through the ceilidh, though, my brothers interrupt the dancing to make an announcement.

Once the music ends, Rory speaks. Without the bullhorn, thankfully. "We have news to share with everyone. Fiona, please come over here. You too, Thane."

Why is a Buchanan involved in my "news"? I wonder about that as I approach Rory. My brother whispers something to Thane when he reaches us. Thane nods.

Then he slings an arm around my shoulders. "We all know Fiona has been unemployed lately, and we brainstormed until we came up with the perfect career for her."

"Don't I get to choose my own career?"

"You're free to disregard our choice. But I hope you'll think about it first." Thane lifts his chin and smiles. "*Collaidh Sgeul-Rùin* offers you a fulfilling new career path as the distillery manager. If you accept our offer, you'll be in charge of the whole operation, supervising all our employees and departments. What do you say, Fiona?"

Every hair on my body stiffens. But it's not fear causing that reaction. No, this is excitement. "Aye, I would love to work for *Collaidh Sgeul-Rùin*."

Everyone cheers.

Domhnall hurries over to me and gives me a firm hug, then kisses my cheek. "Congratulations, *m'eudail*. You deserve this chance, and I know you'll stun everyone at the distillery with how fantastically you run it."

My throat has gone thick. I can't say anything, so I just hold his hand while everyone in my family comes up to me and expresses their congratulations.

After a while, Domhnall leads me out of the long gallery where the others are still having a rollicking time. I don't question why he takes me out into the courtyard or why we go behind the castle. I trust Domhnall without any reservations, and I love him with all my heart and soul. So, when we go through a doorway even I have never seen before, coming back inside the castle via an outside door, I don't question his plan.

We enter a narrow, gloomy stairwell, but I can see well enough that I won't trip over the steps. Domhnall would never let that happen, anyway.

"This is the old tower stair," he tells me. "Iain told me about it. Your ancestor Kieran might have used this tower, but no one knows for sure."

"Are we going up to the wall walk?"

Domhnall slips an arm around me as we continue up the steps. "Aye, we are going to the walkway. It's the most private place for what I have in mind. And it seems appropriate to do this at the top of the castle, where sieges have taken place in medieval times and in this century."

I still can't figure out why he wants to take me up to the wall walk, but I will wait to find out when he's ready to tell me.

We emerge from the tower stairwell, and he guides me down the walkway to the crenellations nearest to the where the old gatehouse had been during medieval times. I know that crenellations are thick slabs of stone placed at intervals along a castle wall so that archers can shoot between them from a place of modest safety.

Domhnall halts and pushes me backward until I bump into the crenellation. "Look at the stars above us, *mo chridhe*. They have existed since the dawn of the universe, and I will love you until the end of time and even longer, after the last stars have faded away."

"I've never heard you say such a poetic and lovely thing."

"Not done yet." He reaches into his trouser pocket and pulls out something that he hides inside his closed hand. And he drops to one knee. "Fiona Sorcha MacTaggart, will you marry me?"

"Aye, of course I will." My eyes burn from the tears that want to flow, and my throat tightens. "I've wanted to be your wife since the day we met. And I would be honored to call you my husband."

"I wish I hadn't waited so bloody long to ask the question."

He reveals the item he'd been hiding—a small satin box. Then he pops the lid up and offers me the shimmering diamond ring inside the box. I raise my hand so he can slide the ring onto my finger.

Domhnall presses his body to mine. The crenellation supports me. He brushes the backs of his fingers over my cheek. "I'm glad ye wore a dress tonight. Makes it easier for me to seduce you up here on the top of the castle with the stars glittering above us."

He palms my breast, massaging it tenderly. "Need to feel you wrapped around my *slat*."

"Make love to me, please."

"No need to beg." He unzips his trousers and pulls his cock out, stroking it lazily. "Dinnae want you to do a thing. Let me give you everything I have and everything I want to show you."

He pushes my dress up to my waist and groans when he realizes I'm not wearing any knickers. I spread my legs, inviting him to take my body, and he slides his cock between my folds. For a moment, he simply glides his length up and down my cleft until I'm gasping for breath and burning for him so fiercely that I think I might come any second. But then he thrusts into me, and I instinctively grasp his biceps. He takes my mouth along with my body, kissing me with such delicate sensuality that it steals my breath away. While he coils his tongue around mine, he maintains the measured pace of his *slat* consuming me.

I plunge my fingers into his hair.

A firework bursts above us, the colors flaring out across the sky just before they begin to fall downward and vanish.

Domhnall grasps my hips, and I lock my legs around him. He punches into me faster, pushing deep, grunting with every thrust. We gaze into each other's eyes while more fireworks burst above us. I throw my arms around his neck and hold on, loving the sensation of his cock pummeling me. My entire body tingles in the most sensual way, and I know I won't last much longer. Domhnall clamps his hands down on the top of the crenellation, using it as leverage to bury himself even deeper inside me.

A series of stunning fireworks erupt overhead, the booms echoing off the castle wall, and Domhnall wraps his arms around the crenellation. He plasters us both to the stone block and fucks me that way, using the unyielding stone as a tool to confine me. The pleasure erupts inside me so quickly and so fiercely that I scream, though the pops of fireworks drown out the sound. Domhnall punches into me a few more times with a ferocity I've never felt from him before. The intensity of our lovemaking sealed a new bond between us. I know it did. I felt it.

Neither of us moves. We just stand her with our bodies melded while the last of the fireworks die away. Then we need a few minutes to recover our wits. Once I've fixed my dress, I notice he seems unsettled.

"What's wrong, Domhnall?"

He winces. "I, ah, forgot to use a condom. Been forgetting a lot lately."

"Doesn't matter. We're getting married, and I might not be too old to have a baby. I'm only forty-two, after all. Keely was forty-one when she got pregnant and nearly forty-two when she gave birth to Joy."

"You wouldn't mind if we had a bairn?"

"No. I would love that."

He grins. "So would I."

We amble back to the tower stair and down the steps, taking our time, discussing the possibility of having a bairn. We both love the idea. Even if I can't get pregnant, adopting is an option. All that matters is that we're together and we will never break up again. We never really did that, anyway. I wanted him back even after I threw him out of the house, but that decision turned out to be the best thing that ever happened to us.

Domhnall's parents will hear about our engagement tomorrow. They were too jeeked to stay for the whole ceilidh, but I know they'll be thrilled to hear the news.

The ceilidh is winding down when we reach the long gallery, but Thane approaches us to ask an impertinent question. "Did you convince her to marry you yet?"

"Aye," Domhnall says. "Can't ye see the ring on her finger?"

"You picked a fine ring for the lass."

Thane's statement surprises me. "How did you pick a ring for me, Domhnall? You've been too busy getting abducted and going through the Three Macs Test."

"I wanted to buy that ring weeks ago, but we'd been arguing so much that I was afraid you'd say no to my proposal. Your family bought the ring for me, for us."

"Was this ring the thing you were hiding from me?"

"Aye."

I clasp his face with my hands. "You silly bull. I always wanted to marry you."

Thane starts to walk away, but Domhnall calls out to him. "You'll be next, Thane Buchanan, mark my words."

"Next for what?"

Domhnall grins. "The meddling. You can't escape the American Wives Club."

"I can, and I will."

Thane turns and walks away.

He might believe he can evade the American Wives Club, but he still doesn't understand how deeply they believe in true love. Oh, aye, he will be married within the year. That's a dead certainty.

Thane Buchanan returns in *Valentine in a Kilt* (Hot Scots, Book 15).

Anna Durand is a bestselling, multi-award-winning author of contemporary and paranormal romance. Her books have earned bestseller status on every major retailer and wonderful reviews from readers around the world. But that's the boring spiel. Here are the really cool things you want to know about Anna!

Born on Lackland Air Force Base in Texas, Anna grew up moving here, there, and everywhere thanks to her dad's job as an instructor pilot. She's lived in Texas (twice), Mississippi, California (twice), Michigan (twice), and Alaska—and now Ohio.

As for her writing, Anna has always made up stories in her head, but she didn't write them down until her teen years. Those first awful books went into the trash can a few years later, though she learned a lot from those stories. Eventually, she would pen her first romance novel, the paranormal romance *Willpower*, and she's never looked back since.

Want even more details about Anna? Get access to her extended bio when you subscribe to her newsletter and download the free bonus ebook, *Hot Scots Confidential*. You'll also get hot deleted scenes, character interviews, fun facts, and more!

Visit AnnaDurand.com to sign up.

9 781958 144237